YOUNG AUTHOR PROJECT

The Art of Giving A Crap

You never know what someone is going through.

The Young Author Project is an independent teacher-led initiative to provide talented youth with the opportunity to showcase their skills and gain real-world publishing experience. All of the following individuals named on this project are considered the original co-authors and receive full credit for the content of this book (in alphabetical order): Olivia DeSantis, Anais Duran, Angel Duran, Taryn Johnson, Kenshin Lee, Kenneth Loder, Michaella Ruiz, Brooklynn Satterfield, and Natalie Wilkinson.

First edition

ISBN: 979-8-9889180-0-4

Editing by Olivia De Santis
Editing by Anais Duran
Editing by Angel Duran
Editing by Taryn Johnson
Editing by Kenshin Lee
Editing by Kenneth Loder
Editing by Michaella Ruiz
Editing by Brooklynn Satterfield
Proofreading by Natalie Wilkinson

This book was professionally typeset on Reedsy.
Find out more at reedsy.com

This is for the voiceless; the kids who feel like their worlds are falling apart and believe they're alone. This is also for teachers, students, and school staff. Let's look out the window and SEE there may be someone right next to us who is worlds away.

Foreword

I have twenty years of experience working with youth and families as a Court Counselor for the Division of Juvenile Justice and Delinquency Prevention and a Child Protective Services Social Worker for a local Department of Human Services. It is truly empowering to be able to share my experiences with a group of young authors who are exploring the consequences of trauma and grief through a young person's point of view. I believe this is truly important work as it gives an understanding that not everyone is born into the same set of circumstances and that trauma can impact individuals in many ways. Our childhood experiences, whether they be positive or negative, can have long-lasting effects, and those effects can manifest in different ways. One of the things that resonated most with me while meeting with the authors of this book is that they have developed characters who come from different walks of life but found a way to support each other through a difficult time. Sometimes all we need is one person to believe in us and help us through a difficult experience in order to achieve better outcomes.

Sarimar Miller

Bachelor's Degree in Criminal Justice and Criminology from Niagara University in New York

Master's in Public Administration from Appalachian State University in Boone, North Carolina

Preface

Dear Readers Young and Old,

DO NOT SKIP THIS PART.

Here is our full disclosure, up front: this novel touches on sensitive subjects like abuse, neglect, self-harm, and drug consumption. The story of Asher and Lucy was written with the purpose of creating a window into a commonly overlooked world - one of pain, trauma, and intense sorrow. **If you are not sure this book is right for you, we ask that you please put it down and choose something else.**

There will be difficult things to read in this book. There will be things some of the characters do that may shock you.

With all that said, this is a *fictional* representation of a harsh reality, written with the expectation that readers understand this up front.

The self-harm depicted in this story is brutal, raw, and realistic. It is also never something that should be done, no matter the reasoning. It is destructive and dangerous, and ***never*** worth it.

I've had students like Asher before and not known it until much later. I've also had students like Asher before where *everyone* knew it and there was nothing any of us could do. For those I could not help: I'm so sorry. For those I could not reach: you have a choice in how this pans out for you. If swallowing your pride for a few uncomfortable moments can change the entire course of your life, then LISTEN, dear child, to those who care and want to help you.

Please seek help if you EVER feel the desire to harm yourself. E-mail me personally if you have to, and if I don't have the tools to help you, I'll find someone that does.

Mrs. Natalie Wilkinson
Young Author Project Coordinator
Email: <u>YoungAuthorProject@SchoolBoost.Online</u>

Acknowledgments

There are *many* whose support helped make this book possible, and we'd like to thank them here with sincerity:

Special Thanks
Renee Roach and Lisandra Taveras for their incredible help with Summer fundraising and their presence for these kids to support them every step of the way. Also to Tryppton, Tamberlyn, and Wesley for jumping right in with us.

Kristy, Russ, Maddie, and Olivia DeSantis for making so many wonderful things for us and showing up in such an awesome way throughout this project.

Elaine Miller for her invaluable input, and to Christy Clary for introducing us.

Sarimar Miller and Shelley Lee for their amazing willingness to help us write a story that was both realistic and compassionate; they took time out of their busy days to allow us to interview them as experts on the sensitive subjects we touch upon. Thank you to Deputy Yang in Concord and to Kenshin Lee for introducing us.

Veronica and Chloe Brown, founders of *Let's Bake Up A Story,* who donated many delicious treats to help us raise money for our ISBN numbers and editing services.

Abdon J. Romero, the unparalleled artist that designed our front and back cover. As always, it's amazing, *maestro*.

The backbone of this project, the parents and families of our authors, for helping us facilitate the countless library meetings:

Kristy and Russ DeSantis
Johnson and Ka Lee
Mike Loder
Sarah Loder
Renee Roach
Emil Ruiz
Sarah and Charles Satterfield
Lisandra Taveras

Locals, Friends, and Family

Atrium Health Mount Pleasant Office for buying lots of chocolates!

The Cabarrus County Schools office in Concord for opening their doors and supporting the kids with warmth and kindness.

Compleat Kidz, Huntersville Branch

Gordon Funeral Home in Mount Pleasant

Madi, who joined our teen literary workshops on Saturdays and quickly became part of the Young Author Project.

Marnie Stoker

The entire Mount Pleasant Middle School staff for your wonderful support. <3

The entire Mount Pleasant Public Library staff for your incredible support as well - we had been showing up so often, we became part of the furniture. Not only did you notice us, you embraced us. Thank you for that.

O'Reilly's in Charlotte

My mom and dad, who are our biggest fans and an endless source of encouragement and love.

Noel Rodriguez and Taylor Maddox

Union Street Public Library in Concord

Ruth Wilkinson for not only helping us sell chocolate, but for patiently reading (and re-reading) this manuscript. I am grateful for your invaluable feedback and encouragement.

Grace Wilson

Matt and Katie Wilson

Also to my favorite person, my other half, my best friend, my husband. I love you forever.

Last but certainly not least: our editor, Miriam Spitzer Franklin, for believing in us, teaching us all, and tirelessly working to help us reach our goal. Thank you so much.

If we missed anyone in compiling this long list, please know we are as extremely grateful for you, too. <3

-Natalie Wilkinson

Praise for The Art Of Giving A Crap

"Through the Young Authors project, these students took on the challenging task of writing a book with multiple points-of-view, somehow managing to weave their stories together in a cohesive project that digs deep into difficult emotions and intense situations." -Miriam Spitzer Franklin, author of *Extraordinary* and *Emily Out Of Focus*

"Reading a book where voices are loud through written word is a sign of something you don't want to put down." -Molly Grantham, 4x Emmy winner

"*The Art of Giving A Crap* transcends the boundaries of a mere story; it emerges as an essential tool for parents, grandparents, educators, and librarians alike, designed to spark and guide profound conversations about the intricate realities of teenage life."
-Suzie Housley, Midwest Book Review

"This is a must-read for adults and teens. It's powerful and carries a message that must be heard. It's worthy of all the stars in the sky." -Carol Thompson, *Readers' Favorite*

"Be warned - this is a hard-hitting emotional rollercoaster and might open your eyes to what the teens around you

face every day...Captivating, compelling, and highly recommended reading." -Anne-Marie Reynolds, *Readers'
Favorite*

"Author Natalie Wilkinson and the Young Author Project
have brilliantly captured the authentic voices of teens
today in this highly engaging book, making the characters'
struggles deeply relatable and engaging for young people
and their families everywhere to connect to." -K.C. Finn,
Readers' Favorite

"The writing style is consistent with the age of its first-
person narrative and, overall, I think this is a solid read for
those looking for a story with extra depth. Recommended."
-Asher Syed, *Readers' Favorite*

"Young Author Project knows how to create a book that will
hold readers' interest and take them on a rollercoaster ride
of emotions. Social issues can be tricky, but the authors
approached these in the right way...I was so deeply affected
by this story that I doubt I will forget the events the authors
described." -Courtnee Turner Hoyle, *Readers' Favorite*

...and many more on Amazon.com.

I

Lucy Mae Clark

1

THE FASHIONISTA

T*hat's me – Lucy Mae Clark: social climber who lives on the Honor Roll and probationary member of the*

popular girls' group at Fountain View Middle School. Come on, I'm practically a shoo-in. (I hope…)

2

The First Day of School

My door creaks. I think nothing of it because my brain is still half-asleep. My mother attempts to walk in quietly, but she has never been the best at that. Especially not with the twins in tow.

She seems bright and smiling today, accompanied by the two smaller-looking blobs. With sudden force, the blobs bounce on the top of my mattress, leaving nothing but cold air under my comforter. They use my bed as a trampoline, nearly knocking my most prized possession to the ground, my uPhone Pro Max with extra storage.

Instinctively, I make the dive and rescue it before it falls. I cannot afford breaking another phone - my parents would kill me. My eyes slowly become more awake and clear, or at least as clear as they could be considering my glasses are still sitting in the same place on my oak nightstand.

"Hi, Lucy!" my chipper little brother calls out a little too loudly.

"Go away Leo," I hiss. I'm trying to keep my cool since he's not being *that* annoying. Besides, Mom is standing right there.

"Your bed is bouncy," Lexi's gentle voice coos.

Lexi is sweet, and that makes it hard to be mad at her, yet all I want to do is snap at everyone and go back to bed. I reach out for my glasses. Though the kids look blurry, I can still tell they're in their PJs. Lexi looks like she has on her pink skirt and white frilly shirt. I also recognize Leo's hamburger t-shirt and checkered shorts through the blur - he practically lives in those.

Before I can reach my glasses, Leo snatches them away from the nightstand and runs around the room like a tiny version of the Dart from Cliffhanger Comics.

I hear thuds and bumps in surround sound from him knocking everything on my shelves to the pink carpet below.

He giggles like a madman the entire time (not that he isn't already deranged)."Woohoo!!!!" he yips.

I cringe, imagining my glasses trailing precariously from his sticky red fist.

Finally, Mom intervenes. "Leo and Lexi, can you head downstairs and get what you want from the fridge to put in your strawberry smoothies?"

"B-but MOM-!" sputters Leo.

"If I hear one breath of back talk then there will be no Danny Cheetah during breakfast!"

"But. But. But-!" Lexi rebuts.

Mom raises an eyebrow. "Is that back talk I hear?"

"No, ma'am." Lexi looks down, unsuccessfully hiding her despair.

Mom turns to me. "It's getting late, Lucy Mae. Let's go."

I robotically rise and pick up my glasses, which fortunately were dumped onto my mattress. I glance at the clock. A cold streak of panic in my belly confirms that Mom is right - I'm running out of time. *Why* does eighth grade have to start so early?!

I quickly brush my teeth, wash my hands, and pop in my contacts. I haven't even started my FreshGirl skincare routine. It's five steps, which is not even close to being enough - I mean, my friends use the Ballanshine skincare routine, which is ten steps! What are you supposed to tell people when everyone else is doing the ten-step and I'm barely scraping by with five!?

3

Rushing

I try my best to get through the routine without rushing. (Rushing pulls on the skin, which leads to wrinkles.)

With my fresh face, I kick off my house slippers and dive into my closet. There's still so much to do:

1. OUTFIT
2. MAKEUP AND HAIR
3. BREAKFAST

OUTFIT

I need to decide on the color. I'm thinking purple with some pink maybe. I walk to my closet and sigh. *Mom promised she would color code my closet, and she never did. I mean, I get you're busy and don't have time but come on, how am I supposed to find clothes if they're all over the place?!*

Ooh, wait a sec.

I hold up a hanger and examine its contents. They're polyester, but these darkish lavender pants are cute and they go with this top. I hold up another hanger. It bears

a crocheted sweater with beautiful purple stripes. I'm lucky enough that they were directly beside each other.
Crisis averted.

The outfit is not even the most important part, though. Without a doubt, makeup and hair are DEFINITELY the most important parts of getting ready for school. Without them, you can't even pretend to be popular. I mean, who's going to take me seriously if I don't look AMAZING all the time?

MAKEUP AND HAIR

I wish my makeup routine was a little longer, but it will have to do for now because it's all my mom and dad will let me buy. If I make the "A" Honor Roll, I might be able to persuade them to take me to Adora (they have all the top-dollar makeup) for my birthday, but it's still a slim chance. I've had my eye on the Adora+ line, which is 100% organic, extra volumizing, AND vegan.

My hair is simple: Straighten, Pony, then Accessory. I quickly sweep my hair up and tuck back the strays.
Perfect.

A quick glance at the clock on my vanity and my breath catches.

8:35.

I'm seriously running late. Before I can look any further, something on the floor catches my eye. That little SNOT knocked my makeup bag onto the floor and STEPPED on it!

This is going to be bad.

I roll my eyes upward, letting out an uneasy breath.

Please, no...

I pick up my makeup bag, and - of course. Not only has my liquid eyeliner spilled all over everything, but my powder broke, too. The inside of my bag looks like an oil spill in the middle of the desert. All my lip gloss tubes are buried in black, goopy gunk, and *forget* about the mascara. How am I supposed to do my makeup now?

UGHHHH!!!!

Could things get any worse than a luck-of-the-draw outfit, a barely passable skincare routine, and an egregious lack of makeup? I guess I'll just use what I have so I can eat breakfast, but I am definitely *not* going to look as good as I did on the first day of last school year.

BREAKFAST

Even though I'm feeling pretty sorry for myself, I know I don't have time for that. I zip up my spine, flash my brightest practice smile, and pad lightly downstairs from my second-story bedroom. Yes, the girls are definitely going to pick on me for this, but I have to keep my poker face up and start to think of comebacks to defend myself with.

My siblings have already started on their strawberry milkshakes and pancakes. They're happily watching their tablet.

I move closer to see their screen. "Hey guys, what are you watching?"

Lexi looks up at me with a sweet smile. "Danny Cheetah, do you wanna watch it with us?"

I want to say no, but how could I when I'm looking at her hopeful blue eyes and tiny outstretched hand? I'm not completely heartless. "Sure Lexi, but only for a few minutes."

Maybe this will help me forget how utterly crap this morning has been.

"Thank you, Lucy!" She leaps out of her seat and dances

around happily. With a few taps on the tablet, she projects the show onto the TV.

All heads in the room swivel upward at the big screen.

I chuckle and grab a smoothie from the fridge. (It's my low-fat milkshake alternative.) The plastic lid gives a satisfying crack when I twist it off. The cold chalky liquid crashes into my lip. It's not as good as the kids' strawberry milkshakes, but if I didn't watch what I ate, I'd never fit in my clothes.

I watch as the eponymous feline comes onto the screen and almost choke on my smoothie. My hand immediately covers my mouth. My eyes grow as wide as saucers and dart away.

He has no PANTS on!

Realizing I didn't say that out loud, I repeat it: "Danny Cheetah has no pants on!"

Leo looks at me like I'm stupid. "He's a CHEETAH."

"Well, his *mom* is wearing pants!" I point out.

Lexi giggles. "Are you gonna tell Harper?"

I clear my throat and smile at her, taking another sip of my smoothie. "Yeah, probably."

My best friend Harper LOVES Lexi because she's always wanted a sibling. Back when we became best friends, she unofficially adopted Lexi as her little sister. They still text each other a lot (Lexi does it with my phone), probably even more than with me. Even though the twins are still very young, they're smart. It's been surprising to me how fast little kids pick up on technology, especially my precocious 6-year old siblings. Nobody had to teach Lexi how to nab my phone and send text messages. Leo automatically gravitated toward streaming video and learned how to search for things he wanted to learn.

The under-dressed wildcat sings sweetly from the TV

screen, "Hey, Meow Meow!" I laugh and shake my head.

There's no way to unsee it, now or ever.

"I should call you that, Lexi - Meow Meow," I joke.

Lexi's face immediately lights up. Anything even close to sisterly bonding makes her as giddy as a kid at the theme park.

I quickly repent. I don't ACTUALLY want to call her that.

Lexi's bright eyes dim a bit when she reads my body language.

Now I feel like a jerk.

Leo turns to look at us and gags. "You guys are weird," he mumbles, turning back to the TV.

I hug Lexi in a feeble attempt to make her feel better. "I have to go now Lex, I'm late."

"OK," she grins. "You're so pretty, Lucy."

My heart melts. *Why can't Leo be that nice?* "Thank you, Lexi."

She skips away contentedly. "Welcome!"

Leo gives Lexi a hurt look. "Hey, where are you going?" With knit eyebrows, Leo announces, "I have to go get ready too!" before following her down the hall.

II

Asher Gryphon

4

Music

Mom and Dad's shouts fill the house. They used to scare me, but they just make me angry now. All they do is hate each other, and it fills the house. I hate feeling this way; losing control never ends well, especially with Dad.

I do the only thing I know to kill time until the bus gets here. I walk over to my stereo and pick through my brother's old CDs. I choose my favorite album by Perturbed and crank the volume until my parents' voices are completely drowned out. I collapse onto my mattress, staring at the dust-covered ceiling fan. Nobody can hear my voice singing along from the back of my throat. This is what peace feels like. Song after song, I eventually drift off to sleep.

My dreams are just getting interesting when Dad's harsh yell slices them open. "Asher, if you don't turn down that music, believe me, you do NOT wanna know what I'll do!" he snarls.

I open my eyes to painful sunlight. "Yes, Sir, I'm very

sorry." I reply politely so as to not anger him more. I slide off the bed, step over to the stereo, and turn down the volume.

Mom pops her head into my room. "What happened to those headphones that you bought?" Her speech is slurred.

I look at her.

She's staring past me at a distant spot on the wall.

"They broke, I'm not sure how though." I lie, preventing myself from saying that Dad broke them in one of his fits.

I watch Mom stumble away down the long, dark hall toward her room. She is drunk off of her mind, again. I go to her just in time to catch her mid-stumble. I guide her back to the chair in my room so she doesn't collapse onto the floor. I hate when she gets drunk.

I glance at her and grab a trash bag.

She is practically turning green in front of me. I hold her hair back as she vomits, chunky green and brown and slime. Drops of it flick onto my socks. It's absolutely disgusting and almost makes me puke, too, but moments like these that are the only times I can tell that she needs me.

When she finally finishes heaving, I tie up the trash bag and take it out back. I lift the glinting metal lid off the trash can. A fat raccoon streaks out from inside it, hisses, and takes off into the woods. The wild bushes quickly enclose behind it, shivering. I'm almost inclined to follow, but I let the storm door slap me back inside the house. I make sure to grab her a glass of water before heading back to my room. I hand her the water and wait for her to say something to break the silence.

"Asher." Mom begins.

"Yes?" I reply.

She hands me a small box. "I thought you might like these.

They will stop you from consistently annoying your father and I." She does not bother to stop the anger seeping into her voice.

"Oh, um, thank you," I whisper as I look at my new wireless earbuds.

I go to the living room and sit on the couch, watching out the window for the bus. I connect the earbuds to my phone and start my favorite playlist. My anxiety melts away as the music plays.

Drowning myself in music is the one way I can feel alive again; no more fear, anger, or sadness plague my mind. The emptiness inside no longer feels so empty when the music plays. Emotions are definitely not my thing, but music makes the bad ones go away. Even if it's only temporary, it provides the relief I need to persevere.

I see the school bus pull up and heave to a stop outside the gate. I go outside to catch it before it leaves.

III

Lucy

5

Only Babies Wear Bows

8:57.

I'm loaded up with my handbag and my first-day-of-school binder. I'm ready to go.

The bell rings at 9:00. Gah. Less than five minutes.

"Mom!" my voice echoes from the foyer.

Mom calls from the next room. "Yes, Lucy?"

"Let's go!"

"Oh honey, your dad is taking you today. You know, it's the twins' first day of school and–"

I put a hand up. "Whatever, Mom. DADDY!"

I smile as he walks quickly into the room.

"Yes, Pumpkin?" he replies.

"Time to go," I urge.

"Of course, Princess," he says.

I nod and follow him to the front door.

Lexi runs after me. "Lucy!"

I stop and turn around to face her. Lexi's pink shirt and new jeans make a good outfit. "Make it quick, squirt," I say.

Lexi takes a big breath and asks, "Can I borrow your pink

bow with the rhinestones?"

I cringe.

I love that bow. Maybe it's time for me to grow out of it. Only babies wear bows.

I nod regally. "Yes, you may."

She beams. "Thank you, Lu! You're the best!"

"I know." I step out the door after Daddy and into the car, headed for a new stage of maturity.

6

THE INFLUENCER

"OH WAIT! *I'M* MONICA!!"

Monica Jersey. She is the newest member of our friend group and is the most annoying. She is not the brightest and honestly, I don't know why she is even in the friend group. I also kind of do. It's because she'll do whatever Meghan wants her to. She's also really pretty (not as pretty as Meghan and Harper, though.) She is basically like a social media influencer because of the amount of followers she has. It's actually pretty cool. I still don't understand how she's passing her classes, though.

7

Late

It's already 9:07.

Late. I'm late. This is NOT good.

I approach the grand front desk emblazoned with FOUNTAIN VIEW MIDDLE SCHOOL in huge block letters. The lady looks at me from behind her computer screen and says, "Good morning. May I help you?"

"Hi, good morning," I reply. "I'm running late today, sorry." I smile like one of those embarrassed emojis with the sweat drop. I don't want to catch *too* much attention on the first day.

The school secretary looks down through her spectacles at the monitor to check the time, then points to the digital kiosk at the far end of the counter. "Alright, punch in your info and print out a pass." She swivels around in her chair and opens a drawer to search for a paper.

I nod like a bobble head. On the kiosk, I tap the screen and follow the prompts. The pass prints out like a ticket at the movie theater.

I wish this was the movie theater.

A familiar figure enters my peripheral vision, and I glance over.

It squawks, "OH MY GOSH! THIS IS ABSOLUTELY SUCH A COINCIDENCE!!"

Oh great. It's Monica. Not such a coincidence, seeing as we go to the same school.

I grin fakely and play along. "OH MY GOSH, TOTALLY! I CANNOT BELIEVE WE ARE BOTH IN THE OFFICE AT THE SAME TIME." I cringe at my own words.

She narrows her green eyes and I take one step back. (She's a little on the crazy side, in case you couldn't tell.) "Why are *you* late anyway? You totally kept Monica waiting."

I stare at her, trying to make sense of what she just said.

She stares back, looking just as confused. It gradually dawns on her. "Oh WAIT! *I'M* MONICA!!" She laughs hysterically and I give her a small smile.

Bless her heart.

"Yep. I was a little confused." She flashes a perfect smile.

Maybe she got in the popular group because of her spotless pearly white teeth.

"Well, I totally meant Meghan," Monica clarifies.

I gawk at her. "Meghan was worried about *me*?"

Monica grins. "Well, not like *totally* worried, but like *kinda* worried – if you know what I mean. Like she wants to know what's taking you so long."

At that moment, the front desk lady swivels back around in her chair to face us. She hands Monica a blue form. "Here's your paperwork, Monica. Have your parents fill this in and bring it back tomorrow." She looks at me and adds, "Go ahead to class, both of you."

Monica takes the sheet from her without saying anything.

I nod and say to her, "Thanks! I mean, thank you, ma'am." It's hard to keep my composure.

Meghan was worried. About me!

Monica skips to the classroom. Though she looks ridiculous, I feel like skipping too.

Maybe this will finally be the year where everyone likes me.

8

THE QUEEN BEE AND THE FAMOUS

THE QUEEN BEE
Meghan Gardener is the most popular girl in the whole school. She's literally a teenage icon. She's been on the cover of *Teen Girl Now* magazine and is the prettiest girl I've ever met. She's kinda smart, but not smarter than Harper. No one dares to disrespect Meghan because of the line of boys dying to do her bidding. Say one wrong thing and they'll be waiting to kill you (not even being dramatic.)

THE FAMOUS
Harper Cimmaron is kind of my best friend. She's absolutely amazing but most importantly now that we're in eighth grade, she's Meghan's right hand. She's also CRAZY smart and can do anything she sets her mind to!

9

Peregrine Falcon

Binder in hand, I cautiously enter the 8th grade hall for the first time. The atmosphere is buzzing with nervous energy, being the first day.

I'm still gushing inside.

Meghan was asking about me.

"Lucy." Meghan's voice snaps my thoughts in half, commanding my attention from across the hall. She's leaning against the lockers in a white skirt, pink top, and perfect white sneakers. Her hair and makeup are flawless; she looks like a supermodel with her brand-new Valentina handbag. She's flanked by Harper and a few other girls. Meghan is looking right at me, so the others are, too.

"Meghan! Hi!" I smile and giggle nervously.

Her crystal eyes give me a once over.

I feel like a fish being watched by a peregrine falcon.

"Why were you late?" she asks.

I stumble for words. "Well um- I had to do my makeup."

"Hm." The eyes streak up to my face and pause, calculating.

I stand stock still, barely breathing.

Her blue eyes flash with realization. She smirks, but not her usual mean one. It looks like a mix of pity and sarcasm. "You don't have any liquid eyeliner on."

"Yeah, it spilled." I cringe and give her a small, helpless smile.

Luckily, Harper sees the exchange and comes to my rescue. She walks over with such a genuine smile that it warms my pounding heart.

I greet my rescuer. "Hey, Harper."

"Hey, girl." Harper gives me a fashionably tiny wave and slips some liquid eyeliner into my hand.

Meghan always makes me nervous; she's so pretty and popular. I want her to like me so much. I have since elementary school - she is everything I want to be.

Harper looks behind her at an unusually rhythmic squeak coming toward us. Upon realizing its source, her eyes narrow and she sighs loudly.

It's Monica, who is just now arriving. She's literally skipping toward us.

Harper proceeds to pick on the sleeve of her orange sweater to try and save face as Monica attracts all eyes in the vicinity. Giggles bubble up around Meghan, who grins wickedly.

Since I was walking like a civilized person, I got to the 8th grade hall a lot faster. Well, to be fair, I more like speed-walked.

Harper and I exchange a quick look.

As Monica catches up with us, I study her carefully.

Her teeth are not worth a spot in this group. She must have blackmail on Meghan or something.

"HEY GUYS - OR GIRLS!" Monica is giggling hysterically

like she actually said something funny. She turns to me. "Hey again, Lucy!"

I smile patiently like I do with Leo when his brain fails.

"Hi, Meghan!" she fawns.

Meghan blesses Monica with a saccharine smile.

Monica turns to Harper excitedly. "Was your summer absolutely FANTABULOUS?!"

Harper blinks slowly. "Yep." She gives Monica an annoyed close-lipped smile.

Absolutely. Fantabulous. Seriously?

The warning bell boops, flooding the halls.

The crowd thins out into different classes.

Harper and I hang back for a second. I shush deviously into her ear, hoping it's funny. "You've gotta give Monica some credit Harper, it must be hard being that dumb."

Harper giggles and nods. "Yeah, you're right." She moves to catch up to Meghan but then stops to say, "I like your sweater, Lucy."

My heart explodes. "Thanks Harper, I really like yours too."

She grins and struts over to Meghan leaving me on the side next to... Monica.

Darn it.

It's okay. Being in this group is worth it. I walk close behind them with Monica, who is talking rapidly about the newest episode of *Keeping Up With Those Kardamoms*.

Harper exchanges tiny goodbye waves with Meghan at the doorway.

I make sure they see me grin.

Meghan takes her heavy presence with her. Everyone in the area visibly relaxes.

Since Harper's in my home room, everything will be okay. She and I go way back, so she's like a bonus sister that's actually my age. If I were in this Homeroom with Meghan, I'd be on pins and needles the entire time.

IV

Asher

10

Free Lunch

I grab the desk in the back corner before anyone else does. I feel safer when I don't have anyone behind me.

I glance around the classroom, taking in the details. There are colorful science posters everywhere. Some of them are about cheese. There's a T-Rex model sitting on top of the cabinets and another poster on the wall with the rules on it.

My Homeroom teacher is an odd man, but he seems relatively good-natured. Seems easily distracted, though - he's been caught up with his clipboard and walking around the classroom for the past 15 minutes.

A few of the popular girls walk in. One of them looks at me and they laugh.

I pull my hood closer over my face and keep scanning the room.

I see Marcus sitting a few rows away. He's probably the only person I might consider a friend.

I wonder if he remembers me. Probably not. I wouldn't if I were him.

When we were in third grade, he and I used to throw bottle caps at the wall to see who could get the closest to a wasp's nest without hitting it. Yeah, we got stung a couple of times doing that.

Before I can fully drift off in my thoughts, I hear the teacher call my name. "Asher Gryphon?"

"Yeah," I reply.

"He can speak?" one of the popular girls chuckles.

The teacher walks over and hands me a huge free lunch application from the front office.

I quickly stuff it in my bookbag.

The snickers continue around me.

V

Lucy

11

Homeroom

I turn to Harper and Monica. "Sit together?"

Monica answers with a squeal and Harper nods, stifling a chuckle at the weird boy in the corner. We pick three seats in the middle of the room. It's always good to be the center of attention, so I eye the seat in the very center of the group. Since she's higher up on the food chain, I ask Harper if she wants to sit there.

She shakes her head no and smiles generously. "This is the perfect way to work your way up."

I nod excitedly. She means working my way up in the, well, order of things. Meghan will probably always be the undisputed Queen Bee, but when you're in middle school, being liked and respected is the most enviable asset anyone can ever dream of.

Then I see someone I never thought I would see again. Marcus! I want to say hi to him, but Meghan doesn't like him very much, so I keep my distance. She always makes fun of him for being too nerdy.

The last time I saw him was in fifth grade, when we were on the Book Warriors team. He was the best, lightning quick, and had a great memory. We studied together all year, and honestly, he's really fun to hang out with. He's grown so much! His brown hair is FLUFFY now, and he looks kind of...really cute?!

Oh my gosh.

I don't say hello. Instead, I look around the room, taking in as many hazy details as I can.

My eyes land on the boy with a black hoodie sitting in the back corner. He's shaded from the fluorescent light, which is dim in where he's sitting. I wave to be polite and he turns away.

How rude. Whatever.

12

Can't

"It's uncertain how he could have crammed his muscles under his bright yellow suit..."

"**H**ELLO CLASS!" bellows the teacher.

The room goes quiet.

For the first time, we actually stop to pay attention to what he looks like - he's standing in the doorway beaming at all of us, and he makes no sense. He's clearly older judging by the wrinkles around his eyes, but he's also strangely massive and looks like a pro wrestler. It's uncertain how he could have crammed his muscles under his bright yellow suit. He has crazy gray hair like Einstein that brushes across the top of the door frame.

We're not sure what to do and all think it might be a good idea to just listen to what he has to say. Everyone settles into their seats, watching him.

In a strong, confident voice, he continues. His words punch us from underneath his thick mustache. "My name is Mr. Cheezers. I'm your Homeroom teacher and we're going to have a great year!"

His smile is so genuine, I can't even bring myself to laugh at him.

"To start us off, we will go around the room and have everyone say your name, favorite color, and the number of siblings you have. Let's start with you, Lucy Mae."

I flash a brilliant smile. "My name is Lucy Mae, my favorite color is pink-"

COUGH COUGH *COUGH*

Is someone seriously coughing?

I swivel around and fix my glare on its origin...*that* boy in the corner.

"Sorry," he chokes out. *COUGH COUGH*

Is he <u>laughing</u> at me?!

He turns away, beet red under his hood.

That helps me. I smile again, turning to the class. "My name is Lucy Mae, my favorite color is *pink,* and I have two younger siblings, Leo and Lexi."

Harper smiles at the mention of my younger sister.

"Lovely," Mr. Cheezers says with a smile. "That's exactly how I want you to do it, everyone. Next should be..."

He pushes his reading glasses up and peers at the attendance sheet. "Harper Cimmaron."

Harper smiles and flips her chestnut hair. "I'm Harper, my favorite color is purple, and I'm kind of an only child."

The teacher laughs a loud cheerful laugh that makes me smile despite myself.

"What is a *kind of* only child?" He grins.

I get the feeling that he's somewhat mocking her, while also genuinely wanting to know the answer. I decide that I like him.

Harper smiles and laughs a little. "Well, I have an unofficial little sister, so that makes me *kind of* an only child. She told me yesterday that she has *two* sisters, including me." She looks at me with a slightly embarrassed smile.

Apparently, nothing could have made Mr. Cheezers happier. He smiles widely and his eyes twinkle. "That's adorable," he says.

Harper laughs sheepishly.

Is she talking about Lexi? Well, I don't know who else she could be talking about. When did Lexi see Harper? Why wasn't I told about this? I'll have to talk to Mom about letting me in on these things.

My mind goes off on a tangent for way too long before I suddenly snap back to Earth.

I've missed most of the information the other students

were sharing about themselves.

Mr. Cheezers is at the end of the list. "Asher?"

I look at the boy who has been rude all morning, now shaking his head.

The teacher frowns but nods. "That's perfectly okay. We have plenty of time for all of us to get to know each other! In addition to this being your Homeroom class, I'm also your Science teacher. I have a background in Agriculture with extensive experience in, believe it or not, cheesemaking. If you think about it, we all have experience with Agriculture because we all EAT!"

Harper and I exchange a glance. I have to bite my lip as hard as I can to keep from laughing.

I know he did not just say he makes cheese.

Mr. Cheezers continues, "We're going to be covering a lot of interesting topics in our class, including river wildlife and chemical reactions. We'll also be doing lots of fun hands-on activities. I expect that we all treat one another with respect and that we all do our best every single time we come into the classroom. When you hold yourself to high expectations, you can achieve anything you set your mind to. Another important rule: the word 'can't' is a forbidden word in my classroom."

I can feel my eyes narrow. Many others have a similar expression.

How is it even possible not to use 'can't'?

"Just don't use it – it's dishonest. With a few actual exceptions, people use the word 'can't' when they really mean 'won't' or 'I don't want to'. They'll say, 'I can't go to the mall with you because I have something else going on.' Well, you COULD go to the mall, but you are currently

UNAVAILABLE because you had a prior commitment, so you're CHOOSING to honor that. Does that make sense? Another example: if you break both your legs, then okay, you probably actually CAN'T walk until you heal, so that is a legitimate use of the word." Mr. Cheezers pauses for a moment and looks across the classroom. "Let me ask you this: can you rob a bank?"

Harper balks and says, "Of course not."

Mr. Cheezers smiles broadly. "Yes, you can."

A wave of shock passes through us all and we stare, wide-eyed.

He continues. "If you really wanted to, you could walk right up and rob the bank. The question is: is it a good idea?"

Oh. I get it now.

The atmosphere relaxes. Some of the kids shake their heads no.

"Let's just say I will not be happy if you use 'can't', so be forewarned!"

One kid's eyes go really wide and he slides down in his chair.

"Now the most important rule in my class is this: BE KIND. If you remember nothing else from what I tell you right now, remember this: you never know what someone else is going through. There could be kids in this school right now that have no idea where they're going to sleep tonight."

He pauses and looks at each of us straight in the eyes, one by one. The energy in the room hushes.

"Maybe there is a kid who doesn't know where his next meal is coming from and only eats when he gets food from school. You may have a colleague who has to go home after school and work a full-time job to help support the family.

Someone might have to take care of siblings by cooking, cleaning, and doing all the laundry because there's no adult at home."

Some of us glance around at each other, then back at him.

"So remember, what I expect from you is that you be a decent human being to others around you. It doesn't cost you anything, and it's easy. One harsh word can destroy someone's day and even linger forever. On the other hand, a kind word can give someone the encouragement they need to help them through a very dark time."

He pauses for a moment to allow us to digest his words, then says, "Go ahead and take a 7-minute break to find your locker number and start getting used to it. Store your book bags - phones included - and take only what you need for Periods 1 and 2. Each of you has your assigned lock on your desk. Do NOT lose it, or you will be charged $5.00 for a replacement. The locker number is written on the back. The bell will ring for class change at the end of 7 minutes, and you'll go to your Period 1 and 2 Elective classes. When we return for Period 3, we'll get into classroom rules and expectations."

Everyone is soon up, scattering like ants toward the door.

13

Stay Cool

I leave the room to find my locker. Meghan saunters over and leans on the one next to me. Harper and Monica listen on from their own lockers nearby.

It isn't long before the owner of the locker walks up, pointing at Meghan with an inquisitive finger. "Um excuse me. That's my locker, if I can just-"

The girl is cut off by Meghan's searing blue eyes. "I'm *using* it."

The girl backs away slowly. "Oh...Okay."

Meghan turns to me and smiles like a switch was turned on. "So, how's Homeroom?"

I nod. "It's pretty good so far. There's this really rude kid, but he doesn't seem like he'll be anybody so-"

I stop in my tracks realizing how mean that sounds. She laughs and my guilt goes away.

"Well, if you need me to take care of him for you, I can do that." A devilish grin brightens her face, which disappears behind a huge pink gum bubble.

I never knew smacking gum could sound so intimidating.

All I can muster is, "Yeah, uh, thanks Meghan. I'll let you know."

Meghan nods. "So like, you don't have my phone number do you?"

My heart begins to pound harder than it did earlier this morning. "No-Nope."

Stay cool, Lucy Mae.

Meghan holds out an expectant hand. "Well, let me see your phone."

I scramble to get it out of my pocket.

VI

Asher

Tip #1: Trust no one.

14

The uPhone 14 Pro Max

Even though I sit in the back corner, I'm good at being the first one out the door and away from everyone. I check the number on the back of my lock. I quickly find my locker, swing open the royal blue door, and toss my stuff in. My backpack is mostly empty, but I bring it to school anyway just in case I have to take something home, like a humiliating free lunch application that lets everyone know how poor I am. The lock crunches shut in my hand.

The other kids are still clumsily making their way to their lockers. Some of them are too dumb to match a number to a locker, so they get confused.

Kids are always fake, and it's always the worst on the first day. I'm already sick of them all.

The hallway is getting louder and my anxiety is rising. I realize that I won't be able to hold off the panic much longer. I turn from my locker, rush into the bathroom, and lock myself in a stall. The close walls of the bathroom stall are my safe place, where nothing can see you or sneak up behind you. It's where I can let everything that I'm feeling out of my system. I can't stop the tears from flowing, it's all too much. Too much noise, too much pain, too many problems, too many jerks, too much everything. It's the first day of school, and people are already laughing at me. I just *know* someone is going to try something to make me mad, but I *need* to stay in control. If I do anything to get in trouble, Dad will be upset and going home will be hell. I'm still healing from the last time.

I hear the bell echo throughout the halls, and I'm still in here.

Crap.

I scramble out of the stall, pump a blob of soap into my palm, and only somewhat run my hands over each other. Water drips behind me as I shake them off, leaving the bathroom.

Suddenly, I feel someone shove me out the open doorway. I stumble into the hall, but my knee catches and I fall onto *her*. Lucy Mae Clark, stupidest girl alive. I hear someone laughing in the background, most likely at me.

Everyone pauses suddenly in suspended animation - we're all watching her brand new uPhone float out of her hand. It slowly turns over in the air in an infinite somersault, then suddenly takes a fast-forward nosedive into the floor. On top of that, she stumbles and steps on it.

The crackle is unmistakable.

The hallway goes eerily quiet.

VII

Lucy

15

Inconsiderate

My phone. My precious pink prized possession, destroyed. I would rather the crunch have been my bones. Hot tears immediately start streaming down my cheeks. I can't help it. I crouch over the mess, gingerly picking up splintered pieces from the case.

Meghan takes a step back and fades away from the noise.

Harper rushes over, but I can't hear what she's saying because everything is muffled and sad. She hugs me.

Before I know it, I'm ugly crying. Not only did I lose my phone, but I lost the chance to get Meghan's number, too.

I look up and see *that boy* again. Did he seriously just knock my phone out of my hand?

I hear myself say to him, "Do you realize what you've done? Now my phone is destroyed, so you're going to have to buy me a new one. You are SO inconsiderate and –"

Too angry to make sense of anything, I stand up and push him.

VIII

Asher

16

Bad Idea

My eyes snap open and fixate on her stupid red face.

Is she doing what I think she's doing? She's really trying to <u>push</u> me right now? Bad idea. VERY bad idea.

She's yelling something stupid at me about buying her a new phone.

I don't hear her over the blood pounding in my ears. I'm trembling. My breath is getting heavy. A spark has ignited and started a deadly fire in me. It fans into a blaze and I punch the lockers once, abruptly, cutting off her insipid monologue. The tin explosion silences the hall.

One teacher comes out of the classroom, looks at us, then rushes back inside. Everyone else seems to melt away but me and this stupid girl.

Consider this a warning. Please leave me alone.

My fist stings and burns. The locker is dented and broken where I hit it.

Broken like me. Who cares, anyway. I hate this place. I despise everyone here. My older brother has the right idea, just leave.

Nobody notices a broken wretch like me, and nobody ever will. That stupid teacher is now calling the office so they can come get me.

I hear myself snarl, "Lucy, you are the biggest airhead I've ever seen in my life. That stupid phone of yours will be outdated in a year, and you can probably afford to get a new one tomorrow." Talking is the only thing keeping me from shoving her into the lockers. "I didn't mean for it to fall, and you know it. All you care about is what makes you happy no matter what it does to anyone else. I swear, you and my Mother are practically the same person!"

I instantly regret my words; she should have never known that, and now the whole school does.

Lucy now looks like someone who can't swim and has floated to the deep end of the pool.

I feel helpless and I can't control my anger anymore. I do the only thing I can think of: break something until the anger goes away. I curse out loud, exasperated, and punch the wall on the way back into the bathroom. I can barely see through the tears that want to pour out.

So much for not getting the hell kicked out of me tonight.

IX

Lucy

17

I have to stop crying

I gape at him. I didn't know this kid even spoke, much less *yelled*.

I watch him disappear into the bathroom.

I have no words.

He has literally <u>no</u> reason to cry right now.

That's when I remember my phone. I sink into a puddle on the floor, probably looking like I'm four. I tap the screen, trying to bring it back to life, but it's too cracked. The light sputters and fades.

My parents are going to kill me.

My eyes well up again and pour. My breath heaves through the tears.

Students everywhere are pulling out their phones to record, which makes it so much worse. Another friend comes and hugs me, which reminds me of my sister and makes it infinitely worse.

I *have* to stop crying NOW before this ends up getting posted.

X

Asher

18

Safe Space

Please don't find me here. Just leave me alone.

I know that's not going to happen. Officer Gruff, our school resource officer, will be here within the next few minutes. I remember how it works from all the other times in 6th and 7th grade. It wouldn't be so bad if they just kept things at school, but they'll want to call home, and Dad won't be happy when he finds out. And when Dad isn't happy, nobody else is happy, either. I just let the walls of the bathroom stall hold me close. I sit on the floor, crunching up as tightly as I can in the back corner behind the toilet.

It doesn't take long. With the hallway mostly empty, I can hear a radio buzz and crackle in the hallway, then the jingling of keys and the squeak of rubber shoes coming toward the bathroom. It's the resource officer, right on schedule. His black shoes stop in front of my stall and he knocks roughly on the door. "Alright, let's go. We're going to the office."

I open the door and come out. I don't want to look at him or talk, I just go with him.

Why can't things just be normal? I wish I could close my eyes and be in a house with great parents that spend money on food and their kids instead of getting high. They would actually love us and would be nice to us. My sister would be healthy and happy, and our home would be a peaceful place of rest.

I know *that's* just a fantasy, though.

* * *

The officer drops me off at the ISS classroom and walks across the hall to the front office where Principal Terry is.

I take my place in the back corner. I can see them both through the glass talking very expressively. They glance at me every so often, so obviously they're talking about me. I feel as though they're judges deciding my sentence and punishment.

Just please don't call home.

19

Verdict

I think I hear the ISS (Indoor School Suspension) coordinator mumbling something at me about completing my classwork in the background, but that's not my priority right now. I'm busy watching what's going on across the hall. I hear her sigh loudly and start typing. I've been here many times before; she's probably emailing all my teachers for paper copies of my classwork.

I watch them check the cameras and stupidly, I dare to hope.

Maybe I won't get punished if they see the truth. This would be over with and I could just go back to class.

I know who shoved me. It was Christian Clawthorne. Ever since 6th grade, it's always been Christian Clawthorne. He's the one that shoved me into Lucy, which caused her to drop her own phone and step on it. I barely had anything to do with it.

*Please just let **them** see that.*

It's hard to see the security footage from way back here. It's just showing flickering, blurry gray and white images picked up from the cameras. Anybody that was there saw that she obviously stomped her own phone.

Principal Terry leans into the screen, squinting through his glasses. It's actually looking like maybe he's seeing some reason...

Wait. Why is his posture changing? Why is he looking right at me?

I watch him let out a long sigh and glance back at Officer Gruff, who is looking on without saying a word.

Now Principal Terry is walking over to the ISS room with a stern look on his face.

Seriously? I'm in trouble?

The door creaks open and he motions for me to come out into the hallway with him.

My limbs are heavy, but I comply. I have no choice.

Principal Terry's brow is red and sweaty, and a strong smell like almonds is coming off him. It's a little bit strange. Then he starts to speak. "Asher, we saw on the cameras that you were horse-playing with Christian and ended up breaking Lucy's phone. Ms. Martin told me what you said to Lucy in the hall. Not only that, you dented a locker and punched holes in the wall. I know you know this is not acceptable."

I spit back before I can stop myself, "WHAT?! Horse-playing? I was just trying to get out of the BATHROOM. Now *I'm* the one who broke her phone? And as far as I know, *Principal Terry,* I actually punched one hole in the wall, not that it makes it acceptable. If you want to accuse me, do it correctly and honestly. What I said to Lucy wasn't even that bad - it was the truth. It shouldn't affect the consequence - it's only words and she'll get over it!"

Principal Terry acts like he didn't hear a word I just said.

He continues, "I'm going to have to write you up and call home."

I knew it.

My stomach catches fire. Principal Terry motions for me to follow him back to the office. There's nothing left for me to do but follow, like a lamb to the slaughter.

I knew this was going to happen.

He tries to call my mom, but he doesn't know that her phone was disconnected three months ago. She'll never update it because the government check isn't enough to cover both their drugs and phone bills.

Maybe the Principal will give up and I'll catch a break for once.

I don't even notice I'm sitting down until I hear the cruel clicks and hum of the office phone as he tries another number. I already know the obnoxiously cheerful keypad tones are singing my Dad's number. My chest feels tight.

Maybe he won't pick up.

Of course, Dad picks up. The phone is on speaker, making the fire in my stomach worse.

The principal tells my father his version of the incident, lying about how the broken phone was my fault because I was horse-playing, emphasizing how I went on to punch a locker and the wall, making a hole in it. Of course, he's sending me home for the day, so Dad will have to come pick me up.

After a long pause, Dad's voice croaks. "Is Asher there with you?"

"Yes he is. Would you like to speak with him?" offers the Principal.

And he says the worst thing possible, "Yes. Would you mind taking me off speaker, please?"

Principal Terry obeys and hands me the receiver. Both he

and Officer Gruff leave the room, listening just outside the door.

Dad yells so loudly that I'm sure everyone within 10 feet could hear him. I have to hold the receiver back a bit. I could swear there is air puffing at me from the receiver.

"Did I really raise a nutjob who thinks he can just destroy whatever the hell he wants without any consequences!? You're a worthless screw-up. Lesson learned: don't have any more kids. I hope Mia doesn't turn out like you. Don't you dare ruin your little sister, don't ever put Duncan's little ideas into her head..."

His voice trails off, I just can't listen anymore.

I'm not sure how much more of this I can take.

Dad pauses for a heady, alcohol-laden breath. A moment passes, and I wonder if he's forgotten what he was talking about. I think he has.

"You're gonna get it when you come home. You're a disappointment to this whole family. What was I yelling for - oh, right - we don't have money to waste on a stupid phone! Guess what, pal, YOU'RE going to have to get a job and WORK to pay off that girl's phone! I'm not going to help you."

Ha. Cute. As if he ever helped me do anything.

Dad coughs, "I need my whiskey."

I really just want to say, *No, you don't. That "beloved" whiskey that you need so much is what makes you such an absolute waste of space.* If I were stupid enough to say that, this whole thing will get a whole lot worse than it already is.

He concludes, "Tell the principal I'm coming to get you."

With nothing much else to say, I just say, "Bye, Dad."

The Principal has no idea what he's just done, and I hate

him so much for it. He's the reason my whole body is going to get crushed again when I get home today. Maybe I'll get lucky and I won't wake up this time. I tuck my feet up under me and roll up into as tight a ball as I can.

The tears bubble over, hot, indignant, and utterly power-less.

This one is going to be bad. Worse than usual.

I hate my life. I wish I could just stay at school.

Maybe I can hide in the bathroom and wait until they close the building. I could sneak around the custodians and sleep over. Nobody would notice I was gone.

XI

Lucy

20

Zombie Princess

From my place on the floor, I finally start to feel my breath stretching my ribs. Cold air fills my insides, and the skin on my face feels tight. I have been feeling better since Mr. Gruff escorted the boy around the corner toward the main office.

I don't care. Serves him right.

My eyes well up again. Harper hugs me again and Monica joins in. Meghan is still conspicuously absent.

We're all pretty much skipping class, and we know it, but this is an *emergency*. I know I'm probably overreacting a little, but I can't stop crying. My parents are going to be so upset with me. It's the second phone I've broken this month. I may not get another one this time.

Mr. Cheezers suddenly comes out of his classroom and looks at us all in surprise. He must be hard of hearing if he didn't hear that locker pop. "Lucy, are you okay? What's going on?"

Harper stands up to address him.

Meghan reappears in front of her, fixing Mr. Cheezers

with a pitiful look. "Mister…" She stops and peers at his door, looking for his name.

"Cheezers," Harper whispers forward into her ear.

Meghan glances back at Harper, raising an eyebrow but not missing a beat. She looks back up at him with shimmering pools of blue. "Mister…Cheezers, Lucy Mae is *not* okay. In fact, someone single-handedly just tried to *ruin her life*."

Mr. Cheezers' eyebrows float upward. The corner of his mouth twitches the tiniest bit underneath his thick mustache. He crouches down next to me and addresses me. "Ruin your life, huh?"

All this attention is too much. I can barely manage a whisper: "They broke my phone."

Mr. Cheezers looks over his twitchy whiskers at the cracked treasure on the floor, then looks in the direction of the bathroom where the boy ran. "Hm."

"*And* he knocked her down," says Harper with a scowl.

"*And* bullied her, *and* said mean things," adds Monica.

Mr. Cheezers sighs. "Do you know who did it? Are you hurt?"

I shake my head. I can't turn him in if I don't know his name.

What is his name?!

The tears resurface and I can feel myself turning red. Mr. Cheezers sighs again, shaking his head.

"Well, phones can always be replaced, and you're not hurt. It looks like you've taken a breather, so get going to your next class." He looks at Meghan.

"Oh, we were just on our way, Mr. Cheezers. Would it be okay if we go to the restroom for just a minute before we go?" She flashes him her best award-winning smile.

He sighs and glances at his watch. "Alright, alright. I have to get back to class. Get going." He disappears, and the girls lead me to the bathroom.

"I'm so sorry that happened, Lucy Mae." Monica really does look sorry, so I nod my thanks, but I know she's already uploaded a video of it. That video she took will probably go viral because of her thousands of followers.

There are two good things about Monica: she's really pretty, like I said before, and also she's great at catching people at their worst. It's good for entertainment, but really bad if you're the victim.

Harper takes it upon herself to retort every single one of the boy's comments for me. "You are *not* an airhead! A year is a long time to wait for a new phone and just because you can afford it and he can't *doesn't* mean he can break your stuff! That's another thing: he *did* mean to break it - he just came flying at you like a *savage!* Just because he has *mommy* issues doesn't mean he can bully my *best friend!*"

I stare at her, probably with the same expression Lexi has when she looks at Danny Cheetah.

She said best friend. I thought Meghan was her best friend now.

She hovers a hand over my face, shushing over me with pity. "I feel so bad - he made your makeup run."

I cringe as I touch the black lines running down my face. I turn to look at Meghan. "I probably look like a zombie."

She smiles and I see something friendly in her face. "Zombie *Princess*," she corrects me.

I laugh.

Her smile expands radiantly. "You can use some of my makeup if you want. I always bring extra. We can't have you looking like *that.*"

Did I hear that right?

While it's true that what's-his-name ruined my life, *I'm also using Meghan's makeup!* I sigh.

Adora+ makeup on the first day of school?

I gush, "That would be great, thanks Meghan."

She dips into her handbag, searching. "Of course, Lucy Mae, that's what *friends* do."

Was that squeal in my head or out loud?

21

Car Riders

At the end of the day, Harper and I walk to the car rider line, like we always did in 6th and 7th grade. Everything is still the same. The car rider line is basically a conga line of parents picking up their kids, drive-thru style, from a huge group of kids waiting in front of the school. There are several teachers and the resource officer out here with us, supervising and directing traffic.

Mom and Dad are both here to pick me up today. Harper and I watch my parents' black sedan inch closer from our place in the mass of floating satellite book bags.

The minivans and SUVs before them gulp up their kids and leave one by one.

We spot Harper's car, too, which is four behind mine. Lexi's hand pops out of the back window of my car, waving frantically.

My family pulls up and Harper smiles cooly at me, hanging back with the other kids. "Bye, Lu."

My car rolls out past the car rider line, away from the crowd. The passenger side window rolls down to reveal Mom in sunglasses. "Hey Harper," my mom calls cheerfully.

Harper runs to my car like she was waiting for that. "Hi, Mrs. Clark!" She sticks her head in the window. "Hey, Mr. Clark!"

Dad waves from the driver's seat with a smile. "We miss seeing you around, Harper!"

She grins. "I miss you guys, too!"

Lexi tumbles out of the car and leaps onto Harper, hugging her like her life depended on it. Like she didn't see her just yesterday.

Harper sings, "HEY MEOW MEOW!"

I feel a sudden stab of betrayal. Just because *I* didn't want to call her that doesn't mean *Harper* can. I harrumph into the car and shut the door loudly. "Hey Dad, I've had a long day, let's get home."

He answers, "Okay Princess. Hang in there for just one second. Help your sister buckle in."

Harper gently places Lexi back in her booster seat. She croons, "Bye, Lexi!"

Lexi chirps from her seat, "Bye Harper, I love you!"

"I love you more, Meow Meow!" Harper backs away, calling through the cracked window.

I reach over and buckle Lexi back in, a little rougher than I mean to.

Lexi's eyes are shining anyway. I haven't seen her that happy with me in a long time. I fight the scowl threatening to appear on my face.

"See you later, alligator!" Harper calls to Dad.

He nods, remembering how we all used to say that to each other. He calls back, "Bye-bye, butterfly!"

Harper turns to look in the direction of a honk and flits

away, smiling all the way to her parents' car.

The scowl takes over my face and the feeling of betrayal infiltrates my mood for the entire ride home. At least we'll have the ride home to catch up. Lexi always talks my ear off with 100 questions and endless stories of things that happened that day.

Except this time, Lexi barely glances at me once and then out the window, humming and clutching her favorite ballerina purse with a tiny hand.

She looks so...happy. She used to get that happy only with me. Why is it that now –

A bump on the road shifts us all in our seats and interrupts my thoughts. *–ugh.*

Whatever. Harper needs to get her own sister and stop obsessing so much over other people's families.

When we finally pull into the driveway, the clicks and whooshes of seatbelts irritate me.

22

Telling on Yourself

I watch as Lexi skips inside, singing something about a girl named Meow Meow. As if I even care. I storm into the living room, sling my backpack onto the floor, and flop onto the couch.

Dad and Mom exchange a look. He pauses in the doorway to listen in while Mom comes and sits next to me. "Hey, are you okay?"

I bristle. "NO."

Mom's eyes widen at the aggression in my voice and I feel a little bad. "Sorry Mom, it's just that Lexi..." I catch myself.

What am I supposed to say? That Lexi loves Harper more than me and I'm jealous? That sounds so stupid.

"...never mind. Sorry about that. It's not important, anyway. This boy ruined my day during Homeroom and nothing has gone right since."

"BOY?" Dad teleports from the doorway to the couch next to Mom with a murderous look in his eye.

I roll my eyes. "A stupid boy. He broke my phone for no reason."

Mom's eyes widen.

Dad scowls deeper. "How did that happen? Let me see it."

"Well…" The pit of my stomach lights up. I hate this feeling, the one where you know you're in trouble but you're too far into it now and you have to finish telling on yourself. I begrudgingly pull the perfectly pink, deeply cracked uPhone out of my backpack.

Daddy's brow tightens and he takes it from me, studying it closely. "Did he take your phone from you? What exactly happened?"

I cringe at his brown eyes, now blazing at me.

"Well, he didn't exactly take it from me. It was during transition from Homeroom to first period and I was about to get Meghan Gardener's phone number. I took my phone out and he slammed into me out of nowhere, knocking it to the floor."

Daddy holds up the phone's soulless husk. "This looks like it was run over by a car, Lucy Mae. Are you telling me the truth?"

I wince. "Yes, Daddy, it's the truth. It was not run over by a car, though. It fell onto the floor and…"

Daddy's eyes have not moved at all.

I sigh, resigned to my fate. "…I kinda stepped on it by mistake."

I catch a glimpse of Mom wincing in the background, but Daddy's face takes up the entire room.

This is going to be bad. Worse than usual.

Here he goes. "Lucy Mae Clark. Do you understand how much uPhones cost?"

I'm sullen. "Yes, sir."

Dad continues, "I understand that given the circumstance,

it was not entirely your fault, but the real world doesn't care about whose fault it is when things happen. The fact of the matter is that you need another phone now, and things in this world aren't free."

I nod penitently. "Yes, sir. I'm sorry, Dad."

"Isn't there a rule at school to keep phones off and in your locker, anyway?"

"Yes, sir."

"So you broke that rule knowingly, and this is the result. I will order a new phone for you, but you will have to do extra chores around the house to pay for it. You're washing and vacuuming the cars every weekend for the next 6 weeks, and as for your replacement phone -"

The jig is up. I'll be lucky to get a Nokia brick. At least they're supposed to be indestructible.

"-there won't be one this time."

The words fall on me like a slab of concrete.

I knew this was going to happen. No phone!? How will I survive?

"But, Dad, what if there's an emergency at school?"

"Your mother and I survived just fine before cell phones. The school has plenty of phones you can use, and you know our phone numbers by heart - you'll be fine."

Mom studies my face. "How does your makeup look even better than it did this morning?"

I smile a little. "I was crying, so I had to redo it. Meghan let me use hers."

"Meghan?" Dad's shoulders tense up even further. "The one who caused you to practically spiral into depression because she didn't invite you to her birthday party in the third grade? THAT Meghan?"

I frown. He's not wrong; I cried for days. "Well yeah, but that was five years ago."

Dad shifts uncomfortably in his seat and looks at Mom. "Well I'm glad you're feeling better, but I'm not sure about this Meghan character, honey. Please be careful and don't get too close."

Part of my heart sinks at this, but I don't say anything.

Mom is still looking at my makeup, but she agrees with Dad. "Maybe we *should* get you that Adora+ line," she murmurs, "But after you've worked off your phone."

I perk up immediately. "Yes please, Mom." We both grin at the same time.

Dad interjects, "So what were you saying that boy did to you, Lucy Mae?" He picks up his phone and starts a search for something, tapping and swiping across the bright slick surface.

What is he doing?

"Dad, you don't have to call the school."

He ignores me. After a long pause, he looks back up at me and Mom. "The new phone will be here in 2 weeks, but you're not getting it until you've earned it back."

"Thanks, Dad," I answer, even though I'm dying inside at the thought of no phone for an entire MONTH AND A HALF.

Mom looks at me closely. "Did the boy do or say anything else to you?"

I feel dumb saying it out loud, but I do anyway. "He knocked me down and it hurt a little, but I'm okay now. He also kinda bullied me, and said mean things, and called me an airhead."

Mom sighs and Dad glares a hole into the wall. "Did the school do anything about it?"

I reply, "Yeah, the resource officer took him to the office."

Dad seems satisfied with it. He says, "Well Princess, you're undoubtedly a lot smarter than him. Just quit breaking phones."

I hug him tightly. "Thank you, Daddy."

That was the best possible way that could have turned out. Why am I still so irritated at Harper and Lexi? I run upstairs and flop onto my bed with my journal. Mom is making me write in it this year.

23

Journal Entry

ugust 12: First Day of 8th Grade, 5:30pm

So my mom is making me do this stupid journal because she doesn't want me to "forget my life." I'm supposed to be doing it every day. Ugh! I don't even know what to write in this!

PLUS, I practically had ZERO time to do anything this morning because my alarm failed to go off at 6:00AM like it should have.

Since I HAVE to do this anyway, I might as well give it a chance. To be honest, I feel a little overwhelmed with the start of the new school year. I know I fit in to a point, but there's always a chance that something will go wrong and all the hard work I've put into making a name for myself could come crashing down with just one little embarrassing moment. All it takes is for someone to post one wrong thing online and your social life is over. Like today, my phone broke and I cried in front of the whole school. I'm lucky Meghan was there or it would have all been over. Then Harper and Lexi are being super annoying, but if I say something, I'll look stupid in front of the girls and they'll kick me out of the popular group.

If my social life ends, then I won't have any friends, which means I won't have any connections to get good jobs in the real world, which will translate to not having any money, which means that I'll starve to death. So I could literally die if I don't fit in.

I'm sure that's probably not true, I guess, but it feels like it. Harper and Monica told me that Meghan will be live-streaming her birthday party invitations on ClockClick soon. If I don't get invited, I don't know what I'll even do.

I just know I need to get it right this year.

XII

Asher

Tip #2
Never open doors if they're closed because
you might see something you really wish you
hadn't seen.

24

Consequences

School ended two hours ago. I've been sitting in the office since Homeroom, so I never went to a single class today. At least I got lunch and they let me get my stuff out of my locker, so that's better than nothing, I guess.

Now at 6 is when my father is finally picking me up. We don't have a car, so he always has to get a ride from someone else. After dismissal ended at 4:30, I had to lie to the teachers that watch the car line and say my parents were right around the corner. I sat on a bench outside to make it more convincing. That was the only way they'd quit making those faces at me and just leave me alone.

Part of me wishes he didn't come, but part of me just wants it over with already. I hear the squeal of brakes from down the road. There's a treeline that blocks your view to the road from here, but I know the sound and the burnt-oil smell. That's definitely Deet's car. The front bumper is always hanging on for dear life and scrapes on the concrete as it gets closer. The fading light makes it harder to see. The geriatric gray Hevy

Alpaca pulls around the corner like a ghost and makes my blood run cold. It shudders to a stop in front of the school.

I stand up, shouldering my featherweight backpack, and walk toward the car. I can feel Dad's beady bloodshot eyes on me. I know he's angry. Very angry.

The car's shocks whine when I sit in the car. I gingerly swing the door shut, avoiding eye contact so as not to draw more attention to myself.

The car ride is sharp and menacing, but Dad doesn't say anything because he doesn't want anyone to see how he "disciplines" his son. That would mean foster care for me and Mia and prison for him, which is honestly what he deserves. The last thing I want is to lose Mia in the system, so I'm trapped. One false move or one false word can make this much worse, so I choose silence.

My mouth has gone dry and my throat hurts.

* * *

I get inside the house, only to be shoved into the office. HARD. I slam into the wall and into my first painful consequence. This is the beginning, so I know that right now, I just need to make it out alive. But it's Dad; his beatings make you wish you weren't alive to feel them. I don't even struggle when I hit the ground, I just take the punishment.

I've learned if you do anything stupid like fight back or try to run away, it just makes the series of kicks, hits, slams, and punches keep going longer. There isn't even a point to protect myself anymore. I made a mistake, and I'm paying the price. I was so stupid to be so mad. I should've just walked away when I had the chance.

The first kick lands, gouging my ribs. Then another on

my leg. I just stay on the floor. He just keeps going until everything from the neck down is bruised and bleeding. My vision fades to black and I fall asleep on the floor. I'm glad for the relief.

* * *

I don't know how long it's been, but the house has gone quiet, so Dad is somewhat calm again. It's finally over, for now. I don't know how much more I could have taken. I stand up slowly, painfully. My face wrinkles. My whole body screams.

I look up to see Mom standing in the doorway, holding the door. I don't think, I just rush to her. She might be a manipulative alcoholic, but at least she doesn't hit me. She looks at me with a worried expression as she walks with me to my room.

I lay down in my bed and she pulls the covers over me. I'm not cold at all - the heat coming from my injuries radiates off me. I just watch her as she leaves the room. I want to cry out to her, but nothing comes. With this simple comfort my Mother has provided, I start to feel a small amount of hope. Things could get better if Dad wasn't around. So much better.

25

Late Weirdo

The next day, 9:35AM.

I have really got to stop spending so much time in the bathroom, but I don't know where else I can find peace and quiet. When the go-go-go of school gets to be too much, I can just come in here, shut the door, and shut out the world with it. These five or ten minutes I get to myself are what's keeping me sane.

I pull my sleeve up to look at one particular scar, the deepest one. I run my fingers over the small patch of marred skin on my arm and dig my nail in.

I wonder how far it can go. Could I actually hit bone?

I produce a small blade from my pocket and press on the spot until a sharp flower of pain blooms. I suck my teeth as quietly as I can. Even though I'm used to it, the grimace is still automatic. The crimson bead of blood that sprouts is predictable, strangely peaceful.

Suddenly, the sound that directs the school goes off, bouncing off the halls and flooding into the bathroom. It's not really a ring, and it's not really a beep, either. It's an annoyingly lukewarm blend of the two. It immediately chops my peace in half.

BOOOOOOOOOOOOOOOOOOOOOOOOOOOOOOOP.

OF COURSE. That means Homeroom is over and I have three minutes to get back to class, pack up, and make it all the way to Art, which is downstairs on the opposite end of the building.

I rip a bandage out of my hoodie pocket as quickly as I can and get it on the cut fast so the blood won't drip through my sleeve. I burst out of the stall, letting the door slam behind me. I run my hands under the water for maybe a second and loudly pump a handful of paper towels out of the machine. I know I didn't do a great job of washing my hands, but I'm in too much of a hurry.

I soon sling my book bag across my shoulder and make for the hallway. It weighs a little more now, since I've got my school Silverbook. It's a standard cheap laptop they give to all the kids.

Last night's "discipline" for the phone incident still stings, everywhere. My legs and ribs ache, but I rush toward the stairs anyway.

2 minutes left.

On every other step, my book bag's momentum sends it slamming into my ribs. The hard rounded edge of the Silverbook pokes through the fabric into my ribs, sending a pounding sting up my right side and forcing flashbacks from last night.

Slam.

I remember the dirty brown carpet fibers.

Slam.

The first kick, right in the ribs.

Slam.

Curling up into a ball, hoping it'll somehow block the voice that loves to remind me of how worthless I am.

Slam.

Looking up just in time to see Mom watching from the doorway with a sad look on her face. Why is she leaving me with him?

Slam.

At least she closed the door, so Mia isn't watching...

The fifth time my book bag hits me, my skin starts to feel tingly and it pulls a small tear out of the corner of my eye, which streaks carelessly off my perfectly intact face. (Dad knows what spots to avoid when he's kicking me so nobody sees.)

I barely make the slippery corner without falling and fly down the stairs, ignoring the shouts of some teacher telling me to stop running. I'm already late. I hate being late. It brings attention to yourself, which is something I hate even more.

BOOOOOOOOOOOOOOOOOOOOOOOOOOOOOOP.

Late. Not good enough.

I finally stumble into the electives hallway and slow to a walk. Room 110, the art room. I catch my breath and grab the door handle. I know everyone is going to stare, but I pull myself into the room. Eyeballs burn into me from all over the classroom. I just focus on getting to the desk as far back as possible. I let my book bag drop to the floor and sink into my seat.

Some kids start whispering, giggling, and occasionally glancing my way, so I know it's all about me. I look at the day's agenda on the screen, waiting for their short attention spans to wane. The teacher will soon circle around.

26

Out of the Clouds

s. Berry is standing over me. "Do you have a note?" she asks.

I snap back to reality. "No, sorry Ms. Berry," I murmur.

Her gaze softens, and she pulls up a chair to sit next to me and help me get my materials in order for class. I think this is her way of silently checking up on me. If it is, I like it a lot. I like Ms. Berry. She is either just a really kind person, or she somehow gets it. I wonder if sometimes I've caught a glimpse of sadness in her eyes, but I could be imagining it. Anyway, she's one of the only people in this whole school I like. She doesn't get mad at me, even though she has no idea why I'm late, and she never writes me up. That's rare for a teacher and it makes me feel really guilty.

I should be better, at least for her sake. It's hard, though. Stress has eaten me up so much that I don't even think about my classes that much. It seems some days that I'm getting hit from all sides, between trying to keep up with my grades while taking care of Mia in that hellhole of a house.

To make things worse, ever since the uPhone incident, there are more people who want to make my life a living hell from the one I currently live in. We're only on the second day, and teachers are already starting to look at me as "that problem kid". When that happened last year, I spent more time in the counselor's office than I did in class.

On top of that, Christian Clawthorne, the giant football player whose side hobby is tormenting me, has been looking way too pleased with himself lately, and that enrages me. Clawthorne knows what he did when he shoved me, he knows he was involved in the uPhone getting destroyed, and he knows he got away with it. Everyone knows it's because his Mom is a higher-up in the school district – it grants him full immunity to any consequences, which means he can tease and torture me all he wants and nothing will happen to him. Not even the principal wants to get involved when it comes to that arrogant piece of –

"Asher?" It's Ms. Berry.

Crap. I forgot she was even sitting there. Must have zoned out again.

Ms. Berry has already placed a brand-new box of colored pencils, a recycled sketchbook from last year, and a pencil in a neat little row on my desk. She opens my "new" sketchbook up to the next available page so I can catch up on the warm-up. "These are the materials you'll need for this activity."

"Thanks, Ms. Berry."

"No problem." Quick as a whisper, she's gone again to check in with other students.

Ms. Berry has always understood me, though. I'm glad I get to be in her class again this year. She's like a second mother to me, even though she has no idea. It all started one day last year when she got me through a panic attack – she didn't even know me back then, but she was still kind enough to notice and help me. I was terrified of having to go home and face my Dad because I'd gotten an F on a math test.

All I remember was sitting up against the wall, barely able to catch my breath. My vision was blurry at the time, because I could already feel the kicks and punches in my mind. What shocked me out of it was a gentle hand on my shoulder. It was Ms. Berry, who had stopped what she was doing to check on me. She looked like she actually gave a crap. Not only that, she went the extra mile to make sure I was okay. Nobody ever does that, because nobody ever cares. I didn't even know how to react to that. That left an impression on me forever that I can never explain and probably never will.

I wish I could just stay here; the art room is nice. Ms. Berry is awesome, and this is the only class that I'm not harassed in. This is one of the few places I actually feel like I belong in.

27

My Hero, Duncan

The art work is easy. All I need to do for the warm-up is sketch an object in the classroom. The main activity is to decorate and personalize the sketchbook. It's just the cover, not the entire sketchbook. I can do that. I recall my older brother helping me make my first sketchbook. I let my mind wander.

I miss him. He was a hero to me... every time I did something wrong, he always took the bullet for me. Duncan was the only person in my life besides Mia that I ever felt comfortable around. He worked a nine-to-five job after he graduated high school just so he could care for Mia and me.

Every time Dad would go off on one of his rants, Duncan stepped in to take care of things. I never knew why he always made sure to close the door when he would talk with Dad. Things were okay for a while, until Duncan seemed to become increasingly sluggish and out of place. At the time, I didn't know why he always seemed so down. I'd ask him what was on his mind, and he'd immediately smile and say something or another to take the focus off himself.

Then one day after a really loud argument in Dad's office, Duncan went to work and never came back. Mia and I didn't know what to do when night came and there was no Duncan to fix dinner and watch over us. I was 11 and Mia was 5, but I decided I'd better help take care of things until he came back.

Mom and Dad didn't even notice Duncan was gone until food started running low. It wasn't long before my turn came to face Dad on my own. I understood very quickly what Duncan was dealing with, and I too began to close the door before the beatings began. I'd rather Mia not see the garbage Dad truly is, so I made a decision to always take the brunt of his fury. It would be best for her to keep her innocence as long as possible.

About two days after Duncan left, I was cleaning up in my room and hit something that sounded like a metallic bang. I noticed a tin box that was hidden underneath all the crap on my shelf. I hesitantly opened the box and was taken aback to see that inside was a small stack of five $20 bills. $100.

That's a lot of money, so I knew my parents didn't leave it there. I also knew that if my parents found out about this money, Mia and I would starve. I took the money out, uncovering a folded note. I still remember reading it for the first time, and I always keep it on me to this day.

I pull my old Arachno-Boy wallet out of my hoodie pocket. From a secret compartment, I pull the carefully folded letter. I make sure nobody's looking and unfold it quietly, hiding behind my sketchbook. I read it again for the hundredth time.

The Letter

ASHER...

If you found this, then you probably already figured out I left to experience the world, but know this: everyone has to take their first leap into the springs.

Some may be lucky, others not so much...Asher, if you're reading this, know that one day I will come for you and Mia but honestly, it won't be soon...if you are careful and smart, this money should last you several months. It's up to you to find a way for you and Mia to eat from now on, because Mom and Dad won't be any help. It took me 6 months to save this up for you.

I know the school breakfast and lunch is not always the best, but we qualify for free food, so make the most of it so you have more money for Mia. When you do have to use money, I suggest buying food that's on sale and stretching it as long as you can so you don't run out too quickly.

The lights will probably turn off again at the end of the month, so buy things you don't need to cook or put in the fridge. Get things you can hide easily like chips, cookies, water bottles, and soda. If you buy sandwiches, eat them outside so Mom and Dad don't see you and start asking questions.

I know you'll figure it out because you're smart. Take care of Mia until I get back. With love, Duncan.

I can't even be angry because I realize now that he left for the better of himself.

A 17-year old kid like Duncan should not have to parent his

younger siblings. Instead, he should be deciding what career to pursue and enjoying his graduation.

I wish Mia and I weren't such a burden to everyone.

The thought stabs like an ice pick in my heart. I've thought of leaving many times, but I have nowhere to go and Mia needs me.

Now that I'm 13 and Mia is turning 7, things are still very hard, but I've gotten smarter. He said he would one day come back for us...

However, he can't help me now. Not with Dad, not with Mom, and definitely not with a meaningless sketchbook activity.

28

Sharpo Markers

I finish the warm-up relatively quickly and start to doodle on my hands to pass time. I love the thick scent of Sharpos. Back before Mom got really depressed, she would have yelled at me and lectured me about ink poisoning if she could see what I'm doing right now.

I prefer to keep my scars covered, so why not use ink? A little Sharpo isn't going to hurt me. However, "a little" Sharpo to me covers my entire arm, and most adults usually disagree.

I start off slowly, swirling lines and pecking dots on all my fingers and nails. I gradually cover my arm so nobody sees my scars. My mind drifts off again, soaking in the colors and lines. Even I have to admit, the felt tip of the marker feels better than a blade.

I love making cool designs, it's fun. I can't wait to get tattoos – I'll probably do them myself, too! I'm saving a little bit of money each week to buy a tattoo gun and some ink.

I'll have to show Ms. Berry and my older brother when I get it. Of course, I'm not going to tell Ms. Berry right away when I get it. She would freak out. Maybe when I complete my first few years of high school, I'll come back and visit. I wouldn't want to upset her with some potentially bad decisions. Ms. Berry and Duncan are the only people I don't want to disappoint. I'll wait to cover myself in permanent ink for their sake.

Once my forearm is mostly full, I look up at the clock and realize class is almost halfway over. I pull down my sleeve and cap the marker.

Let's see about this sketchbook before I forget.

I decide to make the cover about Perturbed and base the creation on their album *MadHouse*. I'm contemplating whether I should draw it or use my Silverbook to trace it.

I'll go with drawing, since Ms. Berry doesn't always like tracing.

I start by making the glowing orange eyes, then follow up on the exposed skeleton teeth, then the chains around the body...

29

Sketchbooks

During the last 15 minutes of class, Ms. Berry asks that students set up their sketchbooks around the classroom for a "look around and admire" kind of presentation. I remember this from last year – she wants us to get comfortable with others looking at our work and learn to accept critiques "gracefully".

Kids are soon wandering around the room, glancing and pointing at each other's work. I also wander around the room, letting my eyes take everything in. There are all kinds of art styles. Cutesy. Anime. Scraggly, twiggy stick figures. Valiant efforts with laborious shading that unfortunately fell flat. I don't really say anything, because I have nothing to say.

When I make the lap around the room and come back to my sketchbook, I hear comments float by. Surprisingly, my sketchbook is getting a lot of compliments.

I can barely hear the first one from the quiet kid (the one that everyone copies off of in Math): "How did you make this without tracing?"

A hulking football player with long black hair chimes in

next. "Teach me how to draw like that," he says from high above my head.

Christian Clawthorne is right behind him. Since he has nothing better to do but pick at me, he takes one look at my cover and says that it's too dark and depressing, like me.

I mean...his is about *The Princess and the Polliwog.* The only reason Christian even knows I exist is because of Mia- she likes to play with his younger sibling at the Y.

To be fair, his cover doesn't look half bad because he traced the villain, but his remarks are so haughty, you'd think his sketchbook cover was a famous art piece hanging in a museum.

Seriously, get over yourself.

Some days I want to throat punch him, but I'd have to be at least 100 pounds heavier and two feet taller so I wouldn't get killed.

Despite Clawthorne, art is still my favorite subject; people come here to have a creative mind and some are even willing to merge our arts together to make an even better piece. The teacher doesn't see me as a weird and troublesome kid - she just sees *me.*

I wish I could say the same of my other teachers, but no such luck. I'll take what I can get at this point.

The bell rings, and the class empties like a drain.

30

Late Bus

The day is a blur after art. Sometime in the middle of Math, my last class of the day, an announcement crackles over the intercom: "Teachers, please pardon this interruption. Bus 772 is running one hour late this afternoon. Please allow students to call home and notify their parents."

I hope that Dad isn't home – he won't like that I'm late. It never ends well when he's upset.

Any Math I hear about after that point goes in one ear and out the other, despite my best intentions. All I can think about is the bus. One hour late is way too long.

I decide to walk home. I can get there before the bus shows up here. All I need to do is concentrate on getting through dismissal and making it home.

The bell boops one final time and everyone pours out of the room.

Normally, I stay behind with the bus riders until we're called, but not today. I merge with the swirl of people flooding toward the front double doors. As I look around to decide what route is best, I see Lucy's head bobbing in the crowd toward me.

Great. She's got company.

I avoid eye contact, hoping she and her friend won't notice me. The crowd funnels out of the double doors and spills out into the front courtyard where the car riders wait. The echoing roar of all the kids disperses into the outside noises – birds, cars, and yelling on the car line.

Of course, the two girls catch up and spot me.

"Isn't that, like, the weirdo in your home room?!" Lucy's friend squawks while pointing at me.

That's got to be the dumb one, I think to myself.

"Yeah, I think his name is Ashton or something," Lucy answers.

I know I shouldn't take the bait, but I'm not in the mood for games. I turn to them. "It's *Asher*," I reply with annoyance.

The phony, offended looks on their faces are my cue to move on. I'm not fighting anyone today, especially not *them*. I just have to get home.

I take a deep breath and walk out to the street. Nobody stops me to ask where I'm going. I look down the long country road.

I have 25 minutes to make it home.

31

Stray

I've been walking for a long time, and I'm just now getting to the old farm that lets me know I'm halfway home. When I'm on the bus, this place is about 5 minutes from home. Walking, though...it's taken me the whole 25 minutes just to get to this point. This is much farther than I thought. My mouth starts going dry at the fact that I'm getting home late, but as I come up on my favorite old farm house, I welcome the distraction.

I usually see this yard while the bus is passing by at 35 miles or more, but I still recognize some of the stuff the old man that lives here has. Since I'm not on the bus, I get to see it up close. I know he's got old paint cans back behind the house, and assorted car parts, and too-tall grass beyond the wood fence stringing along the edge of the road.

I see him out here sometimes messing with stuff, and it's always strangely interesting and familiar. This backyard, even though it has nothing to do with me at all, is one of the very few things in my life that always stays the same, and it somehow comforts me. As I pass the creaky old mailbox,

I can smell rust and oil and grass from here. I wish it was my grandpa's house so I could just walk over and tinker with stuff. Be welcome somewhere like in the movies. Maybe even get a real hug from a grandma. Some cookies and milk.

I wonder if I'd have any real hobbies or skills if I had been born into a good family. I wonder what I look like to the old man if he's watching me from inside the house right now. I probably look like a weird depressed drifter. I decide to imagine him as a nice old man. My pretend grandpa.

I look back over my shoulder at the winding road I just came from. It's been quite a walk so far and my feet are starting to burn, but I have no choice but to keep going. Staying here is not an option, and neither is going back.

I'm kind of like a stray cat, but I know in my heart that I will find home. If I don't find it while I'm young, I'll make it when I'm old. I'll take Mia out of this place and give her the life she deserves. She'll never know hardship again.

My breath catches when I see a deer pop out of the trees. She is full grown and acts almost tame. I'm so taken aback by her largeness and her beauty, I almost don't notice her baby wandering up beside her.

The doe looks me straight in the face. I pause my trek just for a minute. I still have half a muffin I saved from school breakfast in my pocket. I wonder if she'll like something like that. I try not to crinkle the plastic as I bring it out.

The doe watches my hands intently. I wonder if she knows I won't hurt her. I hope she's not so trusting of all strangers, or she and her baby won't last long.

I produce the muffin half, unwrapped, and hold it up to see what she does. It's not much to such a large animal, but it's all I've got.

She looks around, glances at her baby beside her, and takes a careful step forward.

I stay in place, but allow my arm to stretch forward the tiniest bit. I'd hate to scare her off.

After what feels like a century, she lets her lip stretch forward like a finger toward the muffin. She nibbles the tiniest bit, ponders the taste, then takes the rest of it.

That was cool.

She looks at me again, almost as if to say thank you, then bounds away. The baby is very good at keeping up with her and disappears just as quickly.

If I'm lucky enough to find a wife and start a family of my own, I'll take care of them and give them the life I never had. That's probably the only good thing my useless parents have given me. I know exactly what kind of home I want to have – it'll be the exact opposite of the one I'm stuck in right now.

32

Stupid

Then it hits me.

Home. There's no way I'm getting home before dark.

As I walk, the crunch of gravel under my feet shifts to the swoosh of wildgrass. The mosquitoes will start to bite soon. I'll have to sneak in and pray they don't see me.

Then it begins. My phone buzzes in my pocket, then turns off. Buzzes again against the fabric, then dies off. I cringe. I really don't want to look. I shift my backpack uncomfortably on my shoulders and plod on. On the third buzz, I pull my phone out of my pocket. 12 missed calls and 6 texts. All from Dad. I know enough not to mistake that for concern for my well-being. Dad needs something, and I'm not around to get it for him, so he won't be happy when I get home. I look up and see my bus whoosh past, bumbling down the road straight for my street.

It was so stupid of me to think I'd get home faster than a bus.

33

Home

The sun is already setting by the time I reach home. The whole point of walking home was to try and avoid being late, but I ended up taking twice as long. As I come up the path, I look at our broken duct-taped windows, barely covered inside by ratty blinds. In the dim light, our place doesn't look as dirty on the outside. The dead plants just look like plants. The holes in the siding aren't as obvious. The lights are on, and they almost look inviting. Almost.

I take my key out of my pocket and hold it in my hand. I pause, one hand on the screen door handle.

I could just keep walking and find somewhere else to live. It would all be over.

I look back at the road.

Then I hear Dad yell from inside.

Mia.

I yank the screen door open, jam my key into the lock, and rush into the house without thinking.

If he's hurt one hair on her head, I SWEAR...

My eyes wildly scan the empty room. Old, busted up couch. Bean bag chair. Folding table. Stupid crappy chairs. Damned filthy clothes on the floor. I don't see her.

Where is she?

I call for her, trying not to panic. "Mia...?!" My heart is pounding into my neck.

Like a little angel, she stands up from behind the couch and looks at me. She lights up when she sees me.

Thank God.

My whole body sags in a mix of exhaustion and relief. I fall to my knees and wait for her to come to me with my arms extended.

"Asher!" She runs over to hug me, doll in tow. "Where were you? I missed you!" The doll lightly pops my back when she throws her little arms around my neck. I envelop her with my arms and hold her close.

I was hoping to avoid Dad completely, but I've just given myself away. It's okay. Mia's worth it.

As if on cue, I hear him shuffling across the linoleum toward me. His voice drips like sewer water. "So we're big and bad and think we can just show up whenever we want to now, is that right?"

I whisper into Mia's ear, "Why don't you go re-start your puzzle, and I'll come finish it with you, okay? Dad and I are going to talk for a bit, and I'll be right back." I let Mia drift out of my arms to safety. I stand up and lead him away toward the office.

He follows, predictably, his angry shouting filling my head. It's something about how worthless I am and how I don't know how good I have it.

I double check that Mia is far away. She's watching us this

time from down the hall, and she's unsure. I force myself to smile at her with a trembling jaw. I wave at her to go do her puzzle before I close the door, and she happily obeys.

Dad growls behind me through a sticky burp. "I know you got those calls, boy."

Knowing it's a stupid thing to say, I have to get just one word in. "I did. Just didn't want to talk to you."

The first hit actually makes my head ring this time. My eyes vibrate in my skull.

That's a new one...I think I'm passing out.

34

Numb

I wake up on the floor. Same dirty brown carpet. Dad's gone, so he's done with me. I listen for clues to what's happening outside before getting up. I hear snoring drifting down the hall.

Good.

I stand up slowly, minding the painful spots. There are a lot of them. Actually it more feels like just everything hurts, but better me than Mia.

I go to the bathroom. The lights are on this month, which is refreshing. I look in the dirty mirror. I've got some blood pooled right under my nose.

Split lip, he got careless this time.

I take the obnoxious-smelling bar of dollar-store soap from the sink and wash my face with it. The dried blood flakes off and into the water. It swirls down the drain while I pat my face dry with the old threadbare rag we use as a hand towel.

To my surprise, that's all of the damage he did to my face other than my nose. I can still go to school tomorrow without anyone noticing much. I stare at the scissors on the counter and let myself lose a little control. How can this make it any worse?

That's the funny thing about it. We don't feel it like regular people do. I have a really high pain tolerance. People that look at us when we cut ourselves think we're doing it for attention. After a while when bad things keep happening, you just go numb. We're actually just doing it so we can feel SOMETHING. It helps us remember we're actually human, that we're actually alive. I hate that it has to come to this, but I need to know if I am.

I run a quick shower, dry off, and put on my house clothes. I go to my room and close the door. Maybe Mia will forget the puzzle I promised I'd finish with her. I just need to be alone right now.

Almost immediately, there's a tiny knock at my door. It opens.

Mia shuffles into my room, then sees my arms.

"What's that, Asher?" she asks.

"Nothing, now can you please leave me alone?"

"Why?" she whimpers.

"Because I told you to," I hiss.

She ignores me, walking over to where I'm sitting on the bed. She climbs up and quietly curls up next to me.

I wordlessly pull her closer and bury my face in her hair. I love Mia. She's the only good thing in my life. She can be a pain sometimes, but she's my world. I don't know what I'd do if anything were to happen to her.

Mia soon falls asleep. I carefully pull the blanket over her, turn off the light, and snuggle back in with her.

XIII

Lucy

35

Birds, Trees, and Pavement

Student drop-off area, Fountain View Middle School
I glance at the clock on the car's dashboard. 7:42.
I'm just in time before they get started.

Mom pulls her car up to the school's front curb, and I step out. Out of habit, I turn back to smell the warm fuzzy interior of the cabin and give her a tiny wave.

Mom waves back. "Have a great day. Love you!"

"Love you too," I mumble. I look around, hoping nobody heard that cheesy exchange. I close the door, adjust my handbag on my shoulder, and make my way toward the double doors of the school. Even though I'm still a little sleepy, I can hear Mom's car quietly drive off behind me. At this hour, there are not many students yet, except for kids that get dropped off by parents that have to go in to work extra early. It's strangely peaceful.

One of the kids from our team is outside the school, sitting on the blue bench by the front door, accompanied only by his huge book bag in the space next to him. He's got one skinny arm around his book bag like it's a good friend. With his free hand, he's playing a game on his phone.

I thought everyone was supposed to be inside by now. We start at 7:45.

As I get closer to him, he notices I'm headed for the door and calls out to me. "Hey."

What could he possibly want? There's nobody else here.

I point to myself with a questioning eyebrow.

The kid nods. "There's no BW today. I just found out, too. Ms. Constance is sick."

My shoulders droop a bit.

So much for that. What am I supposed to do now?

The doors don't open for all students for almost another hour.

I look around for a place to sit. There's another blue bench, away from that kid.

It won't do me any good to be seen alone with a shrimpy kid like that. I mean, he's nice and all, but just the fact that he's a boy and there's nobody else here is enough for rumors to start swirling. I'm not about to start all that.

I settle onto the bench with a sigh and look around. Pavement. Trees. Brick walls. Glass doors. Birds singing. Slight breeze.

I feel the automatic urge to pull out my phone, but that's not going to happen for a while. It's extremely uncomfortable not having my phone. It's like when you get that funny feeling you've forgotten something and not quite being able to place it - except you know exactly what you've forgotten and are keenly aware of all the things you COULD be doing with your phone if you had it.

My eyes drift around for a second lap. Brick walls. Glass doors. Kid on the bench with his phone. Birds singing. Trees.

Pavement.

I wonder what time it is.

I let out a longer sigh. Then an idea comes to me.

Maybe I can go to the public library next door for a few minutes. It would be much better than sitting here and rotting from boredom. I have to call Mom and see if she's okay with me doing that, just in case. I don't want to take any chances and get in trouble. I could be grounded even more than I already am.

My hand instinctively hunts for my phone, and I realize again it's not here. I roll my eyes all the way up in despair and end up tilting my head back so I'm looking at the overhang ceiling. There's a wasps' nest surrounded by thick cobwebs up in the corner. Now I'm leery and check all the corners, including the one above the kid with his...phone...

I look away from him so I'm not staring.

There's no harm in borrowing someone's phone for just a second as long as I stay far away from him. Ugh. Here it goes.

I mimic how he called me at first. "Hey," I call out to him. I smile politely.

The kid doesn't hear me. No response.

My eyes widen and look around.

Thank God there was nobody else around to see that.

I try again with a bit more volume. I wave a hand at him. "Hey, um – !"

The kid hears me and perks up. I expected he'd be happy that someone like me would actually want to talk to him, but he looks kind of annoyed at the interruption. "What?"

Okay. Rude.

"Could I borrow your phone for a second? I need to call my mom," I ask.

The kid rolls his eyes and does a few quick swiping motions

on the screen to clear out his open apps. Then he stands up and walks a few feet toward me, stretching out his arm with the phone at the end of it. "Make it fast, and don't drop it."

Wow. Low blow. I guess news of THAT traveled faster than I would have liked.

I hide behind my best smile. "Thanks." It's a good thing I have Mom's number memorized. I stand up, leaving my handbag behind, and walk a few steps away from the kid so he doesn't listen in on my call. I dial the number so quickly, the dial tones lag behind. I put the phone up to my ear, trying not to touch it. I can hear it ringing.

Mom's probably suspicious at the strange phone number, but thankfully picks up. "Hello?"

It's awkward to use someone else's phone, and it comes through in my voice. "Hi, Mom, it's me."

She's already suspicious. "Okay. What's wrong?"

Be cool, Lucy Mae.

"BW got canceled today, so I was wondering if I can go to the library next door and hang out until they open the doors at school. There is literally nobody else out here and it's really boring."

Mom pauses to think. "I don't know, you've never gone there by yourself before. Why don't you just - "

Not good.

I interrupt, " - Yes, but I borrowed this phone from a kid in BW and his GPS says it's only 2 or 3 minutes away on foot. It's right next door, there are cameras everywhere at school and at the library, and I can see the Sheriff's car." I try not to sound too desperate, but I think I am probably failing. "PLEASE...?"

Another pause from Mom. "Okay, that's fine.   Go

STRAIGHT over there and STRAIGHT back at 8:20 so you're not late. I want you to call me again when you are back at school so I know you made it. Are we clear, Lucy Mae?"

I'm flooded with happiness but manage to keep it together. "Yes, ma'am."

Mom tests me. "At *what* time are you going back to school?"

"8:20. I'll call you when I get back, I promise. Thanks, Mom. Bye!" I hang up, probably a little too fast. I grimace slightly, but there's no time to waste. I hand the phone back to the kid, who knows I just told a fat lie about looking it up on the GPS.

I smile at him one last time. "Thanks."

"Sure," he says, shaking his head rather judgmentally.

Oh, whatever. Nobody cares about your opinion, kid.

I move past him, grab my bag, and look over at the huge public library building down the street. They open at 8, so it'll be perfect. I'll have a few minutes at least, and I can even get some exercise. It feels so weird leaving the school campus, but cool at the same time.

I didn't expect to feel nervous about this.

36

BW

When I step off the school campus onto the sidewalk, I feel like a completely different person that has other things to do. I wonder if this is what being an adult is like.

I can't wait.

I glance in all directions to make sure it's safe, though I'm not even crossing any streets. The library is on the same side as the school. As I walk, my mind starts to drift back to yesterday.

Of course I'll never tell the girls, but I was curious and happened to poke by the first Book Warriors meeting yesterday. (We call it BW for short. It's a competition that tests your knowledge about a set of assigned novels. Kids read all the novels, then write their own questions and quiz each other for months to prepare for the big competition.)

So when I went yesterday, I was surprised to see Marcus there. Seeing him again after so long made me remember how much fun it actually was back in elementary school, when he and I were on the same team.

Marcus has always been really smart, and whoever had to go up against him was quite unlucky, indeed – he's got a mind like a steel trap and can recall the tiniest details from books, which can give a BW team a distinct advantage in competition.

BW meetings this year are going to be every Monday through Wednesday from 7:45–8:30 A.M., perfect for sneaking into before the girls meet up.

Back on the sidewalk, I see a bearded older man walk past. I immediately tense up, eyeing him carefully.

Stranger Danger is real!

The man walks on, not even noticing I exist. I cringe. I'm not sure whether to feel offended or silly.

Now I'm passing the giant oak trees leading up to the building. I'm almost there. My mind drifts again.

Let the record show that I'm not in Book Warriors JUST to see Marcus, BUT...it is nice to know someone there. How ridiculous, the thought that I'm only going to BW to see Marcus. That COULD be an excuse I can use, though, if Meghan and the girls find out I'm doing something so nerdy. They would never stop making fun of me for it.

37

The Library

I climb up the greenly painted steps to the front entrance of the library. The automatic doors part like curtains and welcome me in. Part of me is relieved I didn't get kidnapped or murdered on the way here. Even though it was kind of scary to walk over by myself, it's really nice to have the place all to myself.

I like this library here in the city better than the River Glade branch Mom and Dad usually take me and the kids to. River Glade is out in the country and it's not bad, but it's so much smaller than this one. The selections over there are more for little kids and older people. This library, though, has been my green-carpeted cathedral for the past few years (especially back in the old days when I needed to be dropped off. How droll.) They have so many great young adult novels, not to mention more spaces to curl up with a book and just be left alone to read.

The shelves stand like sentinels to watch over its peace and quiet. The yawning ceiling always makes me take a deep breath. It's been way too long since I've been here. I know exactly which shelf my favorite book is on, and I make a bee-line for it. *Coldhearted* by Miranda Misenheimer is always to the right of her other black-spined series, *Stories of the Moon.*

Stories of the Moon is not a bad series, but *Coldhearted* is hands-down my favorite book of all time. I snatch my quarry from the shelf and hug it close to my chest, inhaling its wonderful book smell.

Since there's nobody here yet, my favorite poofy chair in the back corner is available. I promptly jump in, and the chair almost swallows me and my bag whole. Perfect. I snuggle up, turning to where I left off last, page 87. The salmon-colored fabric of the chair creates a kind of funnel around my head and deepens the cozy feeling even more.

A few shelves down the way, Ms. Katherine the librarian pops her head out of her tiny office and smiles warmly when she sees me. She must have heard when I ploofed into the chair. Her thick auburn hair and huge owl-eye glasses frame her narrow face. She steps out of her office toward me and clucks, "Hi, Lucy!"

I've always loved the way she dresses. She's got on her practical ballerina flats and gray tweed pencil skirt with the black top, which fit her tiny frame perfectly. I love that outfit.

"The books have missed you around here. "Especially that one." She motions toward my book with her nose, a wry smile playing on her face. She doesn't even have to look at the title - she already knows which one it is.

I grin and loosen my hold on it a little. "It's my favorite."

She nods. "I know. What is that, your sixth time reading it?"

"Twelfth," I whisper, just in case I'm not the only one here.

She laughs loudly, then catches herself. We share a stifled giggle.

I like Ms. Katherine. She and I go way back - she coached both me and Marcus during our Book Warrior days in elementary school.

I hold the book closer to me, feeling slightly defensive since she *did* kinda just laugh at me. "Well, she *is* a great author. I've read all her books. They're amazing, but this one is my favorite because-" I stop and look at her sheepishly. "Sorry. You probably don't care."

Ms. Katherine looks a little offended by that, and takes it as an invitation to perch on the edge of a nearby ottoman. "Why wouldn't I?"

I give her an odd look. "I think the real question is, why *would* you?"

She lets out a sad chuckle, raising an eyebrow. "I like my question better."

I break eye contact and look at the olive green carpet. It has thin beige stripes I never noticed before. "I'm sorry, I guess I just thought you wouldn't care because-" I stop myself. This isn't therapy.

She urges me to continue. "Because why?"

"Because no one else does," I say slowly, waiting for her to laugh.

She doesn't. "Lucy, not all kids like to read, but the ones who do are special."

I scoff. "That's not important in middle school." I sigh, shifting my gaze onto the smooth pages of my book. "Only being popular is important."

She sighs too now. "Sometimes it's good to be different."

"You won't have friends if you're different."

I look up in time to see her face becoming even more somber. "Well, I'm sorry to hear that." Her expression suddenly changes along with the subject. "If you ever want to talk about a book, I'll be happy to discuss any of them with you." She winks at me. "I've read one or two in my day."

The corner of my mouth begins to curl into a half-smile as I glance up at the old wall clock. It's 8:22, so I have to start heading back. Ms. Katherine always knows just what to say. Meghan, Harper, and Monica would completely flip their lids if they learned I was considering joining BW, and that makes a part of me really sad. I hope I don't have to choose. I extract myself from the vacuum pull of the floofy chair. I feel comfortable enough with Ms. Katherine to go right up to her for a hug, and I'm not embarrassed about it. I wrap my arms around her tiny self. "Thank you," I whisper.

She hugs me back, laughing softly. "For what?"

"For caring." I pull myself out of the embrace. I scoop *Coldhearted* up off the chair and reluctantly put it back on the shelf. Ms. Katherine doesn't say anything about it because I always put it back in the right place. (Librarians usually hate when you put books directly back on the shelf because people never put them back in the right place.) I give her a tiny wave, shoulder my handbag, and start to make my way toward the double doors. I catch the quickest glimpse of her reciprocating with a tiny wave of her own. She crosses her arms pensively, looking at me.

As I pass the front desk, I hear Ms. Katherine's voice behind me. "Hey Lucy?"

I turn back to see her scribbling in a book. "Take this, please."

Surely that's not the black and red cover I think it is.

Ms. Katherine is walking toward me and scribbling at the same time. I am both impressed and stunned at what she's doing to a library book.

Writing it in it!? Unthinkable!

That's the ultimate no-no. She catches up to me and extends the book out toward my hand.

Wait, is she actually GIVING this to me? I couldn't –

I look up at her amused face.

She knows I want it. I should just take it. I've wanted this book so badly for the longest time.

I take it gingerly from her hand and hug it to my chest like I did when I first walked in. I wish I could hang out in the school library like this more often.

"Thanks Ms. Katherine." I suddenly realize something and gasp quietly. "Wait a second...is your name spelled with a K?"

She laughs. "Yep. Just like Katherine Tinkerton."

I gasp quietly and her smile broadens.

Katherine Tinkerton is the wonderful protagonist of *Cold-hearted.* I love her because she doesn't let people stop her from doing what she wants, and even though she's rich, she's not spoiled. The love story between her and West is the best one I've ever read, and I've read a lot of books!

As I head out the door, I turn back, risking being late for the girls' daily flagpole hangout at 8:30.

"Good day to you Lady Tinkerton," I say with a dramatic sweep of my hand.

She lets out a surprised laugh and the secretary shushes her.

"Good day to you as well," she whispers with an equally dramatic bow.

I feel proud of myself as I walk out the door. I need to hurry up and get back to school so I can call my mother.

"Me and you are gonna be roomies, West," I whisper to my book, knowing that it's the most uncool thing ever. But no one is here to see me. I let myself marinate in the warm feeling and walk quickly back to school.

As I get to the school entrance I stop, remembering Ms. Katherine scribbling in the book. I open it, revealing her note on the blank first page.

> *Be Lucy Mae, no one else.   With love from Ms. Katherine.*

Does she know about Meghan Gardener?

I stare at the page getting lost in my own thoughts until a girl with short spiked hair comes up behind me.

"Move it Clark!" she barks, shoving me aside.

I scowl at her and move away. As I walk into the building and wait to use the phone, I think about Ms. Katherine's words. They might as well be, *Be Lucy, not Meghan.* I've always wanted to be popular. To just live Meghan's life.

I want to be Meghan... don't I?

XIV

Asher

38

Wise Advice From A Similar Man

Between classes, 8th grade hall. 11:00AM
I'm leaning on my locker, waiting for the classroom door to open.

My whole body hurts. Why am I such an idiot? I knew he was mad, I knew it was going to end badly. Why didn't I just bite my tongue? I shouldn't have snapped, I can't afford to make the same mistake again. I have to focus, I need to survive...

Then a shadow looms over me.

That's not good –

I twist away and look back. My arm flies up, ready to block.

It's just Mr. Cheezers standing in the open doorway. My shoulders relax the tiniest bit and my arm lowers.

His old blue marble eyes roll over my face, calculating.

He's probably going to tell me to sit down.

"Asher –?"

I mumble a quick "yeah" and start to walk toward my desk.

Mr. Cheezers clears his throat. "One second there. Come back."

I turn to look at him.

I hope he doesn't start asking a bunch of questions.

I reluctantly retrace my steps and stand near him.

He asks, "Is everything okay? Something seems to be bothering you lately, and I wanted to touch base with you to see if there was anything I could do to help you."

I knew it.

"No, sir. I'm good."

The marbles roll off into the distance. I hear a sigh coming from Mr. Cheezers, but he doesn't move at all. "I'm going to share something with you. May help, may not, but I want you to know that you're definitely not alone. I've noticed the way Christian Clawthorne and some of the girls pick on you. Here's a secret: most of the time, bullies are looking for a reaction. If you give them that reaction, it's like you're rewarding them. They'll want to torment you all the more just to get a rise out of you. A reaction. There's two ways to deal with this: One, if you ignore them, you deny them the satisfaction and the game becomes boring. They'll leave you alone eventually. Or two: you can stand your ground one good time and let them know you're not afraid of them. They'll lose power over you once you stop giving it to them. Does that make sense?"

I wasn't expecting this.

"Yes, sir."

"Know how I know?" he asks.

"Not really," I reply, trying not to sound rude.

Mr. Cheezers waits for a few students to pass between us into the classroom before continuing. He takes a quick glance at the clock, then back at me. "I had a lot of struggles growing up myself. I won't get into too many details because we're going to have to start class here in a moment, but let's just say my home life was less than ideal. I was hungry all the time because we didn't have any money, and what little we had, my parents would squander gambling. My grades suffered because I was usually hungry and tired. Thank Heaven for the school lunch and breakfast. It was a mess. I did my best to get along with everyone, but with a name like Emory Cheezers, kids were not kind. They teased and tormented me every single day, every chance they got. King Cheese, Cheesy Whiz, Mozzarella, Rat Boy...it was endless."

Why is he telling me all this?

Kids are beginning to fall into their seats like Chinese checker marbles.

Reading my face, he decides to summarize. "-the point is, you're not alone. When I turned 16, I found a job as a farmhand working for a kind old man who taught me how to run horses, tend sheep, bring up crops, and - I find this funny - make cheese."

I nod politely, wondering where this is going.

The others are looking at Mr. Cheezers and murmuring - they're probably thinking I'm in trouble.

He speaks quickly and quietly through an ancient whiskered grin. "Don't worry about me - I do just fine at the farmers' markets during the Summer. The point is: we are all a product of our childhoods, and we have two choices: we can choose to repeat what we lived through or not, for better or for worse. Even if things are not so great at home, we *always* have a choice on how we grow from our experiences. Never forget that, Asher. You have a choice on whether you are a success or not, no matter where you're from or what you've been through. Never be afraid to ask for help. Not everyone shares the same gifts and interests as I do, and I don't need them to. We can embrace our experiences and grow from them instead of living in the shadows of the ones we love."

"Why would you tell me all this? I'm fine, Mr. Cheezers," I lie.

Mr. Cheezers half-winks. "Just a hunch. Hey, if I'm wrong, completely ignore everything I just said."

My ear perks at a new sound. I can hear those stupid girls coming. Their footsteps sound like smug raindrops echoing in the hall toward the classroom. My heart starts pounding.

Meghan detaches from the group, keeps walking and calls out, "Later losers!"

The rest of the girls pass between us, entering the room like they own it. Harper leads the way, flanked on both sides by Lucy and Monica.

Monica looks back at me, smiling venomously. "Hey Asher!"

Mr. Cheezers moves quickly to circumvent the funny business. "Monica, Harper and Lucy please take your seats. I'm currently talking to a student."

They obey.

Mr. Cheezers smiles warmly at me and for the first time in a long time, my frown turns upside down just for a moment.

XV

Mr. Cheezers and Ms. Ami, the School Counselor

A quick glance behind the curtain while students are at lunch.

39

Wednesday, 11:55 AM

Lunchtime

Mr. Cheezers' Einstein hair pops into the darkened office of Ms. Ami's small, empty corner office. The chair sits alone in the dim light of the computer's colorful screensaver.

Muttering through his thick mustache, he muses. "Hm. Must be busy."

A quick glance at his front shirt pocket produces a pen. Taking the liberty of using a sticky note from Ms. Ami's desk, he scribbles a quick note:

> *I have a question re: A. Gryphon. Please call or email me whenever you get a chance. Thanks! :)*
> *-Cheezers*

Lunch is almost over, so he's got to get back. As quickly as he appeared, he's gone. The sticky note stays behind, resting on the keyboard.

40

Wednesday, 12:45pm

Just before transition to 4th period

The classroom phone rings amid the voices and chaos of kids wrapping up their work. Mr. Cheezers adds the new stop to his route, swooping between desks. Given the opportunity, the noise level immediately swells even more in the background as kids chat, pack up, and get ready for the next class.

Mr. Cheezers considers telling them to hush, but looks at the time.

Eh, we're about to leave anyway.

He picks up the phone.

"Hey, it's Ami. Got your note, what's up? Is this Asher Gryphon you're talking about?"

Mr. Cheezers suddenly remembers. "Hey! I almost forgot all about it. Yes –"

He glances up at the students, catches eye contact with one of them, and points to a paper on the floor to get her to throw it away.

Thank you, he mouths.

The student nods and snatches up the paper on her way to the trash can.

Teachers usually take great pains to protect student privacy, so anyone overhearing at this point should not have any idea of who or what he is talking about. That's Mr. Cheezers' goal now.

" – sorry about that. So do you happen to know anything about this person? This individual has been really withdrawn and seems to get defensive very quickly. There's a high level of respect and kindness when addressed, but I just wonder if there's anything else going on at home. Do you know anything about it?"

Ms. Ami replies, "I don't believe so, but I can check in with him this afternoon."

The bell rings. Mr. Cheezers lifts a resigned hand after the crowd flooding out the door. He speaks into the phone, "Cool, thanks."

Neither really has time to be on the phone, so Ms. Ami dismisses first. "Alright, bye."

"Bye."

Click.

Mr. Cheezers puts the phone down and makes his way toward the door. Kids from the next class are already trickling in.

XVI

Asher

41

Balloons

4th period, 12:15pm.

Despite my body feeling numb in a bad sort of way, I continue to my next class. Book bags lull through the hallway like annoyingly cheerful balloons, oblivious to anything outside them. Girls laugh and talk, boys shove each other and guffaw. The assistant principal patrols the 8th grade common area, eyes scanning everything grimly for whatever he's looking for. With a quick lurch, he's on the way to stop something or other on the other end of the hall. I fix my eyes on the doorway and walk a little faster toward it.

Just outside the classroom, I feel myself bump into someone. I look up.

It's Marcus, surprisingly. We lock eyes; his are angry with a bit of sadness mixed in.

That's weird for him.

"Bro, *watch* it," he snaps, throwing up an exasperated hand.

Weirdly, I'm not even mad. I actually kind of feel for the guy. I know what it's like to have too much going on. Marcus is usually really laid-back; I didn't think anything ever really bothered him.

I mumble a quick sorry and slip into class.

42

Fake Smiles

I hate Lunch. It's always the same: too-noisy kids are packed into a too-small area doing nothing but wasting food and making messes. There's always one idiot that thinks it's funny to make the most grotesque mixes in one corner of his tray. It's always the same guy pouring milk, then adding ketchup, swirling in some of the mashed potatoes, then mayo for good measure and God knows what else. There are always particularly thick-headed friends watching this procedure that feel obligated to dare each other to eat from the vile puddle. It's obvious to see which ones have never been truly hungry before; the kind of hungry where you're not sure what you'll do for food over the weekend because there's no school.

I get my lunch from the cafeteria and sit in the far corner towards the back. I always sit with my back to the corner so I can watch what's going on. I can exist mostly undisturbed when nobody notices I'm there.

Today someone does notice me, though. I look up just in time to see something flying toward me. I barely dodge it -

the hard-edged box bounces off my shoulder before falling and bursting open onto the floor. It's a milk carton, bleeding out its chocolate brown entrails. The liquid picks up filth from the floor and carries it in swirls.

This is obviously from Christian and his followers. They usually just hit on girls at lunch, but it seems like messing with me is more interesting to them today.

They're heading this way.

I don't hear his blocky footsteps over the noise of the lunchroom, but I know what they sound like. Christian pauses to kick the underside of Marcus' seat as part of his journey toward me.

Marcus is startled and shoves Christian away, who laughs and keeps walking toward me with his three cronies in tow.

Christian's voice reaches for me through the cafeteria noise. It's pretending to be nice, but comes off overly saccharine. "Whatcha got there, Asher?"

I give him an annoyed glare. "Same thing everyone else has."

They're definitely up to something. The three idiots fan out and form a wall behind him, covering us from the group of teachers sitting together in the middle of the cafeteria.

The teachers are watching now, though. A few other heads begin to turn our way.

How can I get out of this?

I hate that smug look forming in his eyes. They love to do this - Christian wants me to lose my temper, blow up at them, and get myself in trouble. It's happened far too many times. I'm not going to give him any satisfaction today. I'm sick of digging my own grave for his entertainment, so I decide to beat him to the punch.

As if channeling some cooler version of myself from an alternate universe, I push my tray toward him and shrug. "You can have it if you want, I'm not gonna eat it."

The shock on Christian's face spreads like mold.

I take it even further. I pick up my tray and offer it to him with a smile.

Christian takes it absently. "Uhh, thanks?"

Interesting. He doesn't know what to do. I'm actually winning this time.

"You're welcome, glad I could help." I smile at him, basking in his confusion. I take the quickly fading opportunity, stand up, and get out of there. I get permission to go to the bathroom so I can disappear. I watch over my shoulder as I go.

Christian is holding the tray with a confused look on his face. The friends reach over his shoulder and promptly steal everything off it. In the next moment, they disperse; the teachers have stopped staring.

Thank God, if there even is one. I can't believe that worked! Maybe I should do this more often. It'll be nice not have a target on my back for once. Just smile, make them all happy. Play the nice guy and look more alive... Fake it till you make it, or just fake it until it kills you, I guess. All I need to do is survive long enough for me to get out of here and make a better life for me and Mia.

My stomach growls, but it's worth it.

I think I accidentally discovered something with these fake smiles. I want to experiment more with this to see what happens.

After every class for the remainder of the day, I smile at the staff members and teachers to see if they get off my back. I need them to let their guard down. I need them to leave me alone.

It's still out of character for me, so the fake smiles are not really well-received at first. Teachers are doing double takes, and other kids are giving me funny looks. That just tells me I need to keep it up until they get used to it. People tend to get desensitized to things they're exposed to for long periods of time.

I would know.

After a few days, the teachers seem to eyeball me less. Their eyes don't burn into my soul as often anymore.

It's better than nothing. I think this experiment is slowly turning the tide towards me. Put on a happy face and they'll leave you alone. How did I not see this before? Finally, something is going my way. Maybe things will start to get better...

43

Forgery

After my little fake smile experiment last week, I think I'm going to try another one, just to see what happens. Maybe if I look busy, the teachers won't hit me with that stupid quote they love to say: "This assignment is for a *grade*, Mr. Gryphon." I hate when teachers tell me that. It gets really annoying. I know it's for a grade, I just don't care enough to do it.

Today, I'm going to try to "look busy" in Ms. Stein's class to see if she notices. Instead of putting my head down and sleeping like I usually do, I decide to angle my head in a position to where she can't see my work. From the outside, it looks like I'm working, but I'm really sorta scribbling on the notes.

Ms. Stein's shadow falls on my desk, then passes over. She sees my pencil moving, so she doesn't say anything. I hear her blocky heels clack away toward the front of the classroom.

That actually worked...

This is giving me new ideas on how to avoid my problems.

The pretending starts getting easier the more I do it. The next day in Science, I unzip my book bag and bring a form up with my fingers. I tuck it under the folder I have on my desk, only letting the bottom half stick out.

This was supposed to get signed by a parent or guardian, but it's about an upcoming wellness survey we'll be taking. Dad won't care about that. In fact, it might make him angry that they're asking us so many questions, which just translates to problems for me. The only thing that scares him is getting caught; this survey can and will get him investigated if I'm honest.

Maybe I should speak up. No, I don't want Mia trapped in the foster system... I don't wanna be trapped either...

I use an old pen to quietly make a squiggle on the parent/-guardian line. Suddenly, the pressure lifts.

I don't have to show him this. Problem is solved and it was as simple as that.

Mr. Cheezers calls for all forms to be passed to the front of the room. I watch my form get taken by the kid in front of me. It floats away toward Mr. Cheezers.

I think I've discovered something here. My teachers don't hate me, and Christian is leaving me alone. It's working, but who knew keeping a smile plastered on my face would be so hard? I feel so fake and hollow. It was easier to just speak my mind, even though it meant everyone hated me. I'm so tired... I've made everyone happy, so why am I not? I don't feel alive anymore. Where did I go wrong?

I put my head down and let the room swirl away.

Why am I still alone?

I fidget with a small blade in my pocket, and an idea pops into my head as I feel it slice my finger.

One quick ask for permission and I'm soon heading to the bathroom. There's no one in here. I lock myself in the farthest stall in the back. No one can stop me. I roll up my left sleeve and press the blade to my arm. My eyes water as I slowly slide the tiny sharpener blade across my arm. It's so refreshing, so perfect... The blood flows from my arm like a river, dripping on the floor.

Maybe Dad would love me if I was grateful, if I was a better son.

I want to go deeper, I want to feel human. I'm so close, I can see the exit clearly now.

I stop and trace the stinging red line with my finger. Out of nowhere, a thought comes to me.

What about Mia? She needs me. My Mom needs me. She might not show it, but she still cares about me. I can't leave them behind, not yet.

44

Hot Dogs

School is finally over. We've all eaten our microwaved hot dog dinners, no bun this time. I usually serve them on the snack-sized plates because it makes it look like you're getting more food. A lone hot dog on a big dinner plate just doesn't look as filling with all that space around it. One snack-size bag of potato chips as a side for each person rounds it out and fills the rest of the space on the plate. I'm surprised we even have actual plates, to be honest. I wonder if they're leftover ghosts of a past time when maybe our parents were normal. I highly doubt it; they probably belonged to the people that lived here before us.

One by one, we finish our food. Mia licks her fingers and looks up at me, then at Dad. Dad gets up first, leaving his plate.

Mom looks at us from hollow eyes, stretching a smile through tight lips. She looks like she wants to say something to us.

As she takes a breath to speak, Dad's voice cuts her off. "You got the bag?"

Mom jumps like a nervous chihuahua. She pops up out of her seat and scuffles after him. I'm not sure if she's nodding at us or at him, since he's long gone down the hallway. Her timid footsteps always remind me of a mouse. Dad's are heavier, meaner, and rattle the house as he walks into the darkness of the hall.

To distract Mia, I smile at her and say, "Want to help me clean up?"

Mia chirps, "Sure." She dutifully takes a lap around the card table, picking up the dishes.

I take my place by the sink, watching Mom make her way after Dad.

Mia hands me the short stack of dishes.

"Thank you," I say, bringing them up into the sink.

"Welcome," she mumbles, looking around for her doll. She looks like she's trying to retrace her steps, and she wanders off to the living room.

I wash and dry the dishes, then put them back in the dusty cabinet. We may not have much, but it's what we have. I'll wait a few minutes to see what Mom and Dad do. If they do what I think they're going to do, we'll have plenty of time to go out and come back before they notice we're gone. Their poison of choice on weeknights is usually weed, as it helps them to "relax". They'll mostly just sleep and scavenge for food they have hidden in their room.

I find Mia sitting on the floor playing with the rag doll our neighbor gave her two years ago. Its matted blonde hair is filthy and its clothes are ratty, but she cherishes that old thing because it's the only thing she owns. One of the button eyes fell off a long time ago, but it doesn't make a difference to Mia. She can see the good in broken things and still love them. I don't have the heart to take it from her, so she can have it for as long as she wants. I'll have to "accidentally" toss it into the wash next time, though.

On the far side of the house, I hear them rustling plastic and shuffling into the room. The door squeals and clomps shut. The lock clicks. Whenever there's a plastic sound, it's a pretty safe bet they won't be coming back out for a while, unless Dad decides he's mad at something. The bitter earthy smell curls out from under their door like dirty fingers.

45

Settled In

I'm taking Mia out somewhere so she doesn't have to see them being *them*. In other times like this, I've taken Mia out before to play at the park and sometimes on quick walks, but this is her first time going to the library, so I think it will be a cool experience for her.

What I like about the library we're going to is that it's out in the country by our house. It's small, but it's more kid-friendly than the big library close to school. I like that they have a play area, crayons, and a bunch of activities for little kids like Mia.

The bigger library in the city is more for older kids and college students, so they don't have much that we'd be able to really use. Not only that, our library, named after our town of River Glade, is only ten minutes or so away. It'd be ridiculous to walk all the way out to town for an hour with Mia only to have to turn around and come right back. Plus, the River Glade Library is open for one hour longer than the city library. It closes at 8:00 on weekdays, so we should be able to get at least a good hour there before it gets dark. Being out any longer than that is taking a chance I don't want to take with Dad.

They should be "settled in" by now.

I scoop up one of Mia's tiny hands with one of my own. The doll hangs on from her other hand, brushing against the floor. I put my finger up to my lips and she mimics me, brimming with sudden excitement. I glance down the dark, dirty hallway one more time, then lead Mia quietly out the front door. I've learned how to close and lock it without making a sound.

46

What's a Book?

Once we're outside past the rusty chain link fence, Mia whispers, "Asher, where are we going?"

I look down at my precious little girl, my reason for going on. She's smiling up at me and swaying playfully, making her black hair, her doll, and her favorite blue dress all twirl around her. I found that dress for her at Goodwill when she outgrew her purple flower onesie a year or so ago.

I crouch down to her level and look into her big brown eyes. "We're going to the library, okay? Come on, let's get there as fast as we can!" With a smile, I stand up and gently tug on her little hand to get her to follow.

She does, but furrows her brow. As her feet tumble over each other to keep up with me, she puts her free hand up to her chin, doll still hanging on. "What's a libwawy?"

"A library is a place where kids go to read books," I say between furtive glances across the street.

Good. Red light.

I gently pull on Mia's hand to signal her that it's okay to keep walking.

She follows faithfully, voice bouncing with the increased speed of our gait. "What's a book, Asher?" We make it across the street and the cars resume their whooshing behind us. We step up onto the curb of a gas station. There is a patch of tall grass, which parts to let Mia's doll pass.

What's a book? How am I supposed to explain that?

I feel my nose wrinkle. "When making a book, people write important things down and print them out to share with the world. There are many kinds of books. Some are stories and some help you learn new things. Some are like time machines, and some are just for fun. Books are fun to read and they make you smarter."

I realize too late that her doll brushes a little too close to an ant pile, but thankfully nothing sticks to it.

Mia smiles, seemingly satisfied with my answer. "Otay, thank you Asher!" My back and neck are stiff and tense. We walk on quickly, past the shopping center with the Food Lizard and the dollar store.

I love when Mia thanks me. She is the only one who actually cares about the things I teach her. She doesn't understand much yet, but I'm kinda glad about it. I'd rather she didn't know what was really going on with Mom and Dad. I think it would break her heart.

It's only a few blocks to the library from the house, but with Mia, it feels like longer; it seems that something is going to jump out at any second and try to hurt her. I know we're almost there once we pass the old auto parts shop. I can already see the brick library building waiting for us, the American flag waving us over.

47

The River Glade Library

We made it. Only took 10-15 minutes. Not bad.

We cross the threshold and the doors swoosh behind us, kicking up the smell of books and dust. This library is peaceful. I can tell that most of the people are actually happy to be here. It's kinda nice and weird all at the same time.

There are two other kids, a boy and a girl, playing in the Kids' Corner of the library with building blocks and puzzles. They have the same blonde hair and look alike, so they're obviously brother and sister. They look about Mia's age, maybe a bit older. Looks like they've got a pretty decent 2-foot tower going on with the blocks. The little boy shoos his sister away from the base when she wanders too close.

As soon as the little girl catches a look at Mia, she is thrilled to see another kid inside the library. She begins to wave us over, staring imploringly at me. Mia sees her and I can feel her grip begin to loosen, so she obviously wants to meet her.

I think they might be good for Mia to play with, but I better check it out first. I hate that I have way too much experience with things not being as they seem. It sometimes feels like I've had to grow up too fast, but at least it's useful for protecting my sister.

I lead Mia over to the play area, which is pretty much a bunch of little-kid bookshelves fencing off a huge red rug. The rug is covered with yellow numbers and letters, so it stands out brightly against the old green carpet. A few hardcover beginner books and big-piece puzzle boxes also litter the space. The twins and their tower only take up a corner of the giant rug.

Mia looks at the kids, then up at me. "Can I play with them, Asher?"

I postpone my answer long enough for me to get a read on what kind of kids these are. "Hi," I venture, waiting to see what they do.

The little girl pipes up first, grinning at me and Mia. "Hi!"

"Hi. I'm Asher and this is Mia. What's your name?" I ask politely, still holding my sister's hand.

The little girl is the outspoken one. She pipes right up, "MY name is Lexi, and this is -" she turns, realizing her brother is still back behind her, gingerly installing a critical piece of the structure he's worked so hard on. She sighs loudly and yells at him, "COME ON, LEO! Say hello!"

Leo is startled by this and very nearly knocks the entire structure over. The glare he gives his sister could melt an ice cube.

Hm, I don't know...maybe Mia can sit with me over there -

Mia's tinkling laugh breaks through my thoughts. Her little hand squeezes mine, so I pause.

When Mia talks, she sometimes sounds younger than her age. I worry she's not developing right or if she will need extra help when she starts school. She can use all the practice she can get, so I'm going to let her try.

She speaks. "Hallo, Lexi!" She holds up her doll to point at Lexi's flowing locks, which are tied back with a bow. They are so blonde, they almost look white. "You have pretty hair!"

Lexi gushes and twirls so her hair moves with her. "Thank you!"

Mia continues, "Can I play wif you?"

Lexi looks up at me expectantly.

Mia notices and looks up at me, too. "Can I, Asher? *Pweeease?*"

There's no way I can say no now.

"Okay. I'm going to sit right over there. Stay here, okay? I'll come back for you in a little while."

"YAAAY! Thank you, Asher!" Mia hugs me tightly and turns to her new friend.

As soon as Mia enters the red rug area, she immediately forgets I'm there.

That's my cue, I guess.

I feel a half-smile stretch my lip.

I walk over to the computer lab area in the opposite corner of the library and pick the spot closest to the wall so I can see the entire room without having my own back exposed. Being that it's such a small library, I'm still close enough to the kid's area to reach it quickly in case Mia needs me.

I pull out my ancient library card. It's scratched, bent, and barely holding together. Truthfully, it actually isn't even mine. I found it in the dirt by the supermarket one day. I promised myself that I'd never rack up any fees on whoever's account this is, and I've held true to it. It's the least I can do for using it. I use the faded number on the back of the card to log in to the computer and open up VideoTube. A quick search easily pulls up my favorite Perturbed album, which I only have at home on CD. It feels like unwrapping a candy bar nobody else knows about. I connect my earbuds, lean back in the chair, and let the music take over. It's like getting into a warm pool and floating your troubles away for awhile. I periodically open one eye in Mia's direction.

Mia has picked up a block and is being coached by Leo on its exact placement. I can tell she's giggling every time Lexi yells something at Leo. They're a bit intense, but they seem like good kids.

Good enough.

I close my eyes again.

I'll listen to the end of Track 8 and then we'll head back.

48

Spider

Somewhere around Track 6, I glance up and see Mia talking to a couple of adults. She's pointing at me with a worried face, almost as if she's going to cry. I snap out of my chair, dropping an earbud down by my shoe.

Something happened and I didn't see.

I scramble to log off, snatch the remaining earbud out of my ear, grab the other one off the floor, and stuff them both in my pocket on my way toward Mia.

My heart drops when I realize those adults must be the parents of the other kids.

Something definitely happened. Someone probably got hurt with those blocks. I knew I shouldn't have –

The mother sees me coming and smiles, which doesn't match what I'm expecting. I slow down. My eyes search the scene to make sense of it.

Block tower is still up. Nobody is crying. Why did Mia look like that?

The father looks at me, too; he's basically an older version of Leo. A quick shadow of concern passes over his face, but it's very fast. It's probably his kids' reactions to me that make him relax and smile politely at me.

Lexi welcomes me back, "Hi, Asher! We had fun!"

"Hullo," I croak awkwardly. "Is everything okay? My little sister looked like she was going to cry."

The mother speaks up, "Mia was upset because we need to go now, and they were all having such a wonderful time! Your name is Asher, right?"

"Yes," I reply.

Please don't start asking me a bunch of questions.

"I'm glad everything is fine. Thank you."

The mom gushes, "Thank YOU! Lexi and Leo are usually at each other's throats, and your Mia has been such a great influence!"

"Hey!" Lexi calls out indignantly, crossing her arms like an angry little elf.

I nod. "That's good, thank you very much." I turn to Mia and offer her my hand. I'm relieved to feel her tiny hand in mine again. "We also have to go, Mia. Are you ready? Where's your doll?"

She looks behind her and scoops her doll off the red rug. "Got it. Otay, I'm ready now!"

I nod again at the Dad, then at the Mom. "Thanks again."

Before we can start walking away, Leo speaks for the first time. "Are you going to build the next tower with me?"

I feel the corner of my lip pull upward again. "Sure," I concede without thinking.

The mom sees an opportunity and takes it. "Asher, if you don't mind my asking, do you live around here?"

I lie so she doesn't press anymore. "We live like 2 blocks away."

We actually live 4 blocks away, but if I tell them that, they'd get suspicious of two kids walking around alone.

Mom pursues, "Are your parents here? We'd love to meet them!"

Anxiety suddenly crawls up my back like a spider with pinchy claws.

Judging by the Mom's fancy clothes and the Dad's khaki pants, these are definitely the types to report any little thing to DSS. Their kids are cool and everything, but no, thanks.

I lie a second time, "They are in a meeting and dropped us off here so we're not home alone. They already texted me to say they're going to pick us up soon."

I have got to get us away before they ask more questions.

Thankfully, Mia is too distracted by Lexi rambling on about something to hear me, or she definitely would have called out my lie.

I nod my thanks once again and gently pull on Mia's hand, prompting her to walk with me. I begin walking us toward the double doors.

The mother's voice behind me calls. "Hey, hang on a sec!"

The groan under my breath is a borderline growl.

What could they possibly want now?

I turn politely and smile so it'll be over faster. "What's up?"

"Leo and Lexi *loved* meeting Mia. Since we have a teacher workday coming up, do you think your parents would be okay with setting up a play date at the park this Friday?"

Pah. Like they'd give a crap. I don't know about this, though. I don't know these people.

I look down at Mia, who is so excited at the prospect, she's shimmying in her too-big Dog Division boots. She beams up at me.

I guess that's the answer, then.

"Sure," I lie again. "I'll talk to them and see what they say. We usually go to River Glade Park. Will that work?"

"That's perfect. We'll be there on Friday from 2-3."

Mom and Dad always go out with their friends on Friday afternoons and don't usually get back until 2 in the morning.

Without thinking, I say, "Okay. We live by the Food Lizard, so that gives us time to get back out here."

The dad raises an eyebrow and gives the mom a funny look. Then he looks at me again.

My stomach catches fire.

Wait. I said we lived two blocks away, and Food Lizard is way further than that...whatever. I'm sticking to it.

The mother shakes her head at her husband with a never-mind smile. They both look at me, now with pity.

I hate that pity look so much. I'll only endure it for Mia.

"Well, we hope to see you on Friday," smiles the Mom.

"Once you get permission, of course," confirms the khaki-clad Dad.

"Yeah, of course," I lie again. I finally manage to wrench us out of that conversation and we make it back out into the setting sun, Mia bobbing happily by my side with her doll.

That was exhausting.

XVII

Lucy

49

Getting Ready for the Play Date

riday, September 7
11:30am
I've been commissioned to help Lexi get ready for her play date this afternoon, so here I am.

We're in Lexi's room, which to an outsider probably looks like a pink tornado ran through it. Seriously, I always feel like I'm in a little girl's dream house when I'm in here. The walls are pink, the trim is white, and just about every single object in this room is some shade of pink, including bookshelves, lamps, toys, carpets, bedsheets - e v e r y t h i n g. That's just the way she likes it, though, and I can respect that.

Lexi is way too excited about this play date, especially since the other girl is younger than her. It takes me a full five minutes to get her to quit jumping around long enough to let me do her hair.

We finally sit down together on her bed. I set her favorite pink rhinestone bow on my leg to use in a second. I watch the brush glide through her long, white blonde hair, then I scoop it all up in my right hand. Despite its volume, it feels

181

weightless. She's humming something, but I'm not sure what song it is. I suspect she's just making it up as she goes along, because it's mostly just random syllables that are varying in volume and intensity. It must be reflecting her thought process. Her fluffy bunny slippers, which barely reach the edge of the bed, nod in time with her head. Then her song gets louder and she starts bouncing to it.

Finally I just sigh, "This is going to be a really interesting hairdo if you keep moving around everywhere, Lex."

"Lucy, I'm so excited!"

I feel a half smile curl my lip. "Why?"

She bounces on the bed, almost tangling the ends of her hair with the hairbrush in my hand. My face pulls into a too-close grimace as I manage to dodge her in time.

She turns her head to look at me, making it fully impossible to finish brushing her hair. "Can I tell you all about the library?"

I reply, "Of course."

I'm just glad she's excited to talk to me again.

She grins. She talks about the sweet little girl named Mia and how wonderful she is. Her clothes and hair are kind of dirty, her fingernails are long, and her boots are way too big, but she's so sweet. Even her older brother looks like he's mean, but he's actually really nice.

"She needs help! I'll fix her right up. I can't wait to tell Harper, too!"

I giggle, not feeling as sour about it as I usually do. "That's cute, Lex. I know she'll be happy to hear all about it. Now turn around so I can get this bow on you."

She smiles and turns her head. I give her golden white strands one last pass with the brush, then affix the bow.

Not to brag, but it looks perfect. I'm just saying.

It seems the bow has given Lexi another epiphany. "Mia can even be my new little sister!"

With a wry smile, I test her to see what she does. "Does that mean she's my little sister too?" I'm just joking, of course, but there's no hesitation on Lexi's part.

She squeals, "YES YES YES - you HAVE to meet her one day!"

I chuckle, feeling my eyes widen unconsciously to match her excitement.

Lexi bounces out of her pink room out into the hall.

I follow her around the corner into my room. She looks around at my much more conservative (non-pink) decor, then goes straight for my accessory trunk. She looks up at me and thinks a moment before asking. "Can I give her a bow, Lucy? As a present?"

I open the trunk and look at my huge collection of pastel bows.

Eh, why not. I have a ton of them. I'll give her one of my older ones.

"What color is her hair?"

Lexi stops to think, absently teasing the ends of her own hair. "Dark brown. I think maybe black?"

I reach for one of my first bows - the sky blue one with pretty sparkles. "What do you think of this one?"

"It's PERFECT! She has a blue dress just like this!" She hugs me again. "THANK YOU."

I hug her back. "You're welcome." I pause and look at her crystal eyes. They look like Meghan's but lighter, prettier. "Did you say she has an older brother?"

Her eyes brighten. "Oh yeah! He's going today too. You

should come with us, Lucy!"

I shake my head. "No I can't, I have chores."

She smiles sadly. "Alright."

I tilt my head, causing my curly hair to fall to the side.

I need to straighten it again.

Out of curiosity, I ask, "What's his name? The older brother?"

Lexi frowns and wanders away. I hear her voice circling around behind me. "I don't remember."

I flip my hair back again and look over in Lexi's direction. "That's okay, you and Leo have — "

She's already sliding down the banister before I can finish the sentence. "...— fun."

Her voice trails down the stairs. "Okaaaa-a-a-a-y!"

I can hear the front door creak loudly. She's probably gone outside to look at the car. I know Mom and Leo are not out there, because I can hear Mom yelling at Leo from the kitchen to put his socks on.

I'm always fascinated by how easily sounds travel in this house.

A noisy slam signals Lexi coming back into the house. She calls out, "Mom! Where are you?"

Now the sounds of Mom shuffling toward the living room with Leo in tow. "Coming, hon!"

"OH - WAIT!" Lexi suddenly thunders back up the stairs and crunches through clothes and toys to inform me, "I remember his name!"

Mom's voice floats up the stairs to pull Lexi back down. "Lexi? Where did you go?"

Dad's voice follows. "Lex? Let's go."

Lexi is irresistibly drawn to their voices and begins to drift back toward the stairs.

"The older brother is named Asher! Bye Lu, love you!"

My reply is automatic. "Love you, Lex –"

Wait. What?

The voices downstairs swirl together and out the front door, which slams shut and locks behind them. As the car pulls out of the driveway, my mouth stays open.

My family? With him*!*

It's going to take me a while to process this. I have plenty of time to do that, though – I still have to work on my uPhone chores.

XVIII

Asher

50

Precarious

Friday, September 7
12:10pm

Today's the play date, so I have to get Mia ready. Mia definitely remembers that today's the day - she's been singing to herself all morning. It's more like a really cute humming that sometimes goes way off key. It kind of sounds like she's imitating a song she heard somewhere. She's having a pretend tea party with her doll using red plastic cups and an empty beer carton as the table.

I'll be glad to take her to a decent place to play.

First thing's first, though. I've got to make sure Mom and Dad are actually gone. They could still be here, and as long as they're here, the playdate ain't happening. Lydia and Deet (Mom and Dad's weird, slimy friends) usually come to pick them up every single Friday between 10 in the morning and noon. I have no idea where they go, but the earliest they've ever been back is midnight. I've heard Dad talk about how he and Mom deserve some time to themselves to decompress from their hard week.

Sure. Sitting on their ever-widening ones getting high is definitely a hard week's work. It takes a lot of dedication to be that much of a waste of space. Obviously, I wouldn't dare say that to his face, but it's the truth anyway.

Even though it's Friday, I know enough by now not to take any chances. I've got to carefully check the entire house. If I actually do find them, I'll have to come up with some reason why I'm looking for them, or Dad'll get suspicious. I can ask if they want anything to eat as a cover - they never refuse that. The obvious place to start is their main hangout, the bedroom. It's in the darkest corner of the house and gives me the creeps most days. The bedroom door is slightly open, so I pad lightly on experienced feet in case they're still inside.

Once I get there, I press my ear close to the door, but I don't dare touch it. If you so much as breathe on it, this door squeals like a dying rat. I hear nothing. There's just enough of a gap for me to look inside. Holding my breath, I cautiously peek in. All I can really squeeze in is my forehead and my eyes, but that's plenty. The unmade bed is empty. Nobody is sleeping on the floor, either. The closet door is shut.

Room's empty. Good, but I'm not completely convinced.

I slip down the dim hall and stop at the bathroom door. The light is off, but the door is only slightly open. We're used to the power getting cut off every couple of months, so it's a habit to assume the bathroom's occupied even if the light is off. I pause at the bathroom door, listening for any signs of life.

Nothing. That's a good sign.

There's only one more place to check, and that's outside. I'm sure they're probably gone by now, but part of me feels like I should double-check out there, just in case. I need an excuse to go outside, so I grab a trash bag from the kitchen and tie it up, even though it's half empty. It's just a plastic grocery store bag hanging off the cabinet door, so it doesn't take much to fill it, anyway. I reach under the counter for a replacement. The bright blue bag smells like a gas station when I fluff it open and hang it on the cabinet knob where the other one was. The Food Lizard logo hangs askew like a sad, wrinkled flag.

I stop at the only door we have and scan the living room for Mia's location before opening it. She's in her new favorite spot behind the couch, still humming to herself and playing with her doll.

"Stay here, Mia. I'm going outside for a second, but I'll be right back."

Her answer bunches in with her humming. "Otay, Asher! Hmmm–hmmm–hmmm–hmm – "

I open the door. The sudden bright sunlight makes my eyes squint, but it's fine. I see Dad at the end of the driveway. My limbs seize, then go cold. My stomach gets hot even though I'm not technically doing anything wrong.

He's halfway inside a car. "We'll be back," he hollers in my direction. "Don't do anything stupid." I watch his fat sandaled foot ascend into his friend's decrepit Hevy Alpaca. His weight shifts the entire car and makes the front bumper scrape the dust. They're all laughing in there. The door slams shut.

Inside the car, I can see Mom's hair poking up like sad branches. I'm sure she can see me, but she doesn't make eye contact or wave. Neither do I. I proceed with my charade as planned and walk over to the trash can, feeling Dad's eyes on me. The car crunches on gravel before driving off into the distance. I immediately feel my body relax.

The trash can lid is barely on the can, so I already know something's crawled inside. I pick up the metal lid and pause to let whatever-it-is out. When nothing happens, I just toss the bag in and shift the lid out of the way so I can watch the bag fall. Being mostly full of air, the bag bounces lightly off a fat raccoon sitting atop the trash pile. The masked rodent is a regular here, so we're not really afraid of each other anymore.

I keep my voice level and calm as if he were human. "Go on, now. Get."

The raccoon hisses in response and leaps out of the trash can with surprising agility that mismatches his fat hindquarters. He darts to the edge of the woods, then pauses to look back at me. We're nothing more than mild inconveniences to one another, so we've learned to tolerate each other somewhat. Quick as a whisper, he promptly vanishes into the trees.

I wouldn't mind running off into the woods, too. I'd take Mia with me. She wouldn't like the spiderwebs, though. Which reminds me.

A half-smile begins to form on my face. I glance at the driveway. The car Mom and Dad are in is long gone. A thin coil of drifting dust is the only evidence that they were there.

The tiny smile is still on my face, and I carry it back into the house. I call out, "Okay, Mia. Ready to go see your new friends?"

"YES-YES-YES-YES!" comes the giddy little voice from behind the couch. Footsteps thunder toward me and stop suddenly when she leaps up onto me. Mia's got some kind of Kung Fu grip on my shirt and left arm that almost knocks me off balance.

"Alright, alright! Let's get you ready!" I laugh. I'm glad to see her so happy. I manage to ease her off me and back onto her feet. I guide her to the couch, picking up her pink hairbrush on the way. She knows to sit and wait primly for her style. I brush her long brown hair and make sure her clothes are nice and tidy. Mia's one blue dress is starting to look worn around the edges, but I made sure it was clean for today. She insists on wearing it with her Dog Division boots, and I concede. Her other little shoes are starting to develop holes in them, so the boots will work just fine for now since we're walking to the park. I give Mia one last once-over, checking for anything out of place or dirty. She's perfect; face and hair are clean, she smells nice, she has a beautiful smile, and even her doll has had a "bath".

Today should be a good day. I hope it will be a good day...

51

Heavy

I'm kind of on autopilot while we take the walk to the park. Cars, trees, red lights, the Food Lizard. They all drift past us. The only anchor I have to reality right now is Mia's hand in mine. Her hand in mine means I'm responsible. Such a tiny hand is such a heavy weight. I bear it gladly; Mia is worth it. Even so, my mind keeps drifting. It wants to go back to my mom in the car. The way she just sat there. That's all she does, is sit there. While Dad beats me to a pulp. While Mia pulls at her hand because she's hungry. There *has* to be a part of her that wants to love us. That *wants* to be there for us. Why *won't* she?

We arrive at the park, and so does my mind. I don't even remember how we got here exactly, but Mia's hand is still in mine, so that's all that matters. Now I find myself looking at the park's entrance sign. It's got too-fancy letters fuzzed over by years of rain, moss, and rust. River Glade Park. Come to think of it, I've never even seen a river back here. Why is most of everything I've come across so far just been a giant pile of bull-

Mia splinters my thoughts with a squeeze of her hand. "Asher, looky, looky!" She hops impatiently.

52

The Twins

I spot Leo and Lexi a good ways off, chasing each other in the grass. They're probably several hundred feet away, just beyond the playground and sandbox. They're laughing and screaming, arguing over who is "it".

Their parents are sitting on the closest wooden park bench, smiling. The father pauses to glance at his watch, then looks around. It's not long before he spots us, too. They're too far away for me to hear, but he leans over and mentions something to his wife, who soon looks up at us, too.

The twins sense something is going on and look in our direction. As soon as the twins see Mia, they rush to their parents and start to ramble imploringly. The mom and dad wave us over, smiling.

We start making our way to them. Being careful not to stare, I watch them as we walk. They seem so happy. I hate myself for being jealous.

As we approach the sandbox, I scan the area around and behind us. There's only an old man walking an old dog. They're shuffling along slowly and don't seem to mind much of anything.

Should be good.

I lead Mia through the sandbox, which she happily trudges through, kicking up as much sand as she can with every step. She soon steps back out again, relying on my hand to guide her past rocks and anthills. I glance up at the family again.

When the twins don't get their parents' attention instantly, they begin to hop and whine. The father shushes them with just a look. My first assumption is that he'll beat them if they don't comply, but they don't look afraid. In fact, Lexi is trying her best to keep it together, but Leo has actually calmed down. It's kind of weird to me seeing little kids that are not afraid of their dad. It's different somehow. I would even say maybe they respect him.

We pass the playground area and finally make it to where they are. The mom suddenly commands her kids to come close and stay put. It seems random at first, but it becomes clear she's seen something from the look on her face.

53

Stranger Danger

Out of the corner of my eye, I catch a glimpse of a strange individual walking off the path, just along the edge of the woods. The clothes he's wearing are baggy, like they're draped over a skeleton. The stringy hair is messy and matted. It seems like he's looking at the kids a little too much; he's smiling and twitching. I don't like the feeling I'm getting from him. I squeeze Mia's hand tighter and pull her closer. I feel myself bristle like a junkyard dog. My jaw clenches.

I'd love for you to try something. I will end you.

The dad is looking in the same direction as I am, and he grimly stands, squaring up his posture from his old military days. His biceps look strong and full, with his hands clasped neatly together in front of him. Without flinching, the dad stares the stranger down. The weirdo's face changes when he sees he's outmatched, and quietly slips into the trees. The immediate danger is gone, but the uneasiness is not.

Had we not been here, this could have ended badly with someone else's kid. If he has any kind of brain, he won't come here again.

We usually don't have any major problems out here in the country, but they can happen, and we can fix them. My internal radar is now permanently on high in this park forever, peaceful or not.

I've known it for a while, but now I'm positive. People are garbage.

Leo and Lexi see the change in their father's body language and hush more still, like grass. At a quiet word from their father, Leo and Lexi start walking towards us from about fifty feet away. I reluctantly release Mia's hand so she can go to them, too. I stay close by.

Once the girls make eye contact, everything lightens up again. They both squeal and giggle, running as fast as they can toward each other until they almost collide. They're both breathless and exhilarated.

Lexi pipes up first, as always. "Hi, Mia! I brought you a present." She proudly brandishes a blue hair bow.

Mia glows, gently taking the bow in her hands like a treasure. "Wow, thank you, Lexi! So pretty!"

Lexi beams. "Want me to help you put it on?"

Mia nods fervently, hands back the bow, and turns around.

Lexi quickly has Mia's hair swept up and pinned back.

I just watch.

She looks like a little princess.

Mia turns around and faces Lexi, face open and warm. "Wanna play dolls?"

"I didn't bring mine, but we can use yours!" Lexi looks twice at the haggard doll and pauses thoughtfully, but thankfully doesn't make a comment about it. She takes Mia by the hand and they skip to a nice spot in the grass, where they sit down and start having a pretend tea party with Mia's doll.

Leo is not far behind me. Pulling on my shirt, he addresses me. "Wanna build a sandcastle?"

I glance back at him. "Sure," I reply. "Looks like your parents want to talk first, then I'll come over. Why don't you get started and I'll join you in a little bit?"

Leo, who's basically a miniature carbon copy of his father, nods his white blond head solemnly, then makes his way to the sandbox to carry out his task. The first thing he does is take a nearby stick and draw a giant rectangle in the sand where his castle will be.

Smart kid.

The father chooses to remain standing near the bench, arms crossed, so he can keep a good look on the area surrounding his family.

The mom beckons me over so we can all chat while the kids play.

"Please, dear, have a seat." The mom brushes off a spot on the bench and motions for me to sit there.

I can feel the dad watching me, so I nod at him.

I'm surprised that he nods back.

It's so weird. I don't feel afraid of him, even though he's staring right at me.

He breaks the silence. "Guess you saw that...character, too."

"Yeah, I saw him. Didn't like the look of him," I say.

"I think he made the right choice to move along," the dad muses.

I nod again. "I agree."

Dad's face darkens. "I hate to think where he's gone and what he's gonna turn that weird energy on to next. It better not be anywhere near us, for his sake."

The mom adds, "There's a lot of evil in this world. We have to be so careful."

Don't I know it.

"Yeah, it's true." I let out an uneasy breath and scan the treeline again.

54

On a Lighter Note

The mom decides to change the tone of the conversation with a loud cheerful sigh, probably to lighten the mood. "Well, since he's gone, let's talk about nicer things for now." She turns on a huge smile. "We're so glad you and Mia could make it, Asher. Now remember, we'll be here until about 3. Will your parents be available to come pick you up then?"

Did I just roll my eyes out loud?

I try to smooth it over by making eye contact with the mom and smiling. Hopefully, that will make what I'm about to say sound more convincing. "Of course. Maybe you'll get to meet them."

She lights up, an older version of Lexi. "Wonderful! That would be great."

I know good and well nobody is coming. It'll be all too easy to say they're running late when 3 o'clock comes around. If I play this right, they'll easily be persuaded to move along so we can start walking back home before dark.

I turn to watch Mia "walking" her doll in the grass. I love

the way she is. Her little smile, her bright personality, her cute laugh that sounds like a bunny squeaking. She even makes *me* smile. She's my little sunshine.

The mom watches Mia playing with her daughter for a beat, then looks back at me. "I can tell you love your sister very much. Is she your only sibling?"

I shift uncomfortably on the bench.

Here we go with the questions again. I'll just keep it simple and they won't know the difference.

"Yeah."

Duncan is gone anyway, so pretty much, yeah. The details are none of their business.

Dad interjects with the next question. "Are you over at Fountain View Middle?"

"Yeah," I reply.

"How are you liking it over there?" the dad asks.

I think he's just making conversation, so he probably doesn't care to know how it's actually going.

"Pretty good," I lie, nodding and smiling politely for them.

"Who's your Homeroom teacher?" asks the mom. While she waits for my reply, she shifts a backpack onto her lap. With one of those expensive metal water bottles on each side, the backpack almost looks like a spacecraft. She unzips one of its many pockets. Her hand crinkles plastic as she sifts through the contents with her fingers. I catch a glimpse of what's inside the bag - a huge stockpile of snacks. I can't help but stare. She picks out two pre-wrapped brownies with sprinkles on them and sets them on the bench. Once that's done, her hand dives back in and comes back up with two tiny juice boxes. Straws included and everything.

My stomach was okay with the dry cereal we had for

breakfast, but it suddenly growls out loud. I involuntarily clutch at my belly, wide-eyed.

That wasn't supposed to happen.

"I'm sorry, I didn't catch that. What was it?" she says.

I blank. "What was what?"

"Wasn't it...oh, shoot. What were we talking about?" She pauses for a moment, pressing the juice boxes to her chin. She suddenly remembers, pointing at me with a free finger, juice boxes still in hand. "Wasn't it your Homeroom teacher?" She's watching me a little closer now.

I hate my stomach.

I blurt, "Cheezers." I realize how weird that sounds, so I add, "Mr. Cheezers."

The dad continues, "Maybe you've met our oldest daughter, then. She's in his Homeroom."

Probably not.

"What's her name?" I ask.

"Lucy Mae," says the dad.

"Clark," adds the mom.

I suddenly feel hollow. I know to answer quickly so my face doesn't give me away. I furrow my brow, pretending to think. I say, "No, sorry. I think there is a Lucy in my Homeroom, but we don't talk. I'm not sure if it's the same person."

Of course this would be my luck. These are the parents of the idiot with the phone. The one that earned me one of the worst beatings of my life. Now all I need is to get in trouble for this all over again with HER parents, too. I knew they looked rich. They carry around a whole supermarket in their back pocket. Brownies with sprinkles and juice boxes just because you can. Must be nice.

"Are you hungry?" the dad asks me. "Peggy, why don't

you give them both some snacks."

I zap back to reality.

I was staring at their snacks. Wow, Asher, tell them you're a pathetic starving waif WITHOUT telling them you're a pathetic starving waif. Might as well make a sign and stick it to your forehead.

The mom named Peggy catches herself and puts a hand to her chest with an embarrassed gasp. "Oh my - I'm SO sorry I did not offer you some. PLEASE take some. I insist." Without giving me a chance to protest, her hand goes back into the stash and resurfaces with two bags of chips, two brownies, and two juice boxes.

That looks really good...

I feel my stomach begin to burn. I speak awkwardly because my mouth is starting to water. "Well, okay. Thank you."

Peggy calls out to the kids, "Come get snacks! Lexi, Leo, and Mia! Come get snacks!"

Mia looks bewildered at first, but immediately joins in the stampede. All three kids arrive almost instantly, hopping for their rations like baby birds. Peggy gives each of the kids a brownie, then begins to prepare the straws for them on their juice boxes. The piranha promptly dig in and finish in no time flat with chocolate stains on cheeks, noses, and lips. Juice boxes are next, which are quickly slurped dry. Mia is in heaven.

"Mind the trash, kids. Do not throw it on the ground, please. Hand it to us and we'll throw it away," the dad cautions.

"Can I get another one, Mommy?" asks Lexi.

"Okay, but only if you two share it." Peggy pulls out

another brownie, unwraps it, and breaks it into uneven halves with her hands.

Lexi is quick to go after the bigger half, but Leo the budding mathematician isn't having it. "MOMMY, LOOK! She's taking too much!"

Lexi fires back, "DON'T TOUCH MY CRUMBS, LEO."

"BUT THEY'RE *MINE!*" he wails.

Peggy's face has changed. She looks overwhelmed.

The dad looks down at his kids. He uncrosses his arms and walks around the bench to where they are. In a moment, he's crouched down to their level, looking at them both in the eyes. He doesn't wait for an opening. In one deft move, he's somehow got both halves of the brownie in his hand. The next thing they know, both pieces are being shoveled into his mouth. Lexi and Leo look on, horrified, while he chews matter-of-factly, still looking them right in the face. One quick swallow and the brownie, in its entirety, is gone. The kids are baffled. Leo really looks like he's about to cry now, but he dares not.

Lexi asks meekly between sniffles, "Why you do that?"

The dad pauses to swipe the last bit of brownie off his gums with his tongue. "Because you are brother and sister. Do you know what that means?"

Leo looks at his father, bottom lip puckered, eyes brimming with tears. He shakes his head no in the most pitiful way I've ever seen. "No, sir."

"It means that you and your sister are to be best friends for life. I want you to understand how important this is: your mother and I will not always be around to take care of you. We will get old someday and go to heaven. When that day comes, you will only have each other. Leo and Lexi, you MUST love each other and take care of each other always, no matter what. There will be days when you will not get along, and that's normal. It happens. But you must always love each other. Forgive each other. There is nothing more important that you can do for each other. If you are going to fight over things, I will just take them until you can learn to get along."

Lexi and Leo look at each other, then at their dad.

"Do you understand now?" asks the dad.

Both of them sigh mournfully. "Yes, sir."

"We will practice this as many times as we need to until we get it right. Are we clear?"

Both imps nod.

The dad delivers the final verdict. "Now you may go back to your games. No more brownies for either of you until you learn to be nice to each other. Otherwise, more for me."

They comply, walking away with quiet groans.

I'm so taken aback by this display, I don't even notice that I've already opened one of the bags of chips. I hand it to Mia, who has been waiting patiently this entire time. She inhales its contents a little too quickly. I open mine, allow myself to eat one, then give the rest to Mia.

"Thank you, Asher! So yummy!" chirps Mia.

The parents notice and glance at each other.

Peggy quietly gives me another bag.

I don't argue. I'm just glad for the distraction that will probably change the subject again so we don't have to talk about that plague of a phone.

Dad resumes his cross-armed post behind the bench. His eyes have not stopped scanning the area for that weird guy, but he does notice how hungry Mia is, too. "So what do your parents do, if you don't mind us asking?" he asks me casually.

My instincts kick into overdrive.

This is a loaded question. LIE. LIE OR THEY'LL COME FOR US.

I shrug and say, "They stay busy pretty much all the time. They work from home."

Peggy senses my panic and whispers to her husband, "Now, Bill, perhaps we shouldn't –"

Bill once again pauses his sentry work long enough to let his eyes down to look at me. With a nod, he honors his wife's request.

I can see the pity coming again, and it's so annoying. I get that they're at least trying to be nice. I'm just baffled that these nice people are the parents of that obnoxious –

Peggy tries a different kind of question. "What do you and Mia do for fun?"

What do you want me to say? We fly to California and shop for the newest gaming consoles every other Saturday? The only "game" we have at home is catch-the-cockroach.

I smirk at my own sarcasm, but channel it outward as a polite smile for Peggy and Bill. "We like to build puzzles and we play pretend a lot."

Pretend we have parents that love us. Pretend we're not living in a rathole, always on the brink of starving. Pretend we're happy.

That one hit too close. I feel my fists clenching, so I think it's a good time to fulfill my promise to Leo before I say something I'll regret.

I stand up and say, "I just remembered, actually, speaking of fun – I promised Leo I'd help him build his sandcastle. Is that okay?"

"Oh, yes, of course!" says Peggy. "We'll be right here.

We're going to wrap it up and head home in the next 20 minutes or so. Have fun!"

I carefully collect the remaining chip bag, brownies, and juice boxes off the bench, storing them all in the pockets of my hoodie.

We could definitely use these.

I walk over to the sandbox. Leo had a strong start at first with various piles of sand at strategic locations, but he's missing one critical component. I pick up his bright blue bucket and ask, "Mind if I borrow this?"

Leo is just happy that I actually showed up. With a shy smile, he nods.

Keeping an eye on Mia at all times, I take the bucket over to a small pond just off the path.

"River" Glade Park. Okay.

As I kneel to fill the bucket with water, I feel my mind drifting again.

There's no way such nice people could have spawned someone like Lucy. These people actually seem to care about others. They ask real questions about who we are and what we're doing. My own parents don't even give that much of a –

"Asher! Where are you going?" It's Mia, who's watching me, too. She never lets me out of her sight, either. Her little voice carries like a newborn kitten's scream across long distances.

I wave at her and point to the bucket. "Just getting water for Leo," I call out. "It's okay, I'm here."

Mia is satisfied with my answer and turns back to Lexi with renewed excitement. "Wanna play pretend?"

"Okay!" Lexi replies, clapping her hands.

I almost want to tell them what really happened with the

uPhone. Part of me thinks that there's a small chance they'll listen. I would love to tell them how Lucy really treats people at school when they're not around. Who she hangs out with. After what I just saw with this whole brownie episode, I don't think they'd approve of any of it. Only problem is, that would make me a snitch, which would put an even bigger target on my back. With a family like this, it's just not possible for her to be that much of a –

"Hurry up, Asher!" Leo calls from the sandbox.

Oh, yeah. Forgot about the sandcastle.

I pick up the pace and get back to Leo. Within a few minutes, I've poured the water out on one of his strategic piles of sand. At first, he's horrified to see the sand sinking, but I hold up a finger and shush him, signaling him to hang on a second. I use my hands to ply the sand and begin sculpting.

As Leo watches, his face changes as one who has just had a life-changing epiphany. He looks at me, eyes gleaming. "The sand is STAYING!"

Within the span of ten minutes, we've got an entire fortress started, since Leo has now taken the bucket from me and is making quick sprints to the pond and back in half the time I can. We probably won't get to finish it, but Leo is over the moon. I hold up a hand for him to high-five, and he slams it as hard as he can (which is not really that hard at all).

"Come on, kids! It's time to go!" Bill calls from his post behind the bench while Peggy starts packing up.

I raise my hand and wave. "Mia, let's go!"

Leo and Lexi's parents are everything I want my parents to be. They are kind and understand good discipline. They would never do anything to hurt their children. Lucy has no idea how good she has it, and if I ever get the chance to tell her, I will. There has to be some part of her that is good like her family.

Mia bounds up to me and takes my hand. She's hot, sweaty, tired, and beaming. My heart is full.

I turn to look at Lucy's family piling into their car and find myself waving goodbye. Mia waves, too.

Bill is making sure everyone is buckled in before getting in the driver's seat. The sound of the locks activating thumps across the empty field. He watches his wife carefully from behind the wheel as she walks toward me.

"Asher, are you sure you don't need a ride?" Peggy asks, clasping the strap of her backpack over her shoulder. "We'd be happy to help -"

I shake my head and smile at her as if it's the most preposterous thing I've ever heard. "No, Ms. Peggy, we're good. Thank you for offering. They're on the way!"

I kinda wish she'd insist again like she did with the snacks, but these people are too kind for that.

I look down at Mia and ask, "Ready?"

"Ready!" she cries, holding up her newly re-filthed doll.

"Let's do this again sometime," the mom says to us both.

I nod cheerfully. "Of course! This was fun."

Ms. Peggy is warm, but the look in her eyes suspects we'll probably never see each other again. If that's what she's actually thinking, she's right. We don't have each other's phone numbers, and it would be weird to exchange them now. My only contact with this family is through Lucy, and THAT...probably isn't going to happen.

The mom starts to turn from me, but hesitates a moment. I can almost hear her trying to think of a way to reach out, but her face shows that nothing's coming to mind. After a beat, she takes one last glance at us with a sigh and walks back toward the family car, shaking her head. I can tell she wants to care, but has no idea how. It's ironic and kind of sad. What I can do in exchange for her kindness is put on a little show for her.

55

Back Home

I pull out my phone with my free hand and mime checking texts, dialing arbitrary numbers. I hold the silent receiver up to my ear and tell Mia to wave as they pull their car out and start to drive away. They're going slowly, so either something is going on inside the car, or they're waiting around to see who comes for us.

I play along, letting my mind drift while I "talk" on the phone.

The thing is, too: if Ms. Peggy doesn't feel comfortable with us "being okay" right now, she'll definitely be the type to call the Department of Social Services on us. If anyone from DSS were to ever come to our house without warning, Mia and I would immediately be taken away and placed in foster care. That sounds great on the outside; escape the terrible clutches of your crap parents and live happily ever after. However, there are two major problems with that: 1. Being in the system is a crap shoot - you're ripped from your home and flung into outer space, with no idea where you're going to land, and there's a good chance you'll be separated from your siblings if you have any. You might get lucky and land in a nice home with good people. The more likely scenario, though, is more along the lines of my tried-and-true theory: people are garbage. Bad foster homes just want you around for the check. They might lock you up. Starve you. Pretend you don't exist unless DSS comes to check on you. With the added bonus of not having your own stuff, your own bed, your own space. Even though my family and home life are trash, it's still mine. It's a dumpster fire, but it's my dumpster fire, and I'm used to it. This means I still retain some level of control over my own life. So no, I don't want to go into the system, and I definitely don't want that for Mia. I want to take care of her so she can keep her innocence as long as possible, even if it kills me.

I'm pulled back to Earth by Mia pulling on my hand. She looks up at me, one eyebrow raised in question. "What are you waiting for, Asher? Can we go home now?"

I keep the idle phone up to my ear, purely for show, and look around for their black car. I nod, acting like someone cares on the other line.

They're finally gone.

I shimmy the phone into my pocket with everything else and start the walk back home with my sister, her doll, and our new stash of snacks. I'm glad to be rid of the nice people and their endless stream of questions, but my teeth are still on edge.

If we come across that weird stranger again, I'm afraid of what will happen. Not to us, but to him. I'm not sure I'll be able to stop myself if I get my hands on him.

We walk home in relative silence. I scan the horizon for the scumbag in case he decides to make another appearance. Mia is unusually quiet.

Lexi must have really worn her out. I'm impressed.

We crunch across gravel, then swish through tall grass, scurry quickly across pavement for a while, then reach gravel again, walking up the driveway to our dingy door.

I'm good at getting into the house without making a sound. I noiselessly open the screen door, then the regular door. I let Mia in and follow closely, locking the door tightly behind us. My ears open wide of their own accord, grasping for any sounds. They're not home yet, and probably won't be until much later tonight.

Good.

56

Kitten

Ms. Peggy would definitely have a problem with where we live. We don't have much, and what we do have is falling apart. Leo and Lexi's mom reminds me of our own mom long ago, before her spirit died. We had the best days when it was just me, her, and Mia. When it was just us, it actually felt like I was part of a family. She'd fix us lunch and dinner, play with us, watch movies with us. She used to smile.

I look at the TV in the corner, smashed in long ago by the drunk that broke our mother.

Anyway. No point in all that now.

I drop my key in the old brown dish on the counter and wash my hands properly in the sink.

Soap and water. Both sides. Scrub. Under the nails. Rinse completely...funny how I still remember that. That weird teacher I had in 6th grade was a complete germ freak and drilled that into our heads. So random. I never forgot it.

Before Mia can drift off too far, I send my voice around the corner after her. "I'm going to make dinner. Go ahead and take a quick shower. I'll leave some clean clothes in the bathroom for you."

"Otay, I wuv you Asher," her voice trails back from around the corner.

"Love you too, Mia."

I'm glad she thinks I'm worth something. Most days, I don't. Can't even get my sister out of this rathole.

After dinner, we work on her pink pony puzzle for the 150th time. It's weirdly satisfying to see how fast we can put it together every time, since we've almost got it memorized. We get so into it, we lose track of time.

Before we know it, Mia is yawning deeply and rubbing her eyes. I look at the clock on the stove. The red numbers say 11:00 PM, way past her bedtime.

Well, Dad isn't here to get mad at least. I'm glad I got to spend some extra time with Mia. I wish we could have days like this more often. I actually feel okay again. I feel weirdly alive, happy even... it's a nice feeling, but it never lasts.

I scoop Mia up into my arms and carry her toward her room.

I feel her stir. Wrapped around my shoulder like a kitten, she traces one of my bigger scars with a tiny finger. "Hey Asher."

The numb sensation crawls up my back and almost makes me drop her. I clench my jaw and endure it. "Yes, Mia?"

"Why do you always have so many ouchies on your arms?" she asks innocently.

"I'll tell you when you're older, I promise." We reach her bed, and I tuck her in, doll included. "Now get some sleep."

She snuggles in under her blankets. "Otay! Goodnight Asher."

"Goodnight Mia." I lean down and kiss her on her little forehead, then turn off her light.

I'm glad it's too dark for her to see the tears rolling down my face. I need to be a strong big brother, I need to just keep protecting her. Part of me wants to tell her the truth now, but she's too young, too innocent to understand. I can't burden her with my problems, she just needs to focus on being a kid. I want her to have the childhood me and Duncan will never get. It's too late for us, but she has her whole life ahead of her...she deserves to know the truth, but she can wait a few more years. I want her to stay happy for as long as I can protect her. However, I don't know how much more I can take...

I hear the car pull into the driveway at 2:30 AM, right on schedule. I turn over in my bed and try to fall asleep.

XIX

Mia Gryphon

Asher's younger sister

57

Gummy Bears

Saturday, September 8.
4:00am
  It's still dark. The clock's big red numbers say 4 AM. Mama and Dada would be mad if I asked to play because they're sleeping. Asher is a good big brother and always tucks me in at night, so I'll let him sleep, too. I know! I can play with my toys until Asher wakes up. I think I left my toys in the bathroom. I still can't reach that light, but I will keep growing so I don't have to use this box anymore.

  Oof, I got it! [CLICK.]

  Hm. Where are my toys? I know I left them right here. Ooh, gummy bears! I love gummy bears. I have an idea! Mama and Asher would be happy if I got myself ready for the day. They will be so surprised! First I'll have some breakfiss, then I'll brush my teef and get dressed, like a big girl.

  [CRINKLE.]

  This isn't the same box that gummy bears come in. This is a baggie. Hmm. Maybe it's just a different brand, like Asher says. Asher says that when things we buy have a different box but taste the same, it's just a different brand. This looks like gummy bears, so it's probably a different brand. I don't think Dada would be happy if I wasted food, so I need to be a big girl and finish them all.

[THUMP.]

Ow, ow, ow!....My chest and tummy hurt. A LOT. I feel really hot all over. I can't stand up. Where's Asher? My hands feel funny. Why is everything moving?

"Asher?! ASHER!!"

XX

Asher

58

This Can't Be Happening

I shoot up off my pillow and sit up, listening. My heart is pounding into my neck. I scramble to the sound of her voice as fast as I can over clumsy socks and uneven flooring. My limbs are so heavy, I can't get to her fast enough.

[HUARRRRRK.]

Did she just throw up? Here she is. Oh, no, Mia...she's on the floor – this is not good. She did barf. Ugh, let me move her out of it. Wait –

"What is this...?"

[CRINKLE.] A plastic bag.

Cold horror.

Their edibles. They're always laced with something else.

I pick up the bag. It has "fent" scrawled on it in permanent marker.

What if she... No. No. It's not possible. This is not happening. Wait, she's trying to say something. Mia, please. You're going to be fine. You HAVE to be okay, Mia. You're my little sun. My little sunshine...

Her tiny hands are so cold. My face is melting and I can't

stop it.

I can't do this.

"Hey bwother. I wuv you. My tummy hurts a lot, so I'm gonna take a nap, otay?"

Her little eyes are closing–

Her hand droops in mine. Her pale little body sags, taking me with it.

"Mia, NO!!" I cry out, but it just comes out like a strangled sob. I scramble over my stupid self to get back to my room, back to my phone. My heart, my head, my hands, everything is pounding.

Not fast enough. Not good enough.

I clumsily dial 9-1-1, but my thumb hovers over the call button.

Would this mean that DSS would come and take us? Hospitals have to report things like this, and people are garbage. They don't care if you live or die, and Mia might be dying. What do I do? WHAT DO I DO?!

I press the button and the call starts to process, but I kill it before it connects.

Maybe we can fix this. Maybe she can sleep it off. I don't want her to be taken away and stuck in the system without me. She won't make it. She needs to be with me because I can protect her. If they take her from me, I lose my last reason to live.

I. Can't. Do. This.

I run back to Mia. Her little hand has tumbled to the floor. Her hair is spiraled around her head like a halo.

Something's different. Something's wrong.

I press my head to her little chest. Nothing. Nothing. Nothing. She's colder than before.

DAMN IT.

I try to mimic CPR like they made us do in Health class, but I have no idea how to do it. I clasp my hands together, weirdly try to find the spot on her chest, and start pushing down awkwardly. I count a few times, but it feels stupid and pointless because I know in my heart that SHE IS GONE.

59

I'm So Sorry, Mia

The worst blood-curdling howl I've ever heard in my life comes up and out of my stomach like a wraith. It haunts me even though I made the sound. Something very bad surges into my hands. Both fists clamp down and start to smash everything.

NOT THIS. I CAN'T DO THIS.

Anything close, I grab it. I feel the momentum of it sling into the wall.

Book, thump. Lamp, crash. Chair, crack.

I. CAN'T. DO. THIS.

I remember Mr. Cheezers' stupid "can't rant" and it makes me mad. I yell at no one. "YOU HAVE NO IDEA!" I punch the wall once. Again. Again. Both fists. With my head. Over. And over.

It hurts. Good. I need it.

My screams echo down the hall and STILL THEY WON'T COME.

I pause, shoulders arching in time with my panting. My bloodied forehead begins to drip. Sloppy drops fall onto my sister's smiling, one-eyed doll. I pick it up with trembling hands. My face melts again. I'm drowning.

"My Mia is…" my jaw fails. The tears are hot and merciless. I can barely get the words out, but she deserves that I hear them out loud. "MY BABY SISTER IS DEAD." It stabs me in the stomach. I look at her on the floor. I was too late. I howl again, falling to my knees. I hug her cold little body. She didn't deserve to die covered in vomit.

I'm so sorry, Mia. I'M SO STUPID. STUPID. IT'S MY FAULT. WHY DIDN'T I JUST CALL?!

I sit up enough to scratch at my arms as hard as I can. I scream. "I WANT TO BLEED. TAKE ME WITH YOU TO HEAVEN." After this, I don't think there's a way I'll ever get in.

Now I'm really alone. The pain inside is worse than broken glass. There's nothing left to lose, so I'm going to do what I should have done a long time ago. I look around, crazed. My open hands land like eagle talons on a broken stereo, blood flicking. Since I'd rather die anyway, I storm into my parents' room. Part of me is screaming to stop because I may actually die from this.

GOOD. There's nobody left to miss me anyway.

I kick their door open, and the squealing smash startles them awake. They rise from the mattress like poison vines. I take aim and let the stereo fly at them, along with the two words I have wanted to say to them for a very long time, at the top of my lungs. The stereo cracks across my father's head and lands on the floor.

I let them hear the truth, much too late. "I should have called DSS. Mia WOULD HAVE BEEN TAKEN FROM ME, BUT SHE'D STILL BE ALIVE AND AWAY FROM YOU!!!"

My father has been activated and is on me so quickly, I only hear ringing before everything fades to black. While under the black, I hear their idiotic feet going into my sister's room. Then my mother's voice for the first time in way too long. She's howling like me.

I can't help but feel a little bit of satisfaction at hearing her suffer.

ABOUT DAMN TIME. GOOD. YOU DESERVE IT, TOO.

I fade.

60

The Burial

L**ater that night**
8:oopm
I come back from the darkness. My eyes are blurry and my face is in a cold puddle. I have a pounding headache, but I wait on the floor to listen for what's happening. I can somewhat hear my father's fat feet chuffing in his sandals across the carpet. There's an odd noise alongside his steps I don't recognize. It sounds like something heavy dragging behind him.

A streak of panic flares through me.

Is he dragging Mia's body? I swear, I will kill him if he touches her...

Then I hear the wailing. My mother's voice sounds so foreign, so far away. She's the one he's dragging.

She whines, "No..." Then further down the hall, "...my baby..."

Dad cuts her off. "Shut up, come on- we have to get rid of the body-"

A sudden explosion from Mom. "DON'T TAKE HER AWAY

FROM ME! NO MORE! NO MOOOORE!!!!!!" Sounds of a scuffle. Grunting. "NO - MORE!"

A hard, sharp crack. The gasping cry I've heard many times from Mom. Gentle sobbing, but this time, it's deeper than I've ever heard it.

I let my eyes zone out into the dirty brown carpet. There's a dark liquid seeping into the fibers.

I think this is blood, not water. I can't believe that Mia is really gone. It happened so fast. I couldn't even save her when she needed me most. I didn't protect her. I failed. Now I'll never be able to fulfill my promise to her. She was supposed to live a long and happy life. At least I got one part right: she'll never know hardship again.

The thought stabs my throat. Bitter pain bubbles up from my core and exhales into the carpet as a hot, helpless sob. My eyes crinkle shut. All I can do is lay here. All of me pours out in strangled whispers until there's nothing left.

My Mia...my little sunshine...please, no...

I don't know how long I've been laying here. Then I hear it, the whoosh of a big trash bag. My eyes snap open.

That's not what I think it is. That son of a-

"BOY. I KNOW YOU'RE AWAKE. GET YOUR SORRY SELF OVER HERE AND HELP ME. *NOW,*" he growls. I hear the bag rustle. The sound of something small flopping, hitting the linoleum floor. "NOW, DAMN IT," he croaks.

I feel numb, but my body jerks at his command anyway.

Don't tell me he's doing what I think he's doing.

It takes everything I have to drag my body to my parents' bed. Pain screams throughout every part of me. I grab at the sheets and pull myself up as hard as I can. I have to use my knees to prop myself up and pull up the rest of the way. I feel like I've been hit by a truck.

I'm so tired...

I start to black out, but hear the trash bag again.

I have to see what he's doing. There's no way he's putting her in that. I knew you were a lowlife, but this...this is...

My father's words crawl through a sticky burp. "ASHER. LAST CHANCE, BOY."

I hobble down the dark hall into Mia's room. Everything in my body is on fire. Then my eyes fall onto it. A black trash bag, laying flat on the floor and tied off with a sloppy double knot. I fall to my knees. Pain presses down on me like a heavy cloak. My jaw gapes, and there's nothing I can do about it.

I wish it was me instead. It should have been me.

It's happening too fast for me to respond. My body is too weak.

This can't be real.

Dad picks it up, slings it over his shoulder, and walks past me into the hall toward the door that leads outside. On the way out, he kicks the chair I threw earlier out of his way.

I threw that. I'm just as bad as he is. I destroyed her room.

With a sideways glance, he pauses and says to me, "Grab the shovel from behind the trash cans. We have to bury this."

This.

I hear him open the door with a grunt. The screen door slams behind him.

Too slow. Not good enough.

Back in Mia's room, I feel my eyes zone out again for a moment. They refocus, landing on my Mia's bloodstained doll. I choke. I pick it up off the floor and clasp the doll to my chest. More tears fall like bombs around my knees.

Maybe if I hug it hard enough, she'll feel it in Heaven.

A single bang on the wall from outside jerks me back to reality. I stand up, jolted, and soon find myself in front of the trash cans. I don't remember getting here. The shovel is back here, leaning on the house. I pick it up with my free hand. I'm still clutching Mia's doll to my chest.

This can't be happening. Please wake up.

"Dig here," comes the command. The plastic trash bag crinkles lightly as he sets it down with an unusual gentleness. He coughs and sniffs for a second, then wipes his nose with the back of his arm.

I obey with eyes glazed over. I let the doll fall by my foot. I stab the shovel into the ground.

I'm not sure if I'll be able to do this.

I hear a distant kick from across the street, then the sound of a ball bouncing in the empty field behind our lot. I turn to look. The kid from across the street is looking at us. It takes me a few seconds for the cold possibility to creep over me.

We're being watched. That looks like Ozzy from Fountain View...I hope he doesn't make a big deal about this.

Dad's slug voice gropes for me in the darkness. "This stays between us, d'ya hear?" I can feel Dad's eyes searching for me. "Or there may be another accident."

XXI

Ozzy, the Neighbor

61

Bag of Deceit

Meanwhile...

The brothers wait around for the oldest to come back with the ball. It's hard to see where he went with the streetlamp barely doing its job.

The oldest, Ozzy, jogs lightly toward the soccer ball nestled in the weeds. The grass shuffles around his legs. With a quick scooping movement, he's got the ball, but something's different back here. The boy hears the crackling of a plastic bag and the moving of dirt.

Is that a shovel?

It's an odd set of sounds, so he looks around for the source.

It's the depressed weirdo from school and an older, bigger man. Probably his dad or uncle or something. They have a big black bag and are digging a hole.

Ozzy quietly brings a fist up to his gawking jaw.

Oh, snap. What are they burying?

It's not long before Ozzy realizes he's being watched, so he expertly kicks the ball up, catches it, and starts jogging back toward his brothers.

XXII

Asher

62

Too Much

should be digging this hole for you, too, Dad. I hate how weak I am.

I pull up a shovelful of earth, arms trembling and burning. With all my might, I toss the dirt over to the side. My eyes try to refocus on the hole and can't quite seem to find it. My arms are giving out. The shovel bites into the earth by my feet. I'm blacking out again. I'm trying not to, but I'm fading. I can feel my head bounce off the handle of the shovel on the way down.

I deserve it.

Blackness.

XXIII

Ozzy

63

How Rumors Begin

Ozzy's back with his brothers, who have taken the ball and run off with it. He pauses for a second, pulling out his phone. It glares in the dark, giving his chin and brow a creepy blue glow. A few taps and swipes pull up the group chat.

His chat bubble soon floats into the conversation.

```
I just saw Asher and his dad burying something in
the backyard. Maybe it's a body... LOL.
```

Ozzy chuckles to himself and leads his brothers back inside the house. With a sideways glance, he's already refreshing the screen to see if anyone's replied yet.

There's one.

```
Pics!?
```

XXIV

Asher

64

Night

When I wake up again, the shovel is gone. Dad is gone. The trash bag is gone. Between the light of the moon and the yellow street lamp, my eyes can pick out that there's a pile of mangled grass and dirt a few feet away.

I drag myself over and collapse beside Mia's grave.

Part of me died with her tonight, but I wish all of me had. I would give up everything and anything just to go back in time and stop her from dying. It's useless of me to wish, it's too late. I should have saved her...It's over now. Perhaps dying wouldn't be a bad option...

My thoughts continue to grow darker and more demented as I lie in the dirt. I crumple into a ball and just lay there until the sky begins to wake up again.

I feel the morning dew landing on my body. It's hard to tell the difference between dew and tears because I'm getting soaked.

My tired eyes spot a butterfly.

Mia would have loved you...

The butterfly flutters next to the house and suddenly lands on my chest, strangely soothing. It feels like a hug Mia would have given me. I remember the day I walked home after school and the decision I made that night.

I need to be better, even though my family has collapsed. If not, then what was all my bad luck for? It's what Mia would want. I'm going to do this for you, Mia.

I'm going to make sure this never happens again. I take a few minutes to confess my sins to the air. It weighs on me like a boulder that I have to carry alone. Now that Mia has passed, I'm all alone. I let the fact wrap around my mind.

I'm really by myself now. I have no reason to survive. No person to fight for anymore...

I try my best not to think. I don't know how, but after a while, I manage to drift off into a cold, restless slumber.

65

After my Sister

Monday, September 10
8:30am
Walking back into the building as if nothing happened hurts. Just because I need food and a safe place to hide, I am in here acting like my sister isn't buried in the backyard in a trash bag. I don't deserve to eat. I don't know how I'm going to make it through this. Mia would want me to do my best, but I just want to join her.

I take a muffin and a carton of milk from the breakfast line and shove them both into the pockets of my hoodie. I still have one brownie left from the play date in the same pocket. I will never eat it because it's Mia's, no matter how bad it hurts. I hate my body for being so weak. I hate my father. I hate my mother. Even animals know how to take care of their children. Surely it couldn't be that damn hard.

I start walking toward Homeroom again. It's always the same thing every single day. The halls are hollow and meaningless. Everyone here is a zombie follower too stupid to think, and I'm too numb to feel anything anymore.

66

Ms. Berry the Art Teacher

Ms. Berry is rare because she seems to see past the fake walls you put up, but doesn't force you to talk about them or put on an act.

I sit at my desk and look up at the TV screen. Ms. Berry always has the assignment up there for the day, and it's pretty self-explanatory. We're working on our sketchbooks again today. That's easy. This is my favorite class, the only one I have a 100 in. I feel my mind drifting off, but I know it's fine and that I'll come back.

Ms. Berry and I have had many talks, during which she has given me a safe space to vent about my problems with Christian Clawthorne. During some of our conversations, Ms. Berry has shared with me that she also used to deal with bullies herself, so she gets where I'm coming from and how delicate of a situation it is to "snitch". People used to say to her, "You'll never amount to anything!" or "Nobody cares about art anymore, Picasso!" I wonder who she had to help her through it.

If you haul off and punch a bully in the face, you're the one that gets in trouble. On the other hand, once you're labeled the "snitch", the bullying gets so much worse. Ms. Berry makes sure that Christian sits as far away from me as possible, and is always watching my back so he doesn't have a chance to mess with me. Her support is an unspoken thing I'm grateful for and yet can never thank her for.

My mind drifts back to the present. I watch Ms. Berry shuffling around the classroom, bringing materials to one kid, pausing to help another one, and just doing her usual thing. I try to imagine her as a kid getting bullied, but it's kind of hard. Her story gives me hope that maybe I can survive and come out the other side, too.

I've got to get some work done.

I pull out my sketchbook, and a stone falls out of my book bag. The noise startles me and I scramble to pick it up before someone else grabs it. I found it outside when I got off the bus this morning, and I do not want to lose it. It's smooth and round on one side, and flat on the other. I'm saving it so I can decorate it for Mia's grave. Even though she loved her doll more than anything in the world, it got trampled and thrown away once my Dad saw it had blood on it. This rock is all I have for her.

My eyes burn and want to water. I put the rock in my pocket. While my hand is in my front hoodie pocket, I let my fingers twist a bit of skin on my stomach through the fabric. It works to ease my emotions.

I walk over to the materials table, plucking a few different colored Sharpos from the basket. These are my favorite colors because they work on anything, especially skin. I bring everything back to my desk, set the markers in a neat line, and start shading my rock.

Ms. Berry's patrol route soon passes by me. She leans over

and whispers, "This is really interesting. What is it for?"

I look up at her and shake my head no.

Please don't make me answer that.

She says, "Hm. I see." Then she walks on.

* * *

The bell rings and everyone pours out into the hallway. Ms. Berry is kind enough to wait for the others to leave before saying anything. With a gentle hand not quite touching my shoulder, she asks if I have a moment to speak.

I nod.

Ms. Berry motions toward her desk for me to follow her. She sits and begins sifting through things on her desk.

I stand by, waiting to hear what she has to say.

Ms. Berry speaks in a quiet, clear voice. "If I were to be perfectly honest with you, Asher, I worry about you a lot." She continues shuffling her papers as though it were the most commonplace thing in the world to say to someone. What strikes me is she doesn't stare me down or expect any kind of response like the counselors always do.

Despite this, my reaction is automatic. "Don't worry about me, because all that's going to do is stress *you* out. I'm good, Ms. Berry," I chuckle fakely. I glance toward the door.

I'm already late. I'll probably have to ask her for a pass.

I can see her shoulders rise and fall from a mute sigh.

Was that all she wanted? I really need to go.

After a pregnant pause, she replies. "What I'm talking about is not a *worry* like that. I can see that you are strong and capable. I can see that you're exceptionally talented, too, from the beautiful pieces you create. It's clear that your art is not like the other kids' - it has something else behind it that's beyond your years."

My stomach blooms with cold fire.

Strong and capable. Not sure where she got that from.

"The worry I'm referring to is more of a wonder. As I go about my day, I usually see something that reminds me of you and I'll wonder how you're doing, if you're okay. I wonder what may have happened in your life that is causing such a deep sadness in you. I wouldn't ask you to relive it or share it with me if you didn't want to, but I can see it and I can even feel it coming off you in waves. If you ever need someone to talk to, please know that you are not alone. I am here. It is important that you understand I am under obligation to share what you tell me with the counselors if it's something that is putting you in danger. I know I'm just a teacher, but I wanted you to know that someone is thinking of you and cares about you, for what it's worth."

I don't know what to say, so I just mumble a thank you and start making my way toward the door.

"Oh, wait, here -" she blurts.

It cuts off the swirl of thoughts that are already starting up in my head.

"Let me write you a pass. Almost forgot. Don't want them yelling at you for nothing," says Ms. Berry, scribbling on a sticky note and offering it to me.

I look at her smiling face and don't see any sickly pity. I nod and walk out.

Once I'm out, the thoughts begin to swirl again.

One thing I respect about Ms. Berry is her honesty. She taught me that instead of letting her struggles get to her and make her start hurting others, she chose to put that energy into her passion instead, which was Art, and it changed her life.

From what it seems, how you live your life is a deliberate choice, but not everyone makes the right one. It's often said the most dangerous people are broken people, like me. *Hurt people hurt people*, the old saying goes. My own father is a perfect example who takes everything out on us because it was done to him as a kid.

All you need is one person to believe in you to turn things around. To help you see things a little bit differently and change for the better. It doesn't have to be a drastic change, but just a small light switch inside yourself that looks at life a little differently.

67

Gravestone

The bus drops me off at home. The rock I decorated in art class is still in my hoodie pocket. I run my fingers over its surface. It was smoother before I colored it.

The hiss and clank of the bus doors huff hot air behind me. I turn to see it drive off and turn the corner. I take a quick glance at Ozzy across the street. I wait for him to go inside his house.

Ozzy pauses for a second, watching me, too.

I pull my hoodie down and pretend to look for my keys. I listen carefully for the slam of his front door before walking to the grave.

The small mound of disturbed earth waits for me like Mia used to. One more glance at his house, his windows, and everywhere else.

Should be okay.

I produce the rock from my pocket. With my hand, I dig a small hole for it to fit in, then wedge the rock into it carefully. If she can see it, I hope she likes it.

XXV

Ozzy

68

Cruelty

Tuesday, September 11
10:00pm
In the dark of the night, the only thing that can be seen is a phone flashlight bouncing across the grass like a fairy up to no good. It seems to know to avoid the weak streetlamp. It creeps into the yard and hovers over a mound of dirt.

This is its destination. The light turns off for the quickest moment, then blazes brightly.

Ozzy's face is lit up from beneath. His fingers fly across the screen. A text goes out to the group chat.

It's a picture of a smooth stone with Mia's name on it and a date.

Ozzy types.

```
Yooooooo...I think it's really true. There's a
body buried back here...Who's Mia?
```

A text comes back almost immediately from a chat member he doesn't recognize.

    I think Mia is the little sister.

XXVI

Lucy

<h1 style="text-align:center">69</h1>

<h1 style="text-align:center">The Invitation</h1>

Wednesday, September 12
7:35am

I half-wake up and reach for my phone. My hand fumbles blindly on the nightstand, searching. My sleepy brow wrinkles underneath the covers. I reach my arm all the way out and down into the cold to feel around on the carpet in case it fell during the night. Still nothing. A stream of panic surges through me and my eyes snap open.

Where is my phone?

I sit up and raise a questioning eyebrow. Then the leaden hammer drops into the pit of my stomach.

Oh, that's right. I'm grounded. And of course, on the worst possible day.

I slip out of bed, snatch the gray bathrobe hanging from the back of my chair, swoosh it around my shoulders, and dash into the bathroom. I know it doesn't matter what you look like when you're watching a livestream, but I feel paranoid that I'll still be seen through the camera somehow. I flick the bathroom's light switch on. The sudden bright light makes me squint, but it's fine. I splash water on my face, moisturize, slap on a quick foundation, and tie my hair up into a bun. I rush down the stairs towards the computer. Yes, that ancient 2012 one my parents have in the living room as the family computer. I power it on and the load screen flickers to life. I watch the progress bar sputter and heave its way toward 100%.

This thing is so old. I'm surprised it even connects to the Internet.

20%.

My leg begins to shake of its own accord. I lean backwards in the chair and let my head hang backwards so I'm looking up at the ceiling. Turns out we have a chandelier up there.

How have I never noticed that lamp before? Hm. It's dusty.

I let out a huge sigh, sit back up, and look again at the load screen.

53%.

This is ridiculous.

Seriously. How did people even survive in 2012 with prehistoric hunks of crap like this?

78%.

My eyes grow wide and exasperated. I put my head down on the desk. After what feels like an actual century, the load screen finally turns over with a chime and reveals the desktop. I shoot straight up in the chair. My eyes flash down to the clock at the bottom right of the screen.

7:58AM.

Lexi appears behind me out of nowhere. Her little-kid breath on the back of my neck gives me a start. I gasp weirdly, clutching at my chest where my heart is supposed to be. While glaring at her, my throat tightens suddenly. I glance back at the screen and scan it to make sure it wasn't recording somehow.

It's not. I think.

Lexi giggles and asks, "What are you doing, Lucy?"

Not even exaggerating, I tell her, "Today could be the most important day of my life."

Lexi asks, "Is Meghan going to invite people to her party today on ClockClick live?"

I eye her carefully.

There's only one way she'd know about it.

"Harper must have told you when we ran into her at Brooklynn's Pizza the other night."

She nods. "Harper says I should be here so you don't cry." She holds out some spearmint gum, which always calms me down. "Why is this so special, Lucy?"

I don't think. I just take a stick of gum, unwrap it, and shovel it. I don't think my jaw has ever cranked a piece of gum so hard in my life. "So basically, Meghan is doing a live video on ClockClick at eight..."

I check the time. 7:59AM.

I open a browser window, pull up ClockClick, and log in. Chomping on the minty gum helps take the edge off my nerves. The icy flavor comes out of my nostrils and gives me a second to think. It's so awkward to have to do this on the big computer.

Things work so much better on a phone.

Lexi scrunches up her nose. "Eww, why does Meghan do the video so early?"

I try to explain it fast before it starts. "She likes being able to control when people wake up. Anyway, she reads off a list of the invites to the party, that way everyone in the whole school will know whether you made it or not. The first invite is always the most important, because it means that you were the first one on her mind. Every first invite never declines."

Lexi makes things so much worse when she asks, "Are you scared?"

All I can do is nod. I'm suddenly cold. My jaw clenches. My eyes watch the screen helplessly.

8:00AM.

I feel my chest getting tight. My mouth and throat are both drying up fast. The gum is now dead rubber.

Nothing is happening. Did I miss it?!

Lexi sees my panic and hugs me. She whispers, "Well if you don't get in... we could toilet paper her house."

I hug her back, tightly. Her tiny voice draws all the fear back inside of me and hushes it.

Suddenly, there is a notification. It has a red dot on it.

```
GlamQueen started a live video.
```

That's Meghan's username.

I let Lexi drift out of my arms and move to click it immediately.

Meghan's smiling face pops up on the screen. Makeup and hair are flawless. The space behind her is nothing more than a bare white wall and a big-leafed green plant illuminated by the morning sun. She acts like she doesn't know the power she has, which makes her hold on people so much stronger. "Hey guys! I'm just here to tell you who got invited to my birthday party this year!" She eyes the camera coyly, "Listen for your naaaame!"

I suck in my breath.

Please, please, please. If I don't get invited to Meghan's party, I'm officially a nobody. I'll never have another chance at being popular. No pressure!

Lexi stands beside me. She looks nervous, too.

Meghan looks at the camera. Her peregrine falcon eyes seem to look straight into my soul. She enunciates every syllable. "Lucy Mae..."

My stomach catches fire. I gasp, and the gum whooshes into the back of my throat. It feels like sticky webbing wrapping its tendrils around my uvula (that dangly thing at the back of the throat).

Lexi screams. "YOU DID IT?!"

My eyes water and burn, then widen.

Um...this is not good...

After a few very long seconds of not breathing, I finally cough violently. The gray gunk drops onto my sock. Once the air rushes back into my lungs, I manage a nod and thumbs-up for Lexi.

I'm pretty sure I almost just choked to death, but I was the first invite. THE FIRST.

Lexi cheers and bunny hops around my chair. "Yaaaay, Lucy!"

Without thinking, I take a tissue from the nearby box and pick the gum up off my foot. I crumple it all up into a ball and toss it into the bin under the computer desk. I jump up, clear my throat with a grin, and throw my hands up at Lexi. "I DID IT! LEXI, I DID IT!"

Lexi jumps into my arms and we hug. I stand still, carrying her. Looking over her little blonde head at the live stream as it continues in the background, I hear a couple more names, including Harper (of course), and even Marcus.

Cool...

Meghan's voice speeds up as she wraps up, "...and that's it! I'll be texting the deets soon. Hope to get lots of presents! See you all there. Byeeeee!" She winks, holds up her hand for a tiny wave, then cuts the feed. The live stream window disappears, revealing my plain, notification-less dashboard.

Lexi wriggles out of my arms and lands with a thump on her fluffy slippers. She raises both her little hands and sings, "Now life is worth it!"

I take in a breath and frown.

Life?

"That was a little dramatic, Lex."

Lexi shrugs, making a big show of holding her hands out. "But Harper says parties make life worth it. Does that mean that parties are...*super*...*duper*...important?" She punctuates the super and the duper with one hop each. Her platinum hair wisps around her head when she turns to look at me. Her little eyes have that look in them that means she's watching every move I make right now.

I don't like that she said that. "Not always, Lex. Parties are something fun to do, but there is more to life than parties." I pause, hearing my own words sink in as if someone else just said them to me.

But this is a MEGHAN GARDENER party. This is the big one I've been waiting for. Maybe in this case, it's an exception...isn't it?

Lexi grabs my arm and shakes it.

I feel myself drift somewhat out of the haze.

"Helloooo-! " she crows, "Is anybody *listening?*"

I scowl without thinking. "Yeah yeah." I'm drifting off

again.

This is not how I imagined it would go at all. I got picked first, which was the best possible outcome. Why am I feeling like this? I've always wanted to go to one of these, so what's the big deal? Sometimes they're kind of mean at these parties, I've heard. I don't like people being mean, but I really really REALLY want people to like me this year. Really really really. I'm sure it's not as bad as they say...

I drift back to reality. Lexi has wandered off to do something else. I can hear her singing fading down the hall. A noise comes from the computer that sounds like a direct message coming in (DM for short).

That was fast.

It's one of my friends, Emily. Well, she's a kind-of friend. Emily is not really a main character in my book. I am in the same P.E. class as her, but that's about it.

Anyway, Emily DMs me and says,

```
LUCY U R THE LUCKIEST GURL!
```

I sit back down and line myself up at the prehistoric keyboard. I smile wryly, basking in the glow.

```
I KNOW ;)
```

Another message bloops in.

```
I WISH I GOT INVITED I THINK MEGGY FORGOT ABT ME
>:(
```

For the love of all that is good and holy, this girl's abbreviations are killing me.

I reply with some fake sympathy as a courtesy.

```
YEAH, I'M SORRY YOU DIDN'T GET INVITED, EM. :(
```

She shoots back another message almost instantly.

```
DID U JUST USE A COMMA IN A TXT? :0
```

Did you just say "txt" when you could have just put the e?

```
YEAH LOL, I GUESS MY ELA CLASS IS PAYING OFF. :D
```

Emily again:

```
ANYWAY I GTG BUT ILL TOTALLY SEE U LATER <3
```

I decide not to respond to that. I continue to scroll through ClockClick, which I must say is quite a different experience when using an old mouse with a rolling ball rather than just swiping my finger.

It's so much WORK.

As the images float past, I start noticing different weird posts from kids at school. I can see their posts because I follow them, but it's only because they followed me first. It's only right. I find a post that shows a picture of a kid with a black hoodie walking home in the rain. It kind of reminds me of Asher. The kid looks depressed. And it doesn't look like a meme, it looks like a real picture.

The caption reads:

```
WHEN UR BEING EMO AND THINK NOBODY SEES U.
```

Ugh, abbreviations again. Wait, Marcus just commented.
  Marcus' comment reads:

```
Football-is-life: You shouldn't post things like
this of other people. You never know what they're
going through. :( Do you have permission to use
this kid's picture?
```

A torrent of nasty replies crop up, snapping and biting like piranha. The first one sneers:

```
SkibBuddyToilet123: What are you, the bully police?
```

Another one joins in.

```
JustNo2014: Look out, guys, or the hall monitor is
going to get you! I bet you snitch every chance
you get. Get a life, loser.
```

The last one makes the pit of my stomach hot.

```
aN!mEfAn: Nobody cares about getting permission. I
think you should go cry with the emo kid.
```

I re-read Marcus' comment, then look back at the original post. Now I can see that it's obviously an attempt at being ironic or funny, and it's failing; it just comes off as mean.

Would I have noticed that if Marcus hadn't spoken up?

That was brave of Marcus to say, knowing he would catch a bunch of crap for it. The acrid comments obviously came from ignorant idiots who have nothing better to do than laugh at others and post stupid things online. Part of me suddenly feels strangely inferior. I wish I could say stuff like that and have people still like me. I wish I didn't have to work so hard to fit in.

Something that Tess Sariano said on my favorite show, *The Filmores*, is: "I want to be good - life just isn't letting me." He was just kidding, but still. I want to be sweet and kind and stand up for everyone. But I've never been able to stand being disliked, so I guess I just push it down.

Mom's voice cuts through the haze from behind me. "Lucy, are you okay?"

I snap back to reality. "Wuh-?"

70

Getting Permission

I turn around and see Mom's fiery hazel eyes. They're pretty when the sun hits them, but they're also scanning me from where she's standing behind my chair with arms crossed. She looks at my gray bathrobe, then up at my bun. She asks, "What's going on?"

Oh, wait. Meghan's party. This may be the best (or worst) time to ask, but I might as well give it a shot.

I smile at her. "Hey, Mom, can I –?"

Mom's eyes narrow. It's like getting shot at by lasers. She frowns before I can even finish my sentence.

Ugh, she always does this.

I feel myself begin to roll my eyes, but immediately stifle it.

An attitude won't help my case here. I'd better tone it down or I'm dead in the water.

I make a special effort to soften my face, but it's too late.

She's sniffed out something and pursues it like a great white shark. She sits on the couch next to the computer desk. "Can you what?"

I have a sudden flashback to Meghan saying my name on the live stream, and I can't help but grin. "I was just going to ask if I can go to a birthday party. I was invited to go next Saturday."

Mom settles into her seat, but her eyes have not left my face. "Whose birthday? Where is it?"

My grin fades.

Dad wanders into the living room to investigate the conversation he's been overhearing. The glass of orange juice in his hand tells he's coming from the kitchen. He feels the heat waves coming off our conversation, so he comes around the couch, sits down next to Mom, and puts his free arm around her.

She appreciates his support, shifting almost imperceptibly. Her aura softens some, but she still hasn't taken her eyes off me. The computer chair I'm in is a couple of feet away from them, across the blue fluffy rug.

Dad sips his juice and waits with Mom for my answer.

How can I word this? They're not too crazy about Meghan.

"Well, I'd be going with Harper. It's going to be a bunch of us girls from school."

Mom blows by my setup like it's a cardboard box on the street. She repeats herself. "Whose birthday is it? Where?" She even tacks on another question. "When?"

I wasn't quite expecting that answer and I hate when I feel myself fumble. "It's, well, Meghan's...it's at her house with a bunch of us from school. It's a really big deal and everyone is going to be there. She'll be sending the details on the time later." A frustrated sigh betrays me.

This is going to crash and burn for sure.

Dad gently retracts his arm from Mom's shoulder, sets his

juice down on the glass coffee table (coaster, of course), and sits forward, leaning on his legs. Now I have two pairs of eyes on me. "Why are you so nervous, Pumpkin?" he asks, "Is there something wrong?"

"I'm not nervous. I'm just really scared you'll say no." I pause, surprised at my own candor.

The Shark has calmed down and become Mom again.

Wait. Could honesty actually work?

She asks, "What's so important about this party? Is that why you're down here so early in the morning, and all fixed up?"

"All fixed up? All I did was moisturize." I smile and roll my eyes, pretending it was a silly thing for her to say.

I look goooood.

Mom does not give up easily and will ask a question until it is answered. (I'm sure she secretly works part-time with the FBI as an interrogator.) "What's with the computer, Lucy Mae? I mean, I know you're waiting on a new phone, but this just seems desperate. Is it really that hard to stay off the Internet?"

"It's not that, Mom. It's just that – "

She's not going to understand.

I roll my eyes and sigh again.

My whole social future depends on being able to go to this party.

I look at my parents, sitting together on the couch like two parakeets on a perch.

They already have each other and don't need anyone else. They won't get it. It's pointless.

Dad interjects, "It's okay, sweetheart. You can tell us." I'm surprised to see that his dark brown eyes look more concerned than angry.

I have no choice but to just spill it. This is it.

"The thing is, Meghan has a birthday party every year and invites only a certain number of people. If you get picked first, that means you were the first one on her mind, which means you're more important than everyone else." My voice starts speeding up. "So then she does the invitations on a live stream video, which I had to log in to see here because my phone is broken. Nobody sees you if you're just watching a live stream, but you never know so I moisturized just in case. Then Meghan said *my* name first, which is a HUGE deal. I HAVE to be at this party or everyone will judge me because you HAVE to go if Meghan invites you. If I don't go, I might as well change schools." I pause and draw a very deep breath. Then I wait for the verdict.

Come on. Please.

Dad takes in the information and thinks for a moment. "I'm surprised you care so much about this Meghan Gardener kid. She really made you miserable back then, hun."

Mom nods in assent. "I don't like any one person having that much control over you, Lucy Mae."

This isn't going well.

"But Mom, it's *me* that wants to go. Nobody's pressuring me or controlling me. I've been really wanting to go to her birthday party, and she finally invited me. Not only that, she mentioned my name FIRST. That's really rare! Not only that, but all my friends will be there, and they'll wonder where I am if I don't go. I don't want to miss out on this, *please*. There will be grown-ups there." I cringe.

I'm actually not sure if there will be grown-ups there, but I assume so. I mean, obviously, right?

Mom and Dad finally stop staring a hole through me and look at each other instead. They have this really weird way of communicating with just their eyes. Usually it's gross, but this time I find myself staring at their expressions, trying to figure them out.

They seem to be working out the answer I gave them. Mom gives Dad a hard look, then glances in my direction.

I jolt and look away with all the grace of a newborn giraffe. *Ooh, bonus.*

I can see them in the TV reflection. I remain as still as I can and just watch.

On the TV screen, Dad ponders for a moment as if remembering something from long ago. When Mom looks back at him, the look in his eye seems gentle.

He glances over at me, then at his wife. His head moves with the tiniest nod I've ever seen in my life.

I watch Mom let out an inaudible sigh on the TV reflection. She pauses for a moment to remember something from long ago, too, and meets his eyes. She purses her lips skeptically, but returns the tiny nod.

Dad breaks the silence. "Alright, Lucy. You can look at us."

I suddenly feel silly and shift the computer chair so I can look at them again.

He continues. "We're still not 100% convinced about the influence Meghan is having on you, but if it's something all the kids are going to and there will be adults, it should be okay. I'll call Bob later on tonight and check in with him just to be sure he's *aware* he's hosting a birthday party." He chuckles, satisfied with his own joke.

Mom looks at me with softer eyes than before. "Lucy Mae, I will be perfectly clear. I am not thrilled about this party because it's Meghan's. That girl is extremely manipulative, and my only comfort is that you're smart enough to see it. It makes no difference to me if Harper is going or not, because YOU are my child, not Harper. This is a good opportunity for you to practice thinking for yourself. Both your father and I have worked very hard to raise you with love. We have taught you both right from wrong, and how to carry yourself with respect, not only toward yourself, but toward others. We were young once, too, and we remember girls like Meghan. We watched them grow up to be very lonely adults. She is not going to make any meaningful contributions to your life or anyone else's, sadly. My only concern is you. Now that you're becoming a young lady, it's time for us to learn to trust you. Do you understand what that means, Lucy Mae?"

Is my jaw hanging open?

I close it, but I'm still at a loss.

Uh...

"I think so. Kind of –?"

I mean, seriously. Do we really need to go through a whole speech just for a birthday party? It's not like I'm getting married or going on a long voyage across the sea.

My face must be giving me away, because Dad jumps in. He leans in closer to me and locks eyes with me. I'm immediately disabled. I look down at the fuzzy blue rug.

"Pumpkin, listen to your mother, please. This is really important. So far, you have shown us that even though you struggle to keep phones in one piece, you're a good kid."

"Hey!" I can't help but look at him again and smile a little. *Sneaky.*

Dad smiles back, "We know you have a servant's heart, which means that you love to help others. We also know you're at a delicate age where you are learning to balance what you know is right with what your peers are pressuring you to do and think. Having a servant's heart can make a person more susceptible to peer pressure if they're not guarding themselves carefully. We've been around longer than you, and we can see that there is a lot of pressure around this party, and especially around this Meghan character - this should throw up red flags to you. It definitely does to us. However, because you were honest with us, and because we trust *you*, Lucy Mae, we will let you go to this party even though we're somewhat uncomfortable with it. What we ask of you is that you go in with *awareness*. Pay attention to what's going on around you, and if you see something going on that you know is wrong, make a decision to do what's right instead, even if it's not the "popular" thing to do. It will be hard, but you will be able to live with yourself afterward. We believe in you so much, we know you can do it. Fair?"

I suppose so.

"Yes, sir."

Dad hugs Mom, and then comes over to me and hugs me, too.

I look at them both. "Thanks, Dad. Thanks, Mom."

"You're welcome, sweetheart. We love you," says Mom.

Hard to believe she was about to kill me just a few minutes ago.

Now that he's up and about, Dad changes the mood with a loud stretch. "Oooooo-KAY, then." He looks at Mom and me and asks, "All this talk of partying is making me hungry. Want me to make some toast and coffee?"

Mom stands up, smacking his arm gently and shaking her head with a smile. "Sure."

I smile, too. "Sure. I'll be right back. Gotta go to the bathroom first." I watch Dad pick up his orange juice glass, slurp the last bit of it, and put his arm around my mom. They walk together into the kitchen.

I dart into the guest bathroom and lock the door behind myself. I let out the loudest silent scream anyone has ever screamed. I jump up and down as noiselessly as I can, flapping my hands everywhere. It's a total happy dance, and I don't care.

I'm going to Meghan's party!!!

71

Nerves

Saturday, September 15.

I never thought Saturday would get here. It's 7:15, even though I asked them to get me here at 7. I didn't make a fuss about it. I'm finally on my way to a Meghan Gardener birthday party. I've waited for this my whole life and now that it's actually happening, it's surreal.

Is this really me sitting in the car, all dressed up and actually ON MY WAY to MEGHAN GARDENER'S house?

From my dim perch in the backseat of the family car, I look down at myself like Cinderella after her magical transformation. I have on my favorite dress, my new shoes, and my freshly painted nails. They illuminate temporarily when a yellow outside street light whizzes through the car, then up and out to make way for the next one. I try to re-imagine how I did my makeup.

I used my Adora butter eyeshadow, cat eyeliner, extra volumizing mascara, moisturizer, bronzer, powder, blush, and finishing spray. It looked perfect at home, so as long as I don't blow my nose, cough, sneeze, touch anyone, or cry, I should be good.

Even though I'm dressed up and ready, somehow my stomach is so tense, it's actually trembling. I try biting my lip to offset the lockjaw that's settling into my face, but I'm starting to worry I'll bite my lip off.

Am I actually dying right now?

The car goes over a bump, shifting the gift bag sitting by my feet, crinkling the plastic and drawing my attention toward it (thankfully). I got Meghan the rose gold and leopard print Suzie Summer messenger bag. She probably has a hundred, but I hope she likes it. Another bump, and the bag crinkles again. I feel my eyes widen in the dark.

Plastic. How cheap. I'm bringing MEGHAN Gardener a gift wrapped in a plastic bag you can find at the dollar store. I knew I should have wrapped it in paper. It would have been way classier. This is not good.

I sniff at the air.

Does my perfume smell cheap, too?

Now it seems to hang on me like an oppressive cloud of poverty. My voice of reason finally kicks in.

Okay, no. This is Adora+ Envy. There's no way – this is a top quality fragrance.

I take a deep shaky breath and try to escape myself by looking at my parents sitting up front. Well, the backs of their heads, anyway. They look like mannequins from this angle. Dad is driving. The street lights streak across his fresh haircut and his green golf shirt. Long-haired Mom is his silent co-pilot. It's hard to see what she's wearing from back here between street lights. I can see a gold hoop earring peeking through her hair, but that's about it.

They haven't said a word this whole drive, which in a way is just as bad as if they had spent the entire time lecturing me about how they don't like me going to this party.

The thing is, if they go against me, then I have something to strive against and my attending the party is like winning the argument. The fact that they're conceding to me going to this party means that they are allowing the full weight of this decision to fall on me. Nobody is fighting me or trying to keep me from going. This is exactly what I asked for, what I wanted, so all the responsibility falls on me not to screw this up.

To try and escape *that*, I look out the window, halfway exasperated.

Are we having FUN yet?!

I can't rest my chin on my hand without ruining my makeup or wrinkling my dress, so I just lean forward stiffly.

72

Less

My eyes catch the road like a treadmill and finally take my thoughts somewhere else.

This is her street.

It's easy to tell because the street signs change in this part of town; the font on them becomes a little fancier, a little more cursive. These are not common green street signs; the ones in this area are brown and have colorful clip art flowers embossed on them. It's a subtle way for the city to let its residents know they've left Peasantville and are now entering a higher-end neighborhood.

We're slowing down.

We turn right and cross over a small bump, from smooth pavement to crunchy gravel. My eyes grope through dim light and my own reflection in the glass. I can see tall manicured hedges and finally, the sprawling gates. I recognize them from Meghan's ClockClicks.

This is definitely it.

Our car crunches all the way down the long, snaking driveway lined with dark fir trees until the house starts to come into view. We get beyond the trees and I can see everything clearly now. It looks like the White House, only bigger and with way more colorful flowers and shrubs surrounding it. The entire home is bathed in clear, warm light, surrounded by tiny figures laughing and drinking from their cups. The house looks like it has at least 12 rooms. As we get closer, I can see the entrance is made of solid brick and has huge red doors. It's really hard not to think of our simple house. Its main highlight is the big oak tree out back. It has a homemade tree house on it and a tire swing, but that's pretty much it. The rest of our house is pretty common, even though we have two floors. The more I think about it, the more I start to feel kind of....*less.*

The car bumps up again onto smooth pavement. I can feel Mom turning her attention toward me in the dark. "This is it. Remember what we talked about, Lucy Mae. I trust you will make good choices. We'll be back at 11:00 sharp, so be ready." She turns around as best as she can in her seat, reaching uncomfortably around the headrest to offer me her phone. Her hand pauses expectantly in midair, nudging the phone toward me. "Take my phone in case of an emergency." I do and make eye contact with Mom. She looks grimly into my soul with wide eyes.

"Yes, ma'am." I take the phone because I know what's good for me. It's really hard not to roll my eyes right now, but it's best I don't. The plastic bag crinkles again when I pick it up. I wince. "Bye, Mom. Bye, Dad."

Their voices overlap and mirror each other. "Bye, honey."

73

The Party

I open the car door and step out onto the terrace. I shut the door behind me and pause to take it all in. Meghan's parents obviously have enough money to hire several gardeners at least. People's yards only look this perfect in movies or magazines. I guess I wouldn't even call this a yard. It's more like a huge courtyard. Minimalist furniture dots the area like chess pieces that just happened to land in exactly the right places. Long rectangular hedges filled with pink flowers lead the way toward the door.

Once I hear the car crunch its way back up the drive, I start making my way toward the house, clutching my gift gingerly so as not to make noise with it. I have to stretch my legs to climb up the ample brick steps, one oversized step at a time. Some of the other guests glance at me out of the corners of their eyes, then quickly look away except one - a slender, cat-like girl in a blue dress with long black hair and wire hanger shoulders. She's standing halfway up one step with her date, a handsome stranger wearing dark jeans and a dress jacket. I smile politely and give her a tiny wave, but she doesn't acknowledge me or say hello. She just wrinkles her nose and turns to her companion with a snide chuckle. The humiliation burns hot inside my gut, but I keep climbing.

Finally stepping onto the porch, I look up at the massive red doors. My eyes fall upon the beautiful door knockers, one on each door. They're golden lion heads, each biting down on their own golden hoop. My stomach does that weird tremble again when I take one of the golden hoops in my hand and bring it down onto the door. I crack it against the door once, then again, and again.

The latch clicks. I watch one of the doors swing open, revealing almost all the popular kids that I can only dream of being friends with huddled together in the main hall, dancing to dubstep being pumped in from the next room over. Some of them are yelling at each other over the din, trying their best to communicate.

I'm relieved to see it's Harper answering the door with a huge smile on her face. She laughs at me and speaks a little too loudly, "Hey - you're lucky I was near the door when you knocked or nobody would have heard you!" She opens her arms and comes toward me for a hug.

I'm still a little stung about her and Lexi being so close, but I smile back at her and accept the hug for a few moments. Perfume comes off her hair like a flowery wave. I back out of the hug and hold up the gift bag, grateful to the ambient noise for swallowing the plastic sounds for me. "Where do I put this?" I half-yell.

"Here, this way," Harper says. She takes my arm and begins to lead me through the giant house. The main staircase winds up into a gorgeous balcony. As we enter the main hall, I see Monica chatting with three other girls. She might be telling a story; she's making a silly face and shaking her head like a horse. The girls are laughing along with her.

Harper's grip on my arm tightens and we rush over to them.

Monica sees us coming. "OH MY GOSH, HEYYY GIRLLLL!!" Monica squawks loudly, flapping her arms. She leans in for an air kiss, puckering her lips ridiculously.

I visibly cringe but play it off as well as I can, returning her air kiss by pressing my cheek to hers. "Hey, Monica! Great to see you."

Four loud MUAHS, one for each girl, and it's over. I back up carefully to avoid touching any more of my makeup.

Monica clucks, "Go put your gift down and join us!"

"We were just getting to that!" Harper interjects.

Suddenly, there is the sound of a record scratching. The deeply digital music grinds to a halt, then swirls into a different melody - a surprisingly old-timey piano ditty. It doesn't seem to match the pulsing techno from before, but it seems to be intentional because the contrast arrests everyone's attention. The cheerful, airy notes drift down onto the crowd like confetti and hush the crowd. Heads begin to turn in different directions, trying to find the source of the change. The lyrics to the song are sung by a light female voice and are kind of hard to discern, but it sounds like they might be talking about some kind of candle queen. I'm sure I heard that wrong, but then again that happens to me a lot with songs.

Then, one person points at the stairs and everyone looks up. Meghan is emerging. She pauses on the balcony to drink in the moment, looking out over the crowd and waving, a perfect smile illuminating her face. Assorted hands wave back up at her from the crowd. She starts to float down the ivory stairs slowly so everyone can get a good look at her tight black dress. She's wearing heels, but her gait is so practiced, she glides down the steps as though she were barefoot. She holds her head up regally, barely brushing her fingers on the polished oak handrail for dramatic effect. Her hair is in perfect curls cascading down around her shoulders. On top of her head rests a heavily jeweled tiara. Her face radiates confidence and power.

Is it totally corny to say I'm in awe?

I don't mean to, but I keep watching her. Seeing Meghan in her natural habitat is so rare, it draws everyone into a trance. The crowd approaches her at the foot of the stairs, then opens up and surrounds her.

The background music evaporates and morphs back into drippy dubstep. The bass radiates off the walls like a headache. Meghan greets everyone, laughing, answering questions, and making sly faces where there's an opportunity.

That's the thing about Meghan Gardener. She uses her body to manipulate boys to do her bidding by blowing kisses at them and flirting with them. She wears provocative clothing that causes everyone to look at her. Girls want to be her, and boys want to date her. I've wanted to have people like me like that for as long as I've known her. I guess some are just born with it.

I watch her wade through the crowd. Then Meghan's crystal falcon eyes drift in my direction and fixate. The look on her face melts into pure delight.

74

Allure

I feel myself tensing up.

I think she's looking at me.

I suddenly feel like a 5-year-old holding a bad drawing. My hands clutch the plastic rope handles of the gift bag a little tighter.

Meghan is delighted to see the uncertainty on my face. She saunters over to me, wry grin playing on her lips. "Hey, Lucy. Come on back to the living room." She smirks, making her eyeliner look villainous. "That's where all the fun is. Let's leave these losers." She walks ahead of me and stops, looking back at me with a wink.

I laugh nervously, looking around with wide eyes and trying to ignore the sinking feeling that something really bad is waiting for me, but still I follow.

Meghan's pull is irresistible because of her status. She makes you feel like somehow you can attain celebrity status like her just by being around her, so you obey without question. It's the same exact allure that drives people into buying lottery tickets or spending hours trying to make that one viral video hoping they'll strike it big. People love the thrill of the chase and the novelty of it because life can be quite so monotonous. Meghan's influence also causes the same exact terror that makes you bring your hand back down immediately in class if nobody else is volunteering an answer for fear of being singled out. The only thing worse than being singled out is to be made fun of, and Meghan is very quick to do that.

75

Marcus

The asymmetrical fishtail on Meghan's black dress slithers around the corner, and I follow it. As I make the turn into the living room, I see Marcus leaning toward the grand piano, one hand in his pocket and the other absently teasing the keys.

Wait, why can't I breathe? I think this stupid dress is too tight. Why did I pick this again?

Despite my many sudden malfunctions, I'm grateful to see a familiar face that I know to be genuinely friendly, unlike Meghan - you're never quite sure with her.

Marcus notices me, too, and grins at my visible relief. "Hey, Lucy - you look great!" His free hand leaves the piano keys as he turns to greet me. It looks like he's coming in for a hug.

"Hi!" I start to hug him but awkwardly stop, not wanting to be made fun of.

Monica once posted on Instagram that a girl can't hug a guy without having feelings for him, so now everyone is paranoid.

I don't think that's true, but I don't want any rumors either, so I settle for a wave.

He chuckles, knowing what I was going to do, and waves back good-naturedly. Seeing the gift bag in my hand, he points me in the direction of the table that has all the presents. "I think you can set that over there if it's for Meghan."

I nod my thanks, then take a dramatic scurry over to the table. I find a spot for it, let it go at last, and scurry back to Marcus as if I'm dodging some kind of invisible rain.

I like Marcus. Not like THAT, of course. We go way back, and he's a nice guy, unlike some of the other guys here.

I look around, and my eyes stop on Harrison, who's across the room by the china cabinet. I've never understood how he's popular, but everyone knows him, and I guess if you're into cuss words and gossip, he's your guy.

I wave at him.

Harrison winks and wiggles his eyebrows in return.

I turn away quickly.

Eww, that's so gross.

Marcus looks over at Harrison, shakes his head, then turns his attention back to me. *I've never seen Marcus looking so... dapper...before. I didn't know he owned a formal jacket like this, and the way he has his hair swept back suits him really well.*

I suddenly realize I forgot about Meghan, but on the other hand, she disappeared when she went around the corner.

Weird.

Once I come back to Earth, I smile stupidly. "Hi again," I say breathlessly.

Marcus smiles and gives me his version of a tiny wave to tease me. "Hi, again." He motions to a nearby couch and waits for me to sit first before taking a seat himself. I watch his brown eyes drift off in Harrison's direction again. They pause for a moment, then come halfway back to me via a perfect side-eye. "Yeah, you might want to stay away from Harrison tonight."

I make the mistake of glancing over to see Harrison whispering to his friend. Both are now staring at me. I turn to Marcus and gag. Then I wonder. "Hey, what do you mean *tonight*?"

Marcus laughs louder and puts a friendly arm around my shoulder. "This is your first Gardener party isn't it?"

I wince. "Can you tell?"

He smiles. "Not by looking at you."

I grin. "Thanks, Marcus."

He nods, then takes his arm back down, settling into his place on the couch. "So anyway, Gardener parties last till 1 AM at the earliest."

I laugh. "You mean the latest."

He shakes his head. "Nope. The latest we've ever stayed once was 7 AM."

I gasp incredulously.

He nods solemnly.

There's no way I'm going to be here that late. My parents will be back at 11, and frankly, I'm kind of starting to like the idea. I don't want to float aimlessly here. It feels dangerous.

76

Spiderweb

I stifle my discomfort and squeak, "Hey Marcus?"

He had drifted off, but I can see why. It's hard not to watch Monica, who is now hula-hooping with the three girls from before, lined up along the steps of the staircase. Monica is holding out one arm, struggling to keep her phone steady and smile as she records a ClockClick. Marcus takes his unimpressed glance off of them and looks at me. "Yeah, Clark, what's up?"

I smile sheepishly. "Can I just kind of...?"

Now it's my eyes that are carried away. I see Meghan sauntering up to Noah, the newest addition to her collection. Noah, bless his heart, doesn't even see it coming; he's just sipping his punch and bobbing absently to the music. Suddenly, Meghan gets a little too close. She runs her hand along his hair and down his cheek. Poor Noah turns pale and the drink tilts in his hand. He looks like he is either going to pass out or die of dysentery right on the spot.

I'm not even sure what dysentery is, but it's from some old video game my parents used to play. Either way, it doesn't sound good, and Noah doesn't look good, either – he's a fly caught in Meghan's spiderweb.

Her venom has already taken hold, and now he's smiling stupidly at her. She tests her power over him by whispering in his ear, motioning toward the fridge. Noah immediately obliges – he sets his cup down on the nearby accent table and in one swift move, uses his football player arms to gently scoop her up off the floor and perch her on his right shoulder. Meghan giggles, playfully kicking her black stiletto heels with red underneath. Noah walks her over to the fridge and waits for her to stretch out and grab two of the many glass bowling pin–looking bottles collected on top. Meghan gives another command and he obeys, setting her down gingerly. Noah looks at her, waiting for her to say something else, possibly a thank you. Meghan turns and walks away promptly, leaving Noah standing there. Poor Noah's face looks like a confused puppy's.

A lump forms in my throat and I push it down dryly. I turn to Marcus again. "Can I, um...stay with you?"

Marcus smiles, but in a confused sort of way.

My heart starts pounding.

I had better explain this fast. That sounded so wrong.

I can barely get enough air. "Like remember in elementary field trips where you had to stay with a buddy? Maybe you could be that, sort of?" My throat has now dried out.

Marcus watches me, calculating.

I laugh nervously at his lack of reply. It feels like I've just fallen off a cliff and now everything is going to be weird. I try to fix it. "Sorry, that probably sounds weird – you know what, never mind. I'll just suck it up and–"

He puts his hand on my forearm. "It's okay, Clark, I get

what you mean. I wish I would have had a friend looking out for me at my first Gardener party back in sixth grade."

He lets out a shaky chuckle, but it's taking me a while to comprehend his words because his HAND is on my ARM. It's making my blood pressure go even higher, and now I can feel my pulse in my neck.

Marcus seems to wince at the memory of his first Gardener party, removing his hand from my arm. Now that I'm finally able to think clearly, I wonder.

What happened at his first party?

77

Sick

Before I can ask him what exactly he means, Marcus very suddenly grabs my shoulders and steers me off the couch to the other side of the living room. We're now by the china cabinet, near Harrison and his friend.

Okay?

I turn to him for an explanation as a shot of brown chunky vomit sprays the couch we were just sitting on. The splatter is rude and shocking against the expensive white leather. The vomit slimes slowly down the front of the couch and between the cushions. What's not on the couch has flicked into the carpet to be embedded underfoot if it's not cleaned up right now.

The green-faced blonde that hurled is being led away by a friend, who's struggling to hold her upright as the sick one stumbles over her own feet. Her too-short skirt keeps riding up her legs, and she clumsily pulls it down every few steps. Suddenly, the blonde steps out of her shoes and the friend groans, trying to drag her faster. They finally make it to the guest bathroom and slam the door shut behind them. It's for certain she's barfing again, but the thumping music drowns it out, fortunately. The abandoned heels lay a few steps away from each other just outside the door.

"Oh my gosh," I whisper under my breath.

Marcus looks on, stoic.

"Is she sick, Marcus?"

He turns to me with a quizzical look, tilting his head. "You're joking."

I step back, slightly offended. "No I'm being SO serious," I snap, embarrassed that I didn't automatically know why the girl was throwing up.

The look on Marcus' face is equal parts kind and somewhat baffled. He rests his hands on my shoulders this time. He peers into my eyes as though he were looking down a long, hollow tunnel.

He's going to have to stop that if I'm going to survive the night.

In a hushed voice, he explains, "She's *drunk*, Clark." Then he lets his hands float off my shoulders into his pockets. He steps back so he can scan the room again.

I put a hand to my mouth. I can feel my pulse slowing down.

Okay, this isn't funny.

"There are... drinks here?"

Marcus smiles, but it's a pity smile, and I don't like it.

Why am I here?

"Do you want someone to pick you up?" Marcus' intention in asking it is sweet, but it makes me feel lesser.

I furrow my brow as though that was the most ridiculous thing I've heard all day. "Pssssh. No thanks, I can hang." Not even I believe the act myself, but I have to try.

The last thing I want to do is stand out or go against the crowd.

That's practically begging to be made fun of. If I can just blend in for a few more hours, I'll be home free and we can all just pretend this never happened. I hate to admit it, but I think Mom and Dad were right on this one.

Marcus laughs at my expression. "I'm sure you can, Clark."

Be cool, Lucy Mae.

"Where did they even *get* alcohol?" I ask as casually as I can, rolling my eyes. "I'm surprised Meghan hasn't been caught."

He lowers his voice to respond. "Meghan's parents keep so many wine bottles around the house, it's nothing for her to sneak a couple every now and then. They never notice."

I glance at the busy queen bee in the kitchen, who has just finished pouring both glass bottles dry. Red cups are still hovering around her, waiting. She grins maliciously and shrugs at the crowd as if to say, *too slow, losers.* My eyes shoot back to Marcus.

How does he not see the urgency of this?

"She's a MINOR. We're all MINORS," I insist.

He snorts and shrugs. His eyes keep scanning the room in case someone is eavesdropping on us. In hushed tones, he continues, "I know that, and so does everyone else. But it's Meghan. She's really good at getting her way. She acts like she hates the stuff in front of her parents. The truth is, Meghan has figured out how to take the wine slowly enough so one parent assumes it's the other one that's taken a bottle, so they never know. The butler and maid don't really care either way, as long as Meghan doesn't make a mess. It's kind of genius and kind of sad because nobody thinks to ask about it."

I hesitate to ask, but I need to know. "Why do *you* come to these parties if you know what happens, Marcus? I'm honestly surprised."

Marcus shifts uncomfortably, looking around the room. "Everyone on the football team is here, so I'm expected to be here, too. It's just one of those things. I don't really pay much attention to it."

78

Parakeets

I pull out Mom's phone. The one she let me hold because she trusts me. The guilt feels like lava settling in my gut. I check the time.

It's 8:00 PM. I've only been here for half an hour, and it's been a complete dumpster fire. Well, except for Marcus. 11:00 PM seems like an eternity away, but I'm going to have to make do until I can get out of here.

I put the phone back in my pocket and turn to Marcus again. "One more question," I say.

Without thinking, he says, "Shoot."

I respond lightning quick with a quiet, "Pew, pew."

He laughs loudly and points an index finger at me, "Hey, you remembered!" with a gargantuan smile. The pure joy in his voice makes me feel guilty that I haven't talked to him in a while.

I roll my eyes at him. "Of COURSE I remember!"

Marcus and I go way back. Back when we were in Book Warriors together, we often found ourselves in the school library, where we made a lot of great memories. Most of the 5th grade for Marcus and I was spent at the school library, devouring one Cliffhanger comic book after another. The superheroes were Marcus' escape from the things that tormented him in real life. Even though Marcus and I had some great memories growing up, there were some not-so-great ones, too. Back then, 5th-grade Marcus was not only dealing with his dad being in the military, but with the extreme anxiety it caused his little brother, Brody. Marcus' fashion designer Mom was always so busy, Marcus had to step in and take care of Brody most of the time. Sometimes the pressure would get to him and he'd just break. Marcus would cry in school over seemingly small things. These weren't just two-bit tantrums; he would weep. People like Meghan Gardener made fun of him and called him a crybaby. I knew better, though.

We smile at each other for a moment, then he shakes his head as if to clear his mind. "Wait, what was your question again?"

I suddenly snap back to this illegal party and frown. "Where are her parents?"

He frowns in turn. "They go on a lot of business trips. Nobody really knows exactly what they do, but whatever it is, they make a lot of money doing it. Meghan's parents are not exactly what you'd call 'warm and fuzzy', especially with Meghan. It's where she gets her...unique personality."

It makes sense. Meghan learned the art of manipulation from two masters - her mom and dad. It's not surprising she'd turn her skills on them. Maybe it's her way of compensating for the lack of love she got from them. For as long as I've known her, Meghan's parents were always working. I never once saw them involved in anything Meghan did at school or otherwise, but somehow, they made it seem like it was everyone else's fault but theirs.

"Just two more hours," I sigh toward Marcus, almost drowned out by chanting and loud music.

Marcus hears me and croaks cryptically, "...of pure chaos and... fear."

I turn to see if he's joking.

His face is stone cold, and his eyes are moving around the room at almost double time, like he has to be able to see all sides of us.

Is this really what I wanted?

I follow Marcus around the party, saying polite hellos to people and declining invitations to play games that I suspect would have me in the same place as that girl who threw up in the living room. Eventually, Marcus and I sit on a different couch (minus the barf). We both wonder how we got here and just sit quietly like two parakeets being pelted by the flash of pictures, the thrum of the music, and the waves of loud, intoxicated laughter.

From behind us, a hand suddenly slithers between Marcus' head and mine. Its delicate fingers have red claws and burrow playfully into Marcus' hair.

Marcus, startled, stands up, waving an arm around his head for a second as though to get rid of a bug. When he sees the source, his face softens and he half-smiles.

I whip around and see Meghan standing behind the couch, grinning. Her hand retracts, cradling her opposite elbow.

For some reason, my face is getting really hot.

Before either of us can react, she's circled the couch and come face to face with Marcus. She looks dead at me, then at Marcus' eyes and lips. She traces his jawline with a crimson nail.

My face gets even hotter.

What is she DOING?

Marcus flinches, but doesn't move. With a wink and a playful shake of her head, she pulls on the lapel of Marcus' dress jacket and leads him toward the inner rooms. She expects me to follow, too. When we get there, the room is filled with laughing bobble-headed people sitting and laying in clusters around the ivory rug.

I'm starting to regret coming here. I'm getting a really bad feeling.

79

Spin the Bottle

We've entered her bedroom, where there's already a crowd. Meghan walks in and takes control of the room. "Okay, losers! We're going to play a little game of: Spin. The. Bottle. Make a circle."

The partygoers obey, shuffling into place.

Meghan releases Marcus and looks at us both. "Sit," she commands. "Loosen up, little Marc." She smiles wickedly and flits off to find an empty wine bottle for the middle of the circle.

I look over at Marcus. Now that Meghan is gone, the light comes back to his eyes.

Marcus looks back at me, then scans the room. He shakes his head, thinking out loud. "I hate when she calls me that."

I know that all too well. Meghan and her cronies used to call him that in elementary school because he was tiny and scrawny. He's still skinny, but not in a scrawny way.

Meghan's eyes gleam like a cat's in the eerily dim room. She's come back with her prize, an empty wine bottle. Before I can react, she's in the middle of the circle, pointing the bottle at the girl with pink spiked hair from school. "Melanie, you're going to start us off," she says.

Melanie complies. She spins the bottle, and it lands on Harrison.

Harrison smirks.

Meghan smiles widely. "So you can either kiss each other for 20 seconds or go in the closet and promise you'll do something," she says.

My heart pounds aggressively.

What is this?!

I hiss, "Marcus!"

I can feel him shift uncomfortably from behind me.

From across the circle, Monica smiles at me and pats the floor next to her. "Come sit with me."

I look at Marcus, and he looks back at me. As quietly as he can, he whispers, "Will you be okay?"

I nod.

"Yeah, you should go. Who knows what they'll do if you don't," Marcus cautions.

I giggle nervously to save face, realizing how terrifyingly true that statement is.

Melanie looks at Harrison and smiles. A hush falls over the room as she proclaims, "I'll do the 20 seconds; in fact, I'll do another 20 seconds if you want."

Harrison does his infamous wink and begins to stand up.

This is just too much.

I jump up and run to the restroom to hide until the countdown and cheering are done.

Repulsive.

When I come back, Meghan passes me the bottle with a smirk.

"Here you go!"

Before I can object that I don't think that's how you play, Harper bends down next to me and whispers in my ear. "If you don't do this, you can't be in the group."

I visibly cringe and look toward Harper. She's already gone, taking her place next to Meghan and leaving me as the center of attention (which is normally great, but not now).

I wrap my hand awkwardly around the bottle, praying it's not going to land on Christian Clawthorne.

Everyone thinks he's so funny, but his sense of humor really isn't my cup of tea. I don't want it to be Harrison either. Could I get a disease? Oh my gosh, is there ANY way I can get out of this? My first kiss is supposed to be special. Maybe if I just go to the restroom...

"SPIN IT LUC-AY," slurs some girl that I can't see in the darkness.

I spin the cursed bottle, shutting my eyes. Screams and cheers erupt, and my eyes immediately shut tighter. During a pause in all the noise, I hear one voice.

"Open your eyes, Clark." I know that voice as well as my own, although it's gotten deeper since we were kids. I open my eyes.

Of course, it's Marcus. A scruffy smile escapes him and he glances away toward the kitchen. Wolf whistles surround him.

80

The Closet

Now my heart is pounding, I can't breathe, and I want to die.

See, Marcus is amazing, but I'm SCARED. What if this friendship gets ruined? Then how am I supposed to move forward with him?

I think kissing him is better than anything they want me to do in the closet, but as soon as I start to speak, Marcus stands up.

He walks over to where I'm sitting and announces, "We'll do the closet."

People scream around us like he's a celebrity.

Meghan is surprised but pleased. Eyebrow raised, she purrs like a satisfied cat, "Good choice. Right this way." She stands up and leads us to the closet. All heads swivel after us. Everyone's a mess of giggles and elbows.

I'm speechless. I turn to Marcus, mouth open.

He shrugs and takes my hand, leading me to our glamorous cage of doom.

Meghan locks the door behind us, shutting us in the dark.

Her muffled voice teases us from outside. "You'll be there for just a short while. So have fun!"

I sit down on the floor by Meghan's handbag collection, far away from Marcus. "Why would you pick *this*?!"

He steps away from me like I'm going to swing at him.

I actually think I might.

Marcus says simply, "Because we can do what we want." He fumbles noisily around for the light switch.

I frown.

I was not expecting this from you.

I pick a spot to sit down, plopping myself on the floor with an indignant harrumph.

Marcus elaborates. "They won't know what we did or, more importantly, didn't do." He finds the light and clicks it on. It's dim, but it'll do.

I stare up at him. "B-But Meghan said we have to do something."

A different look washes over his face. He walks right up to me. "Fine, if you're gonna cry 'cause we have to do something, *I'll* do something."

I cringe but glare at him with all the ferocity of a newborn kitten. I can barely manage to squeak, "I'm NOT crying."

Marcus grabs my arm, pulling me into a hug. I allow my muscles to relax, hugging him back. He lets go, looking at me with soft brown eyes. His gaze is somehow strong in its gentleness.

I'm definitely going to die in this closet.

Without thinking, all I can sputter is, "That was cute." I gasp at my own thinking out loud.

Marcus chuckles softly in the dimly lit closet. "Is cute a good thing? All I've *ever* done is hug my brother, and even that hasn't happened in a long time." He lets himself fall into a cross-legged seat next to me.

"No, yeah - it's a great thing!"

That was excessive, Lucy Mae. BE COOL.

"I mean, it's a cool thing. I mean... how *is* Brody?" I let out a semi-frustrated sigh and wait for him to fix the silence before it gets awkward.

He laughs. "He's doing all right for an eight-year-old boy, I guess."

I grin and sigh. "I wish there were books in this closet."

He smiles. "*Coldhearted?*"

I gasp and sit next to him. "YOU REMEMBER *Coldhearted?!*"

He laughs again, confused by my excitement. "Yeah, I don't forget things easily. And that's also what got you to read the Arachno-Boy comic I gave you."

I giggle shyly. "Thanks for looking out for me, Marcus."

He grins. "Yeah, Clark. We go way, way back."

Me and Marcus traded books one day when we were younger, saying that if I read his favorite book, he would read mine. Mine was a bit longer, though. By a couple hundred pages.

We smile at each other for a second, then look away so it doesn't get weird.

Marcus raises a palm to emphasize his original point, the one he made before Meghan and her cronies shoved us in here. "See, now we can just hang out until they come back for us. It'll be any minute now."

I yawn. "How long has it been?"

"It's got to have been at least a couple of minutes by now," Marcus hums. He stands up and tests the doorknob.

Still locked.

We exchange a look.

My brow furrows. "Wasn't it just for 20 seconds?"

"I thought so, but maybe that was just for Melanie?" Marcus replies. He knocks on the door, calling through the crack. "Hey, Meghan? Harper? Open the door. Our time is up."

No reply.

Come to think of it, they didn't really specify a time frame. This is NOT good. Mom and Dad will be back at 11:00, and if I'm holed up in a closet with a boy, I will die for a completely different reason.

Marcus presses his ear to the door for a few seconds, then drops suddenly to the floor in a push-up position. He lowers himself slowly to the ground on surprisingly beefy arms.

My eyes go wider than I'd like in the dark.

DO. NOT. STARE. This is SERIOUS. We might actually be stuck in here!

Marcus is doing his best to peer under the door to see anything, but it's not really working. He says to me, "Not much I can see - I think they turned off the light."

"Let me try," I offer, though I'm not sure I'll see much more than him. I scuffle over to the door and do my best to peer underneath, painfully self-conscious since I was just staring at him.

Nah, maybe he wouldn't stare. Let me just get this over with.

From underneath the door, most all of what I can see is just carpet fibers and lint. Faintly, barely, I can see the room beyond. The light is in fact off, and everyone's definitely gone.

Are you KIDDING me right now?

I sit back up and shake my head grimly at Marcus. I pull

out Mom's phone to check the time. 9:45.

Good. There's still some time.

Now it's my turn to call through the cracks. I stand up and call out, "Meghan?! Harper?!"

An unknown male voice seeps through from the other side. "Meghan says you haven't actually done anything because you're calling to be let out, so you now have to stay in there for an hour so you can find your inspiration."

My jaw drops open. "Who is this?! Open the door and let us out!" I try the doorknob for emphasis. Something seems to be blocking the knob from rotating any further.

This has to be one of Meghan's zombies. She won't even come to taunt us herself – she has to SEND SOMEONE?!

I insist, "Seriously. Whoever you are, open this door."

"No can do. Sorry. Have fun'n there," drawls the voice as it fades into the distance, footsteps carrying it away.

Silence.

Marcus and I look at each other.

Now what?

"Well, they can't *make* us do anything, and Meghan said to have some fun," he says, "so we might as well make the most of it like old times."

I stare at him quizzically.

He reaches into his backpack and pulls out a purple box of Cliffhanger ONE cards. "Wanna play a couple rounds? I'm a huge Cliffhanger geek, remember?"

I look up at his smiling face.

I'm beginning to think this might actually be a blessing in disguise.

I giggle again. "How am I ever supposed to forget!"

Every time I saw him at the library as a little kid, it was in the comic section.

Marcus asks, "Do you remember anything about Cliffhanger?"

I smile sheepishly. "I know the basic characters, but nothing about them."

He facepalms, and we both laugh.

After that, we spend about an hour going over the different characters over a game of ONE. I feel like I kind of needed a reminder that a couple of good people are still here.

The pressure I feel with Meghan and the girls is just not here with Marcus. Marcus is simple and direct. He's honest, and what you see is what you get with him. I'm still a little scared by everything that was allowed here, so it's nice to just sit here with someone I know is good-hearted. I can see why he's always liked superheroes and Cliffhanger so much – they are the perfect escape from a less-than-ideal situation. The Chrome Gentleman would just blast his way out of this closet. Arachno-Boy would be able to kick the door down and web-swing out the window with his girlfr–

Marcus drops a Pick 4 and laughs, "Are they never going to come for us?"

I find myself saying without thinking, "It's perfectly fine if they don't."

He doesn't hear, thankfully, and suddenly looks up at all the clothes above us. "Hey!" He sounds genuinely shocked so I scoot over to see what he's looking at. It's a Valentina blazer. Those things are like $2,000 and must NEVER be machine washed unless you WANT to throw your money in the toilet.

I laugh. "You're surprised that she has fancy clothes?"

He points at the blazer and says, "No, it's just that that's my mom's clothes line."

I gasp. "Wait, ACTUALLY? That's so cool!"

He smiles sadly. "Sometimes."

I decide not to push. I change the subject instead. "What should we do now?"

He wordlessly pulls up his movie collection on his phone. A few flicks of his thumb summons the *The Chrome Gentleman* movie. The sounds crackle to life like they're inside a tin can. Soon we're watching Antonio Fizzle build his suit; it's actually pretty cool.

Cooler than I remember.

81

Small Town Rumors

About 10 minutes into the movie, Marcus pauses the video and turns to me.

"I wish you could be a little nicer to Asher," he says out of nowhere.

Random.

I look up from the screen to his now-serious face. "What do you mean?"

Marcus sets his phone on the carpet. "It's just, he's going through a lot right now, and he's trying to make it through one day at a time."

I scoff. "Boys don't have problems; all they do is play sports."

Marcus shoots me a look. "Okay, first, that was really sexist, and second that's not even true."

I challenge him, "Do *you* play sports?"

"You know I do, but that's not the point," he answers.

I roll my eyes and decide to play along. "So what is he going through that's SO bad, Marcus? Asher is rude and even more, he destroyed my phone."

Even though we're locked in a closet and there's nobody around, he lowers his voice. "People are saying that his sister died."

My heart sinks. "His... Mia?" I shift, sitting up straighter. "Are you serious?"

Marcus nods grimly.

It doesn't even make sense. How could she possibly be gone?

"Lexi and Leo had a playdate with her at the park recently and I was actually planning on meeting this little girl the next time that they met up." Then it hits me. "Lexi is going to be devastated. Who told you?"

He goes into his text messages and pulls up a group chat. He pulls the long chain of messages down, searching while he talks. "One of the kids that rides his bus started a rumor about Asher and his dad burying a body in the backyard. At first it was just a joke, but it's turned into a pretty strong rumor. According to this kid, Ozzy, Mia is always running around outside with Asher. But the thing is, Mia hasn't been seen in a long time. People are really starting to wonder, but nobody wants to be a snitch."

"Has anyone actually confirmed that Mia is...?" I don't want to bring myself to say it.

"Not officially, but Ozzy says his brothers play with Mia all the time, too and she just hasn't been around. Plus, he took a picture of a rock with Mia's name in their backyard. It's near a pile of dirt. Everyone thinks it's some kind of grave marker. There's definitely something off." Finally, he finds what he's looking for and taps on it to open it.

With a grim look, he turns the phone to me. It's a picture of a hand-painted rock with Mia's name on it buried in the dirt. The way the flash glares off it in the picture makes it look like it was taken at night.

"How do we know this isn't just something he copied from the internet?" I ask skeptically.

Marcus wordlessly taps on the Info button on the image. The location of where the picture was taken pops up. It was here in Stoneville.

We sit in silence for a while, and I don't know if it's because we don't know what to say or because we are taking some time to respect Mia and Asher.

Every second that passes my heart cracks a little bit more. I look up at Marcus. His eyes are wide open, staring into the distance.

Okay, now it's officially weird, but not in the way I thought it would be.

The time in the closet is now passing by like a sadness bal-loon deflating way too slowly. Watching him shift uneasily against the mahogany dresser reminds me of the silent little boy that would shift unconsciously in his seat while buried in his Book Warrior books.

We went to Bevel Elementary together, where we'd compete in Book Warriors (BW). Those were really the best days of elementary school. We read a brilliant list of books by their even more legendary authors, then memorize every detail about them. By about February, we got to compete with the other schools around us to see who could answer the most questions out of the eight about those books and their details (which could be small or large). Being at this party has been the first time I've really talked to Marcus since we were "Warrior Nerds".

Back in those days, we used to compete to see who could answer the most questions during our practice round. Of course, he always won, but I still tried. Don't get me wrong though, Marcus was cool and all. For some reason, we kind of just split after the last day of fifth grade.

When we made it to middle school there was a total disconnection; I went with the popular kids and he fell into sports. (Which by the way was a total brain teaser because Marcus and sports do NOT add up at all!) How a kid goes from this tiny, shy nerd to a semi-popular closed off jock, is beyond me but it happened and here I am sitting with him. He looks the same and talks the same, but everything feels different. An awkward kind of difference.

Marcus shifts again, jostling me back to reality. This time, he hits his head on what looks to be the diamond and gold handles on the drawers. I chuckle under my breath.

Funny enough, even though Marcus is probably the clumsiest person I've ever seen, he's always been kind. I didn't know he knew Asher.

"Since when have you known Asher?" I ask.

"It's been awhile. When I wasn't at Book Warriors, I would hang out with him a lot, actually. He and I would wait for the bus every day after school and throw rocks at the wasps' nest to see who could get the closest without hitting it."

"Well, that's a stupid idea. You could have been swarmed," I say.

"True. We didn't think it all the way through at the time," Marcus says with a forlorn smile. "Asher is pretty cool, but he's had some hard luck. I think his Dad used to beat him up or something, too. He never took off his hoodie and I sometimes wondered if he was putting a little too much effort into looking like everything was okay. It seemed kind of forced sometimes, but if you would bring it up, he'd look at you like you were crazy. Guys don't usually share that much about their feelings, but I kinda wish he would have trusted me enough to vent once in a while. Maybe I could have helped somehow."

I absently trace the corners of the dresser with my finger. "Wow, I had no idea," I whisper half-aloud.

82

Memory

emory is a funny thing, I guess. I can remember one strange day in exact detail but the minute I try to remember anything else, my memory turns into a fog. Almost exactly three months before the last day of fifth grade, Marcus and I were on our way to a BW meeting and for some odd reason I still remember the exact conversation from that day. Do I mind? Not that much. But this random memory surely is not as important as others could be, right?

* * *

Bevel Elementary, Fifth grade.

Marcus and I were walking down the hall together. His face looked really sad back then.

"Are you okay Marcus?" I asked, genuinely concerned for his well being.

"I'm okay," I remember him saying.

He looked over at a little boy sitting by himself in the corner. He was drawing on himself with a pen.

"Who's that, Marcus?" I asked him, trying not to be too loud.

Marcus turned back to me and replied, "I don't know his name yet, but he is in my class. I don't know why he's so sad, and he won't talk about it."

We continued walking together through the huge empty atrium toward the library for our Book Warriors meeting.

* * *

Present day, Meghan's closet.

It doesn't seem like much of a memory, but I wonder if that little boy back then was Asher.

"Hey, Marcus," I whisper.

"What?" he replies quietly.

I scoot closer to him and drop my head on his shoulder. "I think you're a really good person."

He drops his head on mine silently. "You've always been one of my favorite people. Especially when I didn't have any friends," he says quietly.

I'm surprised that he told me this. Everyone kind of knew he was a sensitive kid, but he never openly admitted it.

I snuggle my head into his shoulder more.

That was sweet of him to say.

"Well, I've always thought you're the best," I tell him.

Then I remember Asher.

Poor Asher.

"Do Leo and Lexi know about it yet?" asks Marcus.

"Not yet. We'll have to tell them," I sigh.

And I dread it.

I feel myself drifting off to sleep. I have a terrible dream about what it would be like to lose one of the twins. It is THE worst dream I've ever had, and I wake up to my own tears. Marcus is shifting his shoulder, checking to see if I'm okay.

Right then, the closet door finally opens. Marcus puts a gentle hand on my shoulder so I'll sit up.

I hear Meghan cooing, Harper gasping, and Monica giggling, but I can't pay any attention to them right now. I feel numb. A streak of light coming in from the kitchen is too bright. I cover my eyes.

I check Mom's phone. It's 10:41 PM.

Thank goodness it's almost time. I'll go wait for them outside.

83

I Won't Go

I walk right out of the house and down the front steps. I silently sit at the bottom. Most party goers went inside long ago, so the ambient sounds of the street keep me company. I glance again at Mom's phone with a tear staining my face.

11 at night...what am I even doing here?

The big front door creaks above me. It must not have shut all the way because the noises from inside are leaking out. I hear Meghan come out from the house and hurry down the steps. She doesn't have her handrail to glide from, which forces her high heels to clack in the most obnoxious way. She chuckles. "You can't leave now, Lucy!"

I don't say anything. I just watch for my parents' car to come back up the driveway.

Meghan begins to sound annoyed. "Look, whatever happened in there can't be SO bad that you want to leave. Come back inside." She loops a finger into the crook of my elbow to pull me back inside.

I yank my arm away, looking up at her through a red haze.

Mia is DEAD, and now I have to break my little sister's heart with the news, you harpy.

As an only child she wouldn't, couldn't understand what it's like to have a sibling.

I KNOW, though.

Siblings are supremely annoying, but they're *your* supremely annoying siblings. With your siblings, you can scream, fight, pitch a fit, and get on each others' nerves from here until the end of time, but you'll always still love and protect each other when things really hit the fan.

Yes, those little snots of mine drive me crazy, but only *I* can call them that. They've pulled my hair, broken my stuff, taken my food, made my life impossible, and driven me crazy almost every single day since they were born. Yet...if someone else ever DARED to hurt them...I don't even want to think about it because it just wouldn't end well.

I didn't lose a sibling, but someone else did. Someone I know, even if I can't stand him. Like it or not, this loss will affect our own family deeply for a long time because Lexi and Leo loved Mia. The intrusive thought comes, unwelcome and dark.

If anything ever happened to Lexi and Leo...

My eyes well up involuntarily, making Meghan's towering figure swim. I still won't say anything to her. I let out a pointless sigh and turn my back on Meghan.

She won't get it, anyway. This whole night has been a waste of time.

I start to wonder how Asher must be feeling, and it makes my stomach feel hot and hollow.

Is this shame?

84

Calling for Backup

Meghan balks at my indifference. She whips out her phone and sends a text. She stares at the red door expectantly. When nothing happens, she calls out in a surprisingly loud voice. "MONICA!"

After a beat, Monica pops her head out from behind the big front door, her dark brown hair swimming over her shoulders. There's an annoyed edge to her voice as she clomps down the steps in her platform sandals. "Like, *WHAT-*?"

Monica stops when she sees me and turns to Meghan. "Oh. I see. Want me to get Harper?"

Meghan nods. "If that doesn't work, we'll grab Marcus."

I'm kind of flattered by how they seem to care about me. It still doesn't make me want to speak, though.

Harper is soon standing in front of me. I can't possibly call her my best friend anymore, but we still have that connection. Her eyes reflect what's going on in her brain. Since I'm upset, she's giving me a weird pity look. It's obvious she has no idea what to say, and she's trying to fix it by rubbing my shoulder.

We both know she can't help me. There's too much of a disconnect for me to trust her like I used to. Harper also doesn't know what it's like losing a sibling either. She was an only child, like Meghan...

I don't want her right now.

My face must show it because Harper receives the message. She turns to Meghan and says mechanically, "She's not gonna speak to me. Go get Marcus."

Meghan sends another lightning-quick text and pauses, watching the front doors.

As if by magic, some unseen force shoves Marcus outside and shuts the door behind him.

Marcus shakes his head and straightens his jacket indignantly on his way down the steps. He sees me and seems to forget about the girls, who are slowly backing away. He takes a seat next to me on the bottom step. "Hey, Clark."

Hearing the same voice that told me the news makes me cringe and curl up into a ball.

Why is this bothering me so much? Mia wasn't even my sister.

All of a sudden I hear Lexi's voice in my head.

...I'm adopting her like Harper adopted me...

All I can manage is, "I can't...I just didn't expect this to affect me so hard –" I flinch at how hoarse my voice sounds.

Marcus looks at me sympathetically. "Are your parents coming?"

I nod my head. More tears stream down my face. "They had drinks, shoved me in a closet, and now THIS. Marcus, I didn't even know Mia. I don't even like Asher!"

Marcus looks up at the girls, who have retreated, crowding by the door to watch us. "Let's go," he says to me.

I turn and look at Marcus the best I can through my watery

eyes.

He puts himself between me and the eye shot of the vultures on the top step. "We gotta get away from these people. Let's wait for your parents somewhere else." We start to walk around the corner toward the back porch where they won't see us.

I'm so grateful for him, but still hear myself laugh coldly. "This will probably be on Monica's Instagram by tomorrow. Marcus, I – "

He stops walking to put a hand on my shoulder. He looks me in the eye. "I know you're confused, 'cause you didn't know the family, and you had a bad experience with Asher, but Lu, it's because you're so pure. You're such a good person."

He pauses and shoots a thumb back toward where we left Meghan and the others behind. "You're better than them." He laughs, embarrassed, and rakes a hand through his hair. "Sorry. That was kinda weird of me to say."

We start to drift absently toward the back steps again.

Before I can object, he starts talking again. "It's that you've always cared. Since we were little. When I was bullied, you would help me. If Harper was upset, you would hug her. When the teacher was overwhelmed in elementary school, you offered to take attendance so she didn't have to. Don't lose that." Marcus stops and looks at me, the warm porch light above us illuminating his amber eyes. "I should probably stop talking now."

I'm touched. I'm not sure what else to say but, "I really needed that. Thank you, Marcus."

We sit down on the steps of the back porch and I glance over at him. He's looking at me, waiting for me to tell him what I need. I hug him, and he wraps both arms around me, holding me still.

It's nice to have someone who cares about how you're feeling.

Then it hits me like a slap in the face.

Does Asher have anybody who cares?

I've started to cry again. Horrified, I bury my face in Marcus' shoulder.

He holds steady.

I cry for my little siblings and the selfish relief that I still have them. I cry for Asher and however he's feeling now. I cry for Mia, and the knowledge that I'll never get to meet her, because she'll never wake back up. I cry for me, because this life that I wanted isn't what I thought. And I cry because Marcus gave me hope that I'm good.

85

Finally

My parents' car finally pulls up in the front driveway. Mom's phone pings immediately.

Marcus gently releases me from the hug and smiles. "Parents?"

I nod. "Yeah."

He nods, too. "Can I walk you to your car?"

I smile despite myself. "Always the gentleman."

He bows gallantly and makes a goofy face.

I chuckle in spite of the last few hot tears rolling down my cheek. I quickly brush them off with the back of my hand.

So much for makeup.

I can see my parents smiling as we walk toward the car. My dad actually steps out and extends a welcoming arm. "Marcus Hall." His smile is practically wider than his face.

An unbearably snotty sound comes out of my nose instead of the sound I intended. I try to gloss it over by talking. "Wow, he looks really excited, Marcus."

Marcus doesn't seem to hear it, thankfully. He walks right up to Dad and shakes his hand. "Hi, Mr. Clark, long time no see."

He smiles widely as my dad pounds his hand heartily on Marcus' back. "Too long, son. I wish Lucy hung out with more people like you."

I glance up, my smile gone. "What?"

Dad looks at me and his smile fades when he sees my face, which is probably red, puffy, and smeared with eyeliner. "Were you-?"

His question is immediately cut off by Mom, who comes out of the car and pulls Marcus' face to her shoulder. "Marcus! Sweetie, it's been too long." She holds him at arm's length, examining him. "You've gotten so tall! And so handsome!"

"Mom," I groan.

She smiles at Marcus. "Sorry, Marcus."

He smiles shyly, face flushing beet red. "Oh no, it's okay." Then his mind seems to change channels. Marcus shuffles his feet and nods toward me. "Um, but you should probably take Lucy home. She's had a rough night."

Dad's face is now grim. He looks at me, then at Marcus. "What happened?"

I can feel Dad starting to get upset, so I interject. "I'll tell you when we get home. It's fine, Dad. Promise."

Mom looks at me, then at Dad. She nods and presses a gentle hand to his arm.

Marcus glances at me and I nod gratefully.

My bottom lip is NOT about to poof out like this. Why is this hitting me so hard? I feel stupid.

The tears begin to swirl again, so I get into the car before anyone sees. I can still hear their voices outside.

My mother's demeanor has darkened a little, too. She turns to Marcus and says politely, "It was very good to see you,

Marcus. Please take care."

She and Dad both get into their seats up front and close the doors. The car wobbles with the snick of the hinges.

Marcus now looks like he may be regretting saying anything. He sounds muffled from outside. "It was really good to see you too." He sends an uncertain wave after us from the rear view mirror as we drive away.

We sit in the car silently. The quiet helps me to catch my breath. I sigh in the backseat.

Mom turns back toward me and scans me. After a calculating moment, she pats my knee. It's as if she somehow knows that what's happening is not an emergency, but it's important to me. She whispers to Dad in the front, probably telling him to wait till we get home.

86

Breaking the News

We get home and go into the living room. Our neighbor, a little old lady named Agnes, stands up from the couch to greet my parents. She's still bent in the shape of a question mark even though she's standing, but she's smiling sweetly as she whispers, "They're sleeping."

Mom hugs her gently and slips money into her hand. "Thanks for watching them on such short notice. We'll see you tomorrow."

Agnes looks down at the money in her hand and shakes her head with a smile, but accepts it gratefully before shuffling out the door.

Mom quietly closes the door behind Agnes and locks it.

I sink into the computer chair, exhausted.

Mom sits on the couch next to Dad.

Dad's eyes are blazing. "Lucy, what's going on?"

I don't want to answer, but the sternness in his voice pulls the information out of me. "It's Asher's sister…"

Mom sits up on the couch. "Mia? She's a sweet girl. What

about her?"

I slide down off the chair onto the blue fuzzy rug. The intrusive thought of what it would be like to lose my own brother and sister haunts me again. The hot tears come back, and so does my stupid lip.

I know what this is going to do to the twins. I hate this so much. I don't even know these people. I shouldn't be crying this much, especially since it doesn't affect me.

Mom pursues, putting a hand on my shoulder. "Lucy, *what's going on?*"

I look at her eyes, then away again. I finally whisper, "She's gone."

"Gone? What do you mean, *gone?* Has she gone missing?" She reaches for her phone on the coffee table, ready to call the cops.

I reach out and cup her hand with my hand to block her from reaching it.

She looks up at me. I shake my head solemnly and repeat, "No, Mom. She's *gone.*"

A soft voice comes from around the corner. "Who's gone, Lucy?"

Mom gasps and covers her mouth with one hand, grabbing Dad's knee with the other.

Lexi emerges from a blind spot behind the corner where the hallway starts.

I cringe. I used to hide there, too. It's a good spot for spying on conversations they don't want you to hear. I should have known. Both the twins have been hiding and listening to us.

Leo's unusually quiet voice pipes up from behind Lexi. "What happened to Mia?"

Leo heard it, too.

It cuts my heart in a hot line. It hurts deeper the more the kids process it. I wish I could shield them from it.

He's trying to make sense of it. Leo warbles, "What do you mean gone? Where did she go? Did she disappear?"

I hear Mom's broken voice. "She's in heaven, baby."

Leo's nose crumples and he begins to cry.

Lexi responds differently. She turns and rips up the stairs, tripping over her feet on the top step. I can see her fall and disappear on the top level, probably landing on her face.

Everyone tenses up, watching her closely. Had Lexi tripped before reaching the top, her nose would have cracked and she would have fallen back down the stairs. She picks her face up off the floor quickly, and looks down at me with wild, tear-filled crystal eyes.

I sit up on the blue fuzzy rug and cross my legs. The rhyme comes to me out of nowhere, offering little comfort.

Criss cross, applesauce.

I wait quietly for her. Lexi's like a wild animal too far gone to be tamed. That's what it feels like. But I understand. I just stare up at her.

As she stares back down at me, I slowly reach out my hand, inviting her back downstairs with me.

It unlocks something in her and she wails. She's soon back downstairs and curling up in my lap, burying her head in my shoulder. She sobs again, gasping for breath. Grappling for control of her senses. Like Asher probably was. After a short while, I can feel her breath pause. "Did it hurt her? When she went to heaven?"

I answer her as honestly as I can. "No, she was not in any pain."

With a heavy sigh, Lexi adds, "You didn't even get to meet

her."

I've never seen her like this. She buries her head back into my shoulder as if to hide from the too-big feelings. "Lucy, I really liked her. She was going to be our little sister."

I nod. I know how much she liked her.

Dad speaks up, addressing me. "Do you know what happened?" He pauses for a deep sigh. "I don't believe this." He leans forward on the couch and puts an arm around Mom. His hand brushes her back and she leans into him, her eyes drifting off of me and into the distance. Leo has curled up in her lap, whimpering.

I answer quietly, cradling my baby sister. "No, I don't know. All I know is that she's..."

The room falls silent.

"She was too young to go to your school, but I'm sure her preschool or daycare knows about it by now," Dad concludes.

Mom sighs absently. "Her poor parents, poor Asher."

I keep wondering why I care, and then wonder why I wouldn't. My feelings are unclear and confusing.

Asher has no one.

The words bounce off my brain and into my heart.

Maybe if someone at least pretended like they cared, he wouldn't be so... unpleasant. So Asher.

I look up at Mom's somber face. She shushes Leo in her arms and pulls him closer. I do the same with Lexi.

My heart hurts. Our hearts hurt.

XXVII

Asher

Tip #3: Just make them think you're fine and they'll leave you alone.

87

Thoughts and Prayers

Monday, September 17
9:00am
I'm starting to get vapid pity looks from some people.

Could they know about Mia?

The thought makes me panic, but I must not show it. That will REALLY make it obvious. As long as I keep quiet, nobody will really know. My thoughts still swarm like fleas, though.

*How can they keep on living as if nothing happened? It's not their fault my world is on fire, but I wish they could feel even a little ember. I bet things would be different. They'd act differently if they got sucker-punched just once by their dads or went hungry for just one night. They'd be less politically correct. Less plastic. Maybe even a bit more human. But they're not, because they're too busy with sports and schoolwork and each other. I **hate** school.*

I make it upstairs to the 8th grade hall and go straight for my locker. Lucy is hovering near my space. She looks like she's waiting for me with a constipated expression on her face. I feel myself tense up, but act like she's not there. She may be waiting for someone else.

Her voice reaches for me through the noise and clang of the halls. It's hurried and breathless. "Hey," she sighs at me, " I just wanted to say sorry for getting so mad at you for the phone. It wasn't even your fault, to be honest. And I'm sorry about your sister. I want you to know that my thoughts and prayers are with you."

A sudden streak of cruelty runs through me.

Ah. The politically correct statement - check.

I turn from my locker and look her straight in the eyes.

Lucy stalls on her feet, unsure how to react.

"Feel better now?" I sneer. I relish watching her expression change.

She falters and gets even more flustered. "What-? Feel better?"

"Yeah. Since you gave me the standard 'thoughts and prayers', you're covered. You can turn around and go back to your perfect life now. That's going to fix everything for me, after all." I add with a note of sarcasm I didn't know I had, "Wow, lucky me!" My voice echoes into my locker.

She tries to fix it. "Asher, I-"

I shake my head with a bitter smile, still looking down into my locker. I tuck my book bag inside it. "Nah. Don't bother. It's okay, really. Look, your friends saw your apology - you're good. Glad I could help." I take out a folder, a pencil, and my Silverbook, and slam the door. I click the lock shut and walk away before she can answer. Back to my dark little desk in my dark little corner where I can hide.

I sit down and feel the darkness shroud me like a blanket. A tiny part of me can't help but feel a tiny amount of regret.

I wonder if Mia saw that. She wouldn't approve if she did.

Part of me knows it's the thought that counts, but honestly I'm not in the mood for sympathy. Besides, I'm not even sure Lucy really does care. Most people are willing to fake an apology to look good, especially girls like that who are trying to become popular.

Either way, it doesn't matter. In my experience, trusting apologies mindlessly has never ended well.

If Lucy knows, then someone's talking. I bet it was that stupid kid that lives across the street.

88

Stitches

Counselors are not always as helpful as they think they are. They come off really fake, force you into coping mechanisms that don't work, and worst of all, they recite everything you share with them, word for word, to your parents. I know they mean well, but it's just not the same as talking to a close friend. I've been burned enough to know to keep my mouth shut.

It sometimes starts when some teacher thinks you're "struggling", then tries to help by putting your name out there for the counselors to "follow up with". The problem is that sometimes, these counselors are not trained to work with you in a sensitive way. They can pry too much at times, and that's uncomfortable.

Now I know for sure someone said something about Mia, because they've thrown me into a grief group. It gets you out of class, but it's better just to go to class and be left alone. Try sitting in a chair and having someone stare at you, trying to get really personal information out of you. It feels more like an interrogation than getting help.

In these grief groups, there are others who have experienced the same thing. All you want to do is sit alone in class and try to move on, but they make you talk about it. It doesn't help bringing it up after the first couple of weeks. Especially if it's fresh - they keep bringing it up, so they won't let you process and heal.

Things you're trying to leave behind and forget are pulled back out into the open, and it's just not helpful sometimes. It feels like they're taking stitches out way too early and all the blood and innards are just spilling out all over again and they just keep poking at your insides despite you screaming in pain.

They sent a letter home to get signed for grief group, but that was an easy fix. As long as they keep assuming everything is OK at home, I should be able to just play along with their little charade until they are satisfied.

Just make them think you're fine and they'll leave you alone.

89

Tweezers

Wednesday, September 19
Lunch

When you get that mark on you, that "troubled kid" target, school staff and counselors around you start handling you with tweezers. Suddenly, you're a poor, fragile creature that needs extra special help. It's idiotic and makes things worse, especially when you're dealing with other things.

Christian has been after me so much lately, I've had to start hiding food in my pockets to avoid him taking it. When the school food doesn't come in a bag or container, I walk my tray straight to the trash can from the lunch line and wolf it quickly before anyone can see.

Long story short, lunch has gone from eating in relative peace in the back corner of the cafeteria to hiding like a rat.

Since it's now known that I'm in a grief group, some of the school staff is worried. They've been noticing that I'm "throwing my food away" during lunch over the past few weeks. I've had a stray teacher walk by once or twice to ask me why I threw the food out.

I'm sure it's not helping that I always put my head down during lunch to try and get a little rest. Honestly, I just don't want to talk to anyone, and I get anxious whenever I eat in a public setting because of Christian. It's just easier not to eat some days.

Instead of pulling me out of class or lunch and talking to me in private, the staff member of the day will now shake me until I put my head up and let them know I heard them. They'll ask me things like, "Are you okay?" "How are you feeling?"

For the icing, they always add advice: "You would feel better if you ate." "Go talk to the other kids." "Just try your best."

The staff people are like parasites; they won't leave me alone until I make them go away. I still have a habit of never talking much, and I never express what I'm feeling most of the time because people wouldn't like what I have to say. If I said what is on my mind, let's just say...I would *upset* lots of people. The school staff would either hate me or ship me off to a mental hospital or something if I ever truly spoke my mind.

The funny part is that the staff never does anything when Christian barks at me to try and be funny, takes my food, or calls me a member of the suicide squad (the fact that he's been saying this doesn't bother me - staff doing nothing bothers me).

It's like being constantly harassed by well-meaning vultures that happen to be deaf and blind. Just this week, I ended up having several panic attacks in the bathroom after they spoke to me because of all the questions and because they kept touching my shoulders. (I hate physical touch in most cases.) So to be honest, I don't like most people in the school system.

* * *

September 25

In order to try and blend in, I've started forcing myself to eat slowly at the table, which makes me feel sick constantly because I'm watching for Christian. As a result, I don't get any rest anymore during lunch, I just I feel tired and sick. I'm becoming irritable and I almost told one of the staff members to F off today. I hate how they treat me, like something that has to be "fixed". It never makes things better. All it does is make me feel guilty and angry.

* * *

October 1

The act is working for the most part, and the school staff has finally started to leave me alone. Even Marcus walks by to say hey once in a while if his usual group is running late.

The other day, he asked if he could sit down with me. I knew it was only because his main friends were on a field trip, but his being there kept Christian off my back for a day. We ended up talking about the old days in elementary school. It was kind of surreal and kind of nice at the same time.

* * *

October 6

On rare days when the coast is clear, I still occasionally put my head down during lunch, but then a bobble head counselor spawns to ask me if I'm okay. They never get that I'm just trying to sleep or block out all the noise.

The only good thing about their irritating persistence is that it helped keep Christian away long enough for the game to get boring for him, so he hasn't been around to bother me anymore.

The way the school staff looks at me, they probably think they are the ones that helped me make friends. They have no idea that all they did was draw unnecessary attention to me, forcing me to become more of a recluse then I already was.

One thing I appreciate about Marcus is that he doesn't treat me as if I'll break. It's been a long time since I joked around with anyone without them walking on eggshells, trying not to "say the wrong thing".

It's obvious he knows about Mia, but he hasn't made it a big deal or forced me to talk about it, which I appreciate. I've almost dared to believe that maybe he just might be looking out for me, but I have my doubts. Mostly we just talk about stupid stuff like things that happen at school or assignments that are coming up.

I'll just enjoy it while it lasts until he gets bored of me and goes back to his regular friends when they get back from their field trip in a couple of days.

90

Getting Steined

October 8
    It's been a month since my sister passed away. I've been keeping track of it every day on my arm. It kind of shakes now when I add a new tally mark because I ran out of space on my forearm, so I've started to go back over the first cuts and break the skin again. It stings more than usual, but it's a nice distraction.

As long as I avoid confrontation, I can stay sane and just get through the day. Christian Clawthorne and his idiots usually hang out around the gym, so I just take a different way to class. There's a path along the outside where I can sneak in the back door without them seeing me. The security guard is always sitting there. Not that it would matter, anyway. Almost every single thing that happens, I'm always blamed for it because I've been labeled "the bad kid" by these adults who couldn't see the truth if it was staring them right in the face.

I pass Mr. Cheezers' class on the way to Math. He's actually cool. I like how he doesn't stress over little things like most teachers and just lets you be yourself. Homeroom is a good way to ease into the day because it gives me a chance to mentally prepare for Ms. Stein, who is the total opposite. Kids call her Mrs. Frankenstein because she's known for being scary. If she's not happy, the whole hallway will know. Walking into her room feels like you're walking into a dungeon catacomb.

I walk into Math class. I start to feel nervous, but honestly I'm just not into it today. I look around at the other kids shuffling to their seats and the feeling fades. I take my place at my desk and set my stuff down. I'm so tired. I'll just put my head down and rest my eyes for a second. I can still hear her, so I should be good...

Sleep feels really good wrapping around my head. My mind soaks it up.

* * *

The voice is muddy and distant like a watercolor painting, but I already know. It's getting louder.

"-ASHER."

I force one leaden eye open. Ms. Stein's polka dot dress is swishing toward me, punctuated by her irritating heels.

She barks, "DID YOU EVEN *HEAR* WHAT I SAID?"

"Um, no, Ms.-"

She cuts me off before I could finish my sentence.

That vein in her neck is twitching again. "That's what I thought. If I catch you sleeping in class again, it will be AN AUTOMATIC WRITE-UP AND A REFERRAL. DO YOU

UNDERSTAND, GRYPHON?!"

"Yes, ma'am." I sit back up, feeling like an old creaky ladder. It's pointless to start a confrontation now because it'll just drag on. She'll go away eventually.

Satisfied with my compliance, she walks back to the front of the classroom.

The only thing that helps is I know she has no idea why I'm so tired. Part of me wants to tell her what is going on in my life. Why I'm so tired and what happened with my sister. She doesn't have time to listen, and I don't think she would really care, anyway. Besides, that would just bring attention to myself, and I don't need that happening.

I hear Bobby Finkle and Roy Hayman snickering, "Oh snap - Asher got *Steined!*"

Idiots...

That's what everyone calls it when somebody gets on Ms. Stein's bad side, which doesn't take a lot. Today was my turn. I can never seem to go one day without having problems.

I zip up my spine and sit up straight. I'll do what I can to look busy so she'll leave me alone. Looks like we're working on Pythagorean Theorem again.

Mia would love all these shapes...

* * *

The time slips by quickly, and the bell soon rings. It's not over, though. My stomach gets hot when I remember I still have to talk to Ms. Stein, and she'll probably ask why I dozed off. What if she's actually nice and understanding, like Mr.

354

Cheezers and Ms. Berry?

Yeah, okay.

The room immediately clears out and the next class begins to trickle in. Ms. Stein is standing at the door, handing out worksheets. She glances icily at me between papers. "Hello, Asher. So tell me, why did you think you could sleep in my class?"

"Oh, it's just because I'm tired. I had a lot on my mind and had trouble sleeping last night," I lie.

The truth is, my dad remembered what I said to them about Mia after she died. He was drunk, so he stormed into my room by surprise, yelled at me for sassing my parents, punched me in the ribs, and knocked down everything in my room. He then demanded that I clean it up. So I guess it was partially true that I didn't get a lot of sleep last night.

Ms. Stein doesn't need to know about that. I do not want to go through therapy again and endure more fake sympathy.

"Okay. That's no excuse though. Get some sleep tonight. Goodbye, Mr. Gryphon." Her eyes don't leave the papers in her hands.

I silently exit the math room. I honestly don't want another burden to be added on to my shoulders.

I can barely walk with how many I already have anyway.

91

Great Expectations

After Ms. Stein's class, I have Mr. Brockley, the Social Studies teacher. His class isn't as bad as Ms. Stein's, but he can get annoying sometimes.

Mr. Brockley lifts himself up on his tiptoes and stands tall at the front of the room. "Okay, class! Today we are going to review the causes of World War I. Now remember the acronym M.A.N.I.A. Who can tell me what the first A in M.A.N.I.A. stands for?"

I'm in the 2nd row from the front (assigned seat, not my choice) so I can hear Mr. Brockley say to himself, "Hmmm. Who hasn't answered yet?" His eyes scan the room looking for his first victim.

Mr. Brockley is an introvert's worst nightmare. I swear, I think he gets a kick out of torturing kids who don't want to talk. His eyes land on me, and I accidentally make eye contact. I try looking away, but it's too late. I know he's going to call me.

"ASHER!" he exclaims with great joy, except he's the only one who's thrilled.

The truth is, I wasn't really paying attention to the question. Now 29 pairs of eyes are staring at the quiet kid, waiting to see how he'll mess up this time.

I take a wild guess. "Achievements?"

Mr. Brockley pursues. "No, that's not right. You're confusing the causes of World War I with the main components of a civilization. Try again!"

Seriously? People are starting to laugh...

"Uh. Abolition?"

Mr. Brockley lets out a loud huff. "NO, ASHER. THAT'S THE UNDERGROUND RAILROAD. WE JUST LEARNED THIS YESTERDAY. YOU SHOULD *KNOW* THIS."

Kids are cracking up at this point. This is getting stupid.

I lose it, yelling a little louder than I mean to, "Look, I don't know, okay?! I DON'T KNOW! Call someone else! I'm sorry I'm so stupid! I'm sorry that I'm not this 'special honors wonder child' you want! I'm sorry, but *I don't know!*"

An uncomfortable hush falls over the room. I instantly regret saying that, and now my heart's pounding.

I don't need to draw any more attention to myself, and that little show brought so much of it.

Mr. Brockley promptly goes off on a tangent, launching into a 10-minute lecture about peer respect and safe spaces. It's awkward. Since the moment is now thoroughly killed, Mr. Brockley has us work on our study guides in teams instead of reviewing. People working in teams promptly move their chairs to sit with their friends. The chatter begins to swallow the quiet, and I can hide in it.

I watch Mr. Brockley walking toward me.

Great. Here we go. He's probably going to chew me out and tell me how a kid has no right to talk to any adult like that. Heard it a million times before.

Then his eyes do something surprising. They're not annoyed anymore. They have somehow softened. It's almost a pity look, but not quite. He reaches my desk, leans toward me, and speaks in a quiet voice so the others don't hear. "Asher, may I speak with you after class? I promise, you are not in trouble."

I'll believe that when I see it.

I nod as though I had a choice.

Class drags twice as slowly now because I'm dreading the conversation. I try to distract myself with my work, but my brain feels like a chaotic scribble. I let out a sigh and put my head down. I come back up when the bell rings. The herd sweeps past, colliding with each other out the door. I stand up, scoop my backpack off the floor, and wait for Mr. Brockley in the open doorway.

"You wanted to talk to me?" I ask.

"Yes." Mr. Brockley stands up from his desk and makes his way to the doorway. "Asher Gryphon. Let me start out by saying, you are NOT stupid. And I'm not looking for some 'special honors wonder child', as you put it. I am just looking for your best work. I'd better NEVER hear you say that about yourself again. Okay, Asher?"

I'm not quite sure what to say other than, "Yes, sir."

"I can definitely see that you're very stressed," he continues. "And I understand why. The counselor, Ms. Ami, gave your teachers a quick heads-up that you're part of the grief group now. We don't know the details about why, I won't ask, and you don't have to tell me, either. Long story short is: if you have any more problems with anyone in this school, you come let one of us know. Am I clear?"

I look at the floor, then at the whiteboard behind him. "Yes sir."

Word travels fast. I wonder if he actually doesn't know anything about Mia. At least he's not going to make me talk about it.

He continues, "You're a great kid, and you have so much potential. You just need to give yourself some grace. I can help with whatever you need, but nobody's perfect, Asher. I just want to say that I enjoy having you in my class."

"Thank you, Mr. Brockley." I don't know what else to say, so I motion toward the door and pause. I don't want to be rude, but I have to get to my next class.

Mr. Brockley suddenly realizes he's made me late. He glances at his watch and holds up a finger at me so I'll wait. He pulls a pad of sticky notes from his front pocket, scribbles on the top one, and peels it off, reaching toward me with it.

I step forward and nod my thanks.

Mr. Brockley turns to his computer and bids me to have a good afternoon. He opens his desk drawer to grab a bag of chips.

Since the hall pass bought me a few minutes, I make a quick stop in the bathroom. The fact that my safe haven is a bathroom stall hits kind of differently today. As soon as the door clicks shut, hot tears well up and spill over onto my face. I clench my jaw, refusing to let it tremble. I focus my eyes on the scratches in the door and take a long, shaky breath. It makes the tears jiggle and I'm soon underwater again.

It's weird to think that somebody actually SUPPORTS me, no strings attached. Mr. Brockley just expects the best work out of us, which is understandable. He's a far cry from the usual nattering nitwits nagging us about talking in class.

Those are always the same teachers that write you up for the stupidest things.

Nattering nitwits. That was dumb. Where did I even get that from?

In spite of the tears, I feel the corner of my mouth turn up into a tiny smile, my first one in a very long time.

XXVIII

Lucy

92

Journal Entry

O ctober 10, 9:57pm

I never knew how bad it really was. Asher never deserved any of it. I shouldn't have been so awful to him. It was just a stupid phone. Was fitting in really worth hurting him?

I've made a decision. I am going to start being nice to Asher. Like super nice. He's not even gonna know what hit him. I need to make things better and help him. If there is even a hair on his head that falls out of place, I will be there to fix it. I will be there to fix everything. I won't let him get hurt again.

93

Late Again

ctober 13, 7:55am.

Once again, I did not wake up on time.

Once again, I'm in a frenzy, running into my closet. The alarm clock I started using instead of my phone flashes as though it has been going off for a while. Even though I've had my phone back for a couple of days, I just kind of got used to the old clock.

I have no choice but to get it together and focus; time is of the essence. I *might* be able to make it to school before the bell.

My closet has been getting progressively messier over time, which is weird for me. Of course, there is nothing on the floor and all my shoes are perfectly lined up on their rack, but its structure has somehow gotten...*looser.* I used to have each color perfectly coordinated so I could quickly and easily put together my outfits for our girls' group.

Nowadays, I have to actually hunt for things like an old lady hunting and pecking out letters on a keyboard. It's definitely not helping me right now since I'm running late, but the strangest part is that it doesn't bother me as much as I thought it would. In fact, it feels kind of nice not to have to worry about it for once and just have a normal closet. (Whatever that means, I guess.)

I'm not going to make it, especially with today's outfit. Meghan texted us last night that we have to wear pink dresses and baby blue ribbons, but...what if I don't want to?

I realize I'm pawing anxiously through my clothes and stop for a second. Who said that clothes were something mandated? For the past eight years, right up until I started trying to join this stupid group, I have managed to go without needing anyone to tell me what to wear or when to wear it. Why should I start to care now?

I look to the right and find something better than what Meghan wants. Not only is it more comfortable, but it also *looks* a lot better. I pull the hanger off the rack. It's a pink Blossom and Bloom t-shirt. I hold it up to myself, scanning the clothes rack for a bottom. I quickly find a pair of soft purple pants to go with it. No bows, but maybe a claw clip. That's so much SIMPLER.

I suddenly feel a slight twinge of panic that wants to intrude on my thoughts.

Meghan will definitely have something to say. They won't let me sit with the group today because of this.

I turn to look at myself in the mirror, still holding up the shirt and the pants. It looks cute and I like it. I decide to breathe the thoughts away.

No. This is nice.

I'm tired of being some little dog following her around. This is all I need, simple and easy. I should not have to look a certain way for them to decide to be my friend.

Besides, when has being their friend gotten me anywhere? I mean, they had ALCOHOL at a party full of middle schoolers! Those are the types of people that you see in those crime show documentaries. Kids like that end up choosing to waste their lives on drugs and alcohol, and it's really sad because nobody seems to step up to stop them.

Mom told me once that girls like Meghan end up alone and lonely, and I think she's probably right. Sometimes a little tough love is the best medicine, and Meghan could definitely use some in her life – she actually thinks she rules the world. Sure, my parents are slightly terrifying on the wrong day, but I know they love me and would always have my back no matter what. Meghan doesn't have anyone in her life like that. It's actually kind of sad.

I know what I need to do, and I know the girls are not going to make it easy on me. I quickly run through my skincare routine, scoop my long, thick hair up into the claw clip and adjust my earrings.

*Perfect. Just as **I** like it.*

I run out my bedroom door, nearly forgetting my socks and handbag. I look at my old backpack sitting in the corner and realize it would be way more comfortable to fit my stuff in. After a quick transfer, I'm soon flinging one of its straps across my shoulder while also trying to not ruin my hair.

I thunder down the stairs and run to the kitchen counter. I grab a protein bar from the basket and a quick orange juice from the fridge. Dad's keys are on the counter, so I swipe them. I'll start the car to make it easier.

My white Trebella sneakers, which have managed to *stay* white, sit perfectly by the front door, but before I get there, my body stops.

I hear my dad nearly yelling his lungs out in the other room about what I think was alcohol. The sound is ugly and fills me with dread. Suddenly, getting to school on time is not so urgent. I can feel my pulse start to pound a bit in my throat. My stomach ices over as I put on my socks.

I stand still, listening.

Is he talking to Meghan's dad?

My mind drifts back to the conversation mom had with me just the other night about alcohol. My uncle was over for dinner, and he'd offered me a sip of wine to try and be funny. Let's just say Mom was *not* amused, and we ended up having a long talk afterward. At that time, I promised her never to fall to peer pressure and to always be open and honest if I were to ever run into it, especially when it came to alcohol or drugs. I knew good and well I should have spoken up then about Meghan's party, but I didn't want to be a snitch. Now it's caught up with me; Mom *and* Dad will know I hid it from them. I look at the grandfather clock in the hallway.

Crap, it's 9:05. I won't get there until at least 9:20 now with traffic.

I rush to the door, carefully put on my sneakers, and bolt to the car, leaving my half empty orange juice on the floor by the door.

Mom will definitely kill me for that one, but it would be worse if I came back into the house with outside shoes.

I unlock the car doors and jump into the front seat. The dread is still very much with me. All I can do is sit up primly and gingerly nudge at my backpack like a suspect trying to look innocent during the trial.

Dad gets into the car and slams the door.

Yep, I'm dead.

His face is stern and closed off. I don't say anything because I don't want to make it worse. I don't think he's ready to talk to me about it yet. Usually he likes to talk to Mom first. I'm okay with that - it'll buy me a few more hours to live. The drive to school is more silent than those viral silent rooms. I break the silence when I get out of the car at 9:35. I'm REALLY behind today.

I speak meekly. "Bye, Dad...!"

Dad doesn't respond. He doesn't even move.

This is something I'll have to deal with later.

94

Spineless

After electives, just before Science class.
It's about 11:18 when I spot Asher in the 8th grade hall. He's buried in his locker, getting ready for Science.

I skip up to him. "Hi Asher!"

He sticks his head out long enough to see who it is, frown at me, and go back into the locker.

No hello back? Geez, tough crowd, but I kinda get why…

I push the hot feeling in my stomach down, now more determined than before.

Everyone shuffles through the door into Mr. Cheezers' room and disperses to their seats. Monica smiles at me from her perch in the middle of the room. I smile back and wave without thinking.

Right as I sit down, Monica suddenly pipes up. "GUYS. YOU REMEMBER THE WEIRDO THAT BROKE LUCY MAE'S PHONE? HIS SISTER IS DEAD."

My face goes up in flames. How did she even find that out? I mean she's Monica, so I guess I shouldn't be that surprised.

Asher looks like he wants to sink through the floor.

I lean over to her and whisper loudly, "MONICA. Why would you *do* that?"

She sneers at me like I'm an idiot. "'Cause everyone should know. He doesn't get to keep secrets." She shrugs unapologetically as I gape at her.

"That was so mean," I hiss, glancing subtly back at Asher.

He still looks like he wants to die. There's nowhere for him to go, so he puts his head down on his desk and covers himself with his hood. Rightfully so, everyone in the class is staring like he has two heads. Poor thing. I'm really starting to hate the way he's treated.

How did Mr. Cheezers not HEAR that?!

I can feel my ears glowing hot red. They usually do when I'm angry. Dad is always telling me not to take on other people's offenses, and I never thought I would take on Asher's, but I have to do something. The other kids are now pointing and talking about him.

I've had it. "STOP STARING AT HIM." I state it loudly and firmly.

Asher takes the tiniest peek from underneath his hood but remains hidden.

Harper looks incredibly surprised.

"TURN BACK AROUND NOW." I almost growl it. People are used to my small, gentle voice, so it's jarring. Surprisingly, they obey. There are still a few mumbles and whispers, but *they listened.*

They listened to me.

Mr. Cheezers has finally organized himself enough to begin the class. He stands up from his desk and looks out over the room, starting his lecture where he left off yesterday.

"Good morning, all. Let's not sleep, please, Asher. Sit up. And no hood, please. Thank you. Okay, everyone, let's turn to the next available page in our notebooks and get ready to take some notes."

I watch Asher pick his head up just enough to count as compliance. He looks slightly relieved, (very slightly) but also suspicious and confused.

I turn back around. Now *I'm* a little embarrassed. I might have overreacted a bit.

Harper snaps her fingers at me and I flinch. "HEY. What the heck was that?"

I look down and shrug. "I just wanted them to stop staring at him." I pause to meet her eyes. "It's rude."

She gawks at me like I'm an alien from outer space.

Monica sniffs injuredly.

Something inside me panics, and I find myself giving her an apologetic smile. I don't want Asher to hear my excuses for defending him, so I whisper. "Sorry Monica, I didn't mean to yell. I'm just tired."

Monica nods. "I guess I understand. I get angry when I don't have my Enorme pink coffee from StarShucks every morning, too."

I kind of hate myself for being so spineless.

Science seems to go by quickly. I don't look back at Asher anymore.

I have to do better.

As soon as class ends I run to the door and open it for him. As he walks through the doorway he stares at me, like he doesn't know what to make of this.

XXIX

Asher

Tip#4
Wear sweatshirts.
Say you're cold. Don't forget the bandages.

95

Tryhard

Has this girl lost her mind? She's smiling like a lunatic and holding the door open for me. Everyone sees this. Everyone is laughing.

I get out of the doorway as fast as I can and walk around to where she is. Her smiling face follows me like a haunted painting. I try to get her attention to get her to leave me alone. "Lucy."

Lucy is staring a hole through me, complete with the pity smile.

She's making me anxious...

She finally replies, but is still clueless. "Hi Asher! Here, let me help you carry your stuff." She reaches out her hands toward my sketchbook and I step away.

Trying to keep my voice down, I say, "What are you *doing*?"

She pursues. "Helping you, of course! It's what friends do."

I don't like this at all. If she wants to fit in with the popular girls, why is she bothering me? Maybe it's just one very cruel joke, but that expression on her face seems genuine. Maybe I should let her help, at least until she doesn't feel guilty anymore. Wait, why should I help her? She's probably only doing this to make herself feel better, not to help me...

I feel my eyebrows knit together. "Friend? I'm good, I don't need help. I carry my own stuff, I don't have maids or anyone to do it for me." I turn and leave so I'm not late, stuffing my sketchbook under my hoodie as I walk.

I can hear her flat black shoes padding behind me, following me down the hall. She says loudly, "HEY."

I look back at her, slightly amused.

She takes her hand uncertainly off her hip and says in a quivering voice, "I do *not* have maids."

I roll my eyes. "Okay, I really couldn't care less though."

I start down the hall again. I hear her infuriating shoes start to follow me again.

She's really beginning to piss me off.

I don't hide my anger. I turn and blaze at her, "WHAT ARE YOU DOING?"

She flinches at my reaction, then frowns at me. "I'm being a kind, nice person. And you're being very rude."

Some of my hair falls in my face, obscuring my vision. Before I can swat it away, Lucy beats me to it. She uses her hand to brush it off my face.

I automatically step far away from her. "*Hey!* What are you doing? I don't know what you want from me, I'm not some charity case just because my sister died." My voice cracks slightly on that part.

"Sorry, Asher," she says quietly. "My siblings really loved her."

It catches me by surprise. I don't have anything to say.

"I just want to help, Asher," she continues.

I look away. "Thanks, but I don't need your help." I start to walk away again, and this time I don't hear her follow.

"ASHER," she yells from behind me.

I heave a big sigh and turn back around, exasperated. "*What*, Lucy?!"

She looks down sheepishly. "I'm sorry."

I've never heard her say those words. I wait for her to continue.

"You probably had a lot bigger things to deal with than breaking my phone. And you probably didn't do it on purpose." She turns red, searching my face for a reaction that doesn't come. "Don't worry about it, though," she adds quickly to fill the silence. "My dad got me a new one."

I hear myself mumble under my breath, "Must be nice," but I nod. "Fine, apology accepted. Now please let me get to class. I'm already late as it is."

She nods, too, backing away. "Yeah of course, sorry."

I start to jog down the hall, leaving her standing there. "Cool drawings, by the way," she calls from behind me.

"Thanks," I reply.

XXX

Lucy

96

Journal Entry

Octber 14, Evening.

Dad was really upset with me for not saying anything about the alcohol at Meghan's party. I feel really bad about that. The only thing that made it worse was Mom's disappointment.

We all had a long talk about it last night over dinner. I really should have just come clean and told them, because now I broke their trust. They let me go to the party even though they weren't 100% sure about it because they trusted ME to do the right thing. THAT was the part that hurt Dad the most, and it feels worse than anything else. During our talk last night, Dad told us how it all happened.

The only reason Dad even found out about the alcohol at Meghan's party was because he knows Meghan's father from work, so he has his phone number. (I think their companies work together sometimes on projects or something like that.)

When I first asked permission to go to the party back in September, Dad called him that night to confirm the details and make sure it wasn't going to be some kind of rager. Meghan's parents had been off on a trip during the party, so Dad didn't hear back until yesterday morning. Meghan's dad was NOT aware there was a party going on.

When Meghan's dad checked with the butler and maid, they assumed he knew about it. It really hit the fan when Meghan's dad noticed the missing bottles of wine from the top of the refrigerator – he had bought a new brand to try and it had disappeared. That's when he started counting back and realizing that bottles have been disappearing for awhile now. Meghan's father was so furious, he called Dad back, thanked him for reaching out, and told him that he would definitely take care of the problem.

If my Dad was that angry, I shudder to think how nuclear Meghan's dad is right now.

97

Viral

O**ctober 17, 8:57am**
Homeroom is starting, but there are still a lot of kids drifting in the hallway. They're all staring at their phones.

They seem to be looking at the same thing, but there are many different reactions to it. Some are laughing uproariously and high-fiving each other. Others look at their screens in stunned silence, watching the video on loop.

It's got to be something on ClockClick. I whip out my phone. With a few flicks of my finger, I'm checking my news feed.

ClockClick recommends I watch something Monica posted last night - it already has over 500 likes and 126 comments. Considering our school only has around 800 kids, that's pretty close to everybody.

It's a video of a blonde girl at Food Lizard putting on a green apron. It's hard to tell who it is because she's wearing a cap that covers her face. The video suddenly cuts to her bagging groceries. She looks vaguely familiar, but it's hard to tell who it is. She turns her face toward the camera and suddenly, it's obvious. A caption flashes across the screen:

WHEN MOMMY AND DADDY CUT YOU OFF AND YOU SUDDENLY
HAVE TO WORK...

Another caption quickly takes its place:

R.I.P. MEGHAN GARDENER!

I don't believe what I'm seeing. I immediately tap on the comments section and start scrolling for more context. I quickly learn from the growing grapevine that not only has Meghan been cut off completely from her allowance and her phone, even her makeup has been taken away and thrown in the trash.

Suddenly, the answer to that nagging question becomes clear to me.

Monica is not in the popular girls' group because she's got a pretty smile, a winning personality, or even half a brain. It's because the power she wields on social media is great. That's actually pretty terrifying.

I look back up and see Meghan coming out of her Homeroom class at the end of the hall. She's walking right toward me, and she does *not* look friendly.

98

Venomous

I t's a lot to process in a very short amount of time. Here is Meghan Gardener herself, and she's coming straight for me. Her crystal eyes burn into me, but the rest of her is really distracting. She's got on a regular pair of tennis shoes and plain blue jeans. Her hair is swept up into a ponytail, which accentuates her rather plain face. There is not a trace of makeup anywhere. Even her t-shirt is just plain old white.

Whoa...I didn't know Meghan had freckles. She kind of looks like...a soccer mom...

The thought overwhelms me so much, I don't even realize she's given me a hard shove, sending me to the floor. The cold, hard tile snaps me back to Earth.

Meghan snarls venomously at me, digging her nails into one of my arms. "I invited you to my party, welcomed you into my house, practically GAVE you Marcus, and you SNITCHED." She takes a fistful of my hair and pulls it, hard. "You will *never* have friends again."

I don't have time to explain anything. My hair pulls my

face back and up, ripping tears out of my eyes. My arm is on fire.

This is not funny. She's actually going to kill me.

I instinctively raise my free arm to try to relieve the pressure, but it's not working. I try to twist, flounder, get out of her grasp somehow. She's got one foot on mine and is pinning me down with surprising force.

I find the strength to shove her backward a little, but that just jerks my own head, since she's still got my hair. The nails pierce deeper into my flesh.

Ow, ow, OW!

I hear Mr. Cheezers' voice cut through the growing noise. "MEGHAN Gardener, that's ENOUGH!" Using his imposing size, he pushes his way through the gathering crowd, shoves a beefy arm between us, and easily separates us. He stands between us and holds out his arms to create more space. He looks around for another adult to take action and call for an administrator.

Meghan glares at me, vitriolic. Her ponytail is now askew. She paces anxiously against Mr. Cheezers' forearm as one who would definitely jump me again if a chance appeared.

I glare back at her, breathing hard. My heart is pounding into my throat, and my entire body is numb and heavy.

What the hell was all that!?

Then comes Monica's voice, but I don't see her face. She's standing with her back to us, holding her phone up in the selfie position. She's recording a live ClockClick. "Like seriouslyyyyy -" she drags out the last syllable with an impressive vocal fry that would infuriate a speech therapist, "-it looks like SOMEONE needs to take a five-minute break. Meghan, sweetie, let it go. It's OVER."

The kids in the crowd giggle and start making fun of Meghan. Any notoriety or influence Meghan had is officially dead.

Principal Terry comes thundering down the hall, radio and keys bouncing on his belt for dear life. The crowd parts to let him through. Most disappear back into the classrooms for fear of getting involved.

Monica cuts the live feed and vanishes into the crowd.

My breath finally starts to even out a little. I look at Meghan again, at least as best as I can see around Mr. Cheezers' bicep.

You know, come to think of it, she's not really all that pretty. She needed all the clothes and makeup to make her look some-what interesting. If she hadn't been so manipulative and nasty, maybe people would have been kinder to her. Instead, everyone is thoroughly enjoying her downfall.

Principal Terry leads her away to get suspended, no doubt, being careful to keep his guard up in case she tries something again. Meghan now looks more like a plucked chicken than a peregrine falcon.

Mr. Cheezers looks at me and tells me to go to the bathroom so I can wash my face.

I guess that's the end of Meghan Gardener.

99

Journal Entry

O**ctober 17, after school**

Sooooo...I did NOT see that one coming with Meghan. I'm actually kind of relieved that the great Queen Bee has been dethroned. I feel like I can actually relax and just be myself so I can think about more important things.

For one thing, I'm really worried about Asher. Lexi and Leo still get really upset whenever Mia's name comes up, so I think about him a lot.

It's been so hard because I know there's nothing I can really do to fix it for anybody. I wish so badly I could.

Dad says I have a servant's heart, but maybe I was trying too hard to befriend Asher...he always gives me awkward looks when I try to be there for him.

Maybe he's not used to having friends since everyone sees him as weird. I just want to help. I'm only trying to be his friend. Why does he get so annoyed?

I don't care about fitting in, I just want to give him actual hope and make a real difference. I want him to believe that things can get better.

This has been a lot more difficult than I thought, but I won't let that stop me, though. Dad says nothing comes without difficulty.

I will become friends with Asher if it's the last thing I do!

XXXI

Asher

100

Awkward

October 20, Homeroom.

We're all waiting for Mr. Cheezers to start attendance. Most have found their seats, but a few kids linger around their friend's desks to chat in the last few moments. Lucy strategically drops a pencil that rolls over by my feet. It's obvious she's just using it as an excuse to come talk to me. She makes a show of groaning, standing up, and going after the pencil, which brings her to the back of the class, directly toward me.

Harper and Monica eye her, then each other, and turn around with a snicker.

Oblivious, Lucy fishes her pencil off the floor and hangs back by my desk for the tiniest moment. She's trying to act casual and it makes me cringe inside. "Asher -" she whispers.

"*What?*" I hiss.

"Is it really true what you said to me the day my phone broke?" she asks.

I feel my eyebrows knit together. "I have no idea what I

said to you that day. That was a long time ago."

She glances at Mr. Cheezers, who's still in the doorway with a clipboard, waiting for stragglers to come in from the lockers. She looks down at her pencil as if something is wrong with it. "You said I'm just like your Mom. What was that all about?"

What a randomly stupid question at such a bad time.

"What are you talking about?" I shoot back.

Lucy quickly changes the subject. "Can I sit with you at lunch tomorrow? I was hoping we can talk about something important."

Is she nervous?

"I guess-?" I say, incredulous at my own answer.

101

Scars

October 20, Social Studies.
I haven't had my head down for even a minute it feels like, and Mr. Brockley is already shaking me awake. I have a lot of respect for Mr. Brockley, so I sit up and stretch my sore arms a bit to try and keep myself awake. Something seems off, though. I feel like someone might be watching me. Then cool air curls around my arm.

My sleeve was rolled up and I was sleeping on it.

Wide-eyed, I clap my hand onto my crumpled sleeve and yank it back down. My stomach surges inside me.

Mr. Brockley must have seen the scars.

I look up immediately to see what he's doing.

Mr. Brockley walks on, stopping at his desk to write something down right as the bell rings and everyone starts to crowd the door.

I really hope that's not what I think it is. If I make it a big deal, it'll just be worse.

XXXII

Intermission

102

Mr. Brockley, Required Reporter

October 20, 4:45pm.

Once the kids are gone for the day, Mr. Brockley quietly shuts the door of his classroom. He lets out a long sigh and walks to his desk, sitting on the rolling chair. It drifts a bit, carrying him with it. Gathering his resolve, he scoots the chair up to the computer and takes the mouse. He picks up his scribbled note from earlier and sets it aside.

We'll try the parents first.

He thumbs over to one tab out of about 37 he has open. It's the parent contact log he has to fill in every time he contacts a student's home for something. Quickly, he taps in the date and the name of the student. He plans out what he's going to say in the reason box. It's easier to just write it out as a script and read it back while on the phone. Helps with the nerves, and it keeps things brief.

The digital letters populate in a neat little line, thinking out loud for him:

```
Good evening, Ms. Gryphon, this is Mr. Brockley
from Fountain View Middle. (Is this a good time?)
I just wanted to reach out with a concern I had
regarding Asher. Asher seems very tired lately and
has been sleeping a lot in class. I'm sure you
know he always wears his favorite hoodie... |
```

The letters stop for a second and the thin black bar appears, punctuating the silence. Mr. Brockley's fingers hover over the keyboard as he tries to word it. He ventures forward to see how it turns out.

He starts with:

```
...and it's getting really worn and dirty...."
```

No, no. That's not the reason for the call.

He taps the backspace button way too many times and tries again:

```
...but today when he was sleeping in class, his
sleeve was rolled up, and I saw his arm.  Asher
has very deep scars on his right arm, and quite a
bit of heavy bruising.  I wanted to bring that to
your attention just in case he might be getting
bullied outside of school or participating in
heavy contact sports.  Asher is usually
well-behaved here in school, so I'd be surprised
to hear of him getting into a fight.  Anyway, if
there's anything I can do to help, please let me
know.  Do you have any questions for me?  Thanks
```

and have a great night.

That seems to be enough, so Mr. Brockley pulls up Power-School (the 12th tab in the collection), finds Asher's student information page, and uses one finger to peck at the numbers on the classroom phone.

It rings. And rings. And rings. Then an automated reply. "I'm sorry, this user has a voicemail box that has not been set up yet. Goodbye." The call clicks off.

That's always a good sign. Trying the dad.

Looking at the next set of numbers, Mr. Brockley gives it another shot.

This time, it doesn't even ring. It just gives a series of error beeps, the kind a landline phone makes when you leave the handset off the hook for too long.

I could have sworn that number was working before.

Mr. Brockley sighs tiredly.

Surely there has to be SOMEONE else.

Nope. There is a Duncan Gryphon listed as a brother/-guardian, but there's no contact information.

Of course.

Mr. Brockley looks out across the empty desks and his eyes land on Asher's usual seat in the back corner.

Those scars were really deep, and there were a lot of them. I've never seen anything like that.

After a moment, he takes a deep breath and blows it out hard. He leans back in the chair, rubbing the inside corners of his eyes with his fingers.

Something is off here. If I make a report, it can cause more problems than good, but what if he really needs help?

His eyes now look a little sadder than before, searching the screen for a place to open yet another tab.

I hate this.

A quick Google search brings up the number he's looking for. In one movement, he picks up the phone receiver with his left hand. It hovers as he alternates looking at the screen and the phone, dialing the numbers carefully.

It rings.

An automated message clicks on. "Thank you for calling the Department of Social Services. Please listen carefully, as our menu options have changed. If you know the name of the person you're trying to reach, please dial 1 for our staff directory. *Para español, oprima* 2. For child services, please press 3. To be connected to the operator, please press 0 or stay on the line."

Mr. Brockley accidentally presses two buttons at once. He holds his breath, hoping it would still go through.

The machine replies, "I'm sorry, that is an invalid entry. Please try again."

Mr. Brockley's brow sinks into a straight line. He mutters under his breath while he waits for the entire message to play again. This time, he very deliberately presses 3.

The machine accepts his entry like a jukebox coin and continues to the next set of prompts. "To make a report, please press 1. To follow up on an existing report, please press 2. To go back to the main menu, please press 3."

Mr. Brockley presses 1. It rings a few times, and someone picks up.

"Department of Child Protective Services, this is John. Are you calling to make a report?"

"Hello, good evening. Yes, I'm a teacher at Fountain View Middle. I'm not 100% sure on this, but I wanted to mention it just in case. One of my students doesn't seem right - I've been observing him and have noticed that he seems more tired than usual. His sleeve was rolled up while he was sleeping in class today, and I saw that his arm has several very large scars and heavy bruising. I've tried contacting the parents without success - they don't have working phone numbers."

John replies, "Thank you so much for reaching out and providing this information. What is the child's name and age?"

"Asher Gryphon," says Mr. Brockley. "PowerSchool says he's 13."

The voice on the other end buzzes again. "How many scars did you see on his arm, and what did they look like?"

"At least 10-12. They looked like straight lines and they overlapped, almost like tally marks. I don't know if I saw that right, though."

John doesn't say anything, only clicks the information onto his keyboard. The clicks subside and he asks, "What were the approximate size of the scars? You also said there was bruising? Would you please describe it in as much detail as you can?"

Mr. Brockley sits up in his chair looking absently in the direction of Asher's desk, trying to remember. "The really big scars had to be about 2-3 inches long each. There were some half-inch ones that were scattered around the bigger ones. The bruises I saw were mostly around the wrist, and it made me wonder if there are more."

John's nod on the other end is almost audible, but only

more keyboard clicks come. Soon, a follow-up question: "Have you seen or heard anything specific that might indicate a threat to the child's immediate safety?"

Mr. Brockley holds up a questioning hand. "Other than what I've mentioned, I don't have any other evidence that this is happening. This is a suspicion I have based on his scars and behavior."

After answering another 20 minutes of questions from John, Mr. Brockley's eyes are bleary gray and drying out in the light of the computer screen. The automatic lights in his room have long flickered off. Mr. Brockley's hand wanders into the snack drawer and begins scavenging for something decidedly unhealthy. Trying his best not to make noise, he opens a bag and mutes the crunch of the chips as much as he can.

John finally starts to wrap it up. "Do you have anything else to report or add?"

Mr. Brockley sits, crunching pensively until he remembers he has to answer out loud. "No, that was all." After a quick gulp, he adds, "Thanks." Mr. Brockley pauses and adds, "Is there a way for this to be sent in anonymously? I don't want to cause problems for him or make it a big deal, but I did want to say something just in case there is something going on." He shovels another couple of chips in his mouth, less worried about the noise.

John's answer sounds kinder than expected. "I know it can be hard to make these reports because you're just not sure about potential repercussions, but we do thank you for upholding your obligation as a required reporter. For your peace of mind, information contained in this report is confidential. If you have any further questions, comments, or concerns, you can always reach us at the same number you called today. We appreciate you calling the Department of Child Protective Services and making a report. We will contact you if we need further information."

"Okay, thanks very much. Have a good evening." Mr. Brockley sets the phone back on the hook and looks back toward Asher's chair.

I hope it's not what I think it is.

Resigned, he eats the last chip and tosses the bag in the trash can, wiping his hands on his pant legs. Then he stands up, takes his coat and backpack, and leaves for the night.

XXXIII

Asher

103

Unfair

October 21

It's 6:45 AM. I'm sitting on a big rock on the edge of the sidewalk where I live, waiting for the bus and drawing in the dirt with a stick. I miss Mia. I wish she would just wake me up in the morning, prove to me that this was all just a bad dream. I know there won't be any waking up from this nightmare for a while yet, but hope has this bad habit of coming back.

I don't see an easy way to just pick up and leave for something better, but I can leave this house.

Maybe I can go live with Duncan...

My older brother is still alive, he still takes care of me despite not being here with me. He sends me about 100 bucks to buy food every month, so he's doing much better than when he first left.

I always find the cash in a paper bag, carefully tucked under the same rock in our backyard. It's never enough, but it's better than nothing and probably the best he can do right now. I hope he knows how much I appreciate him, wherever he is. I have no idea where he is or how to find him, which some days hurts even more than knowing Mia is dead. I can't help but wish he was here. I miss him, too.

I look up to check for the bus, squinting through the wind. I can feel it ruffling my hair.

Nothing yet.

I resume my stick drawing of nothing in particular.

Duncan would come back if Dad disappeared.

There's nobody else around to hear me. I scream. "THIS ISN'T FAIR!" The stick snaps in my hand.

I just want everything to be okay again. I feel as though my heart has been ripped out and stomped all over until it wasn't beating anymore. Mia was the only hope I had left. Everything feels so hopeless and alone. Maybe if I disappeared, no one would notice. Maybe I should go be with Mia in the peaceful place. It is not fair the way our lives turned out.

The bus pulls up in front of me with a hot heave. I get up and adjust my book bag, waiting for the doors to hiss open. I step on what's left of the stick, grinding it into the dirt, and begin the climb.

XXXIV

Lucy

104

Small Talk

October 21, Lunchtime.

Come lunchtime I sit in my usual spot at the corner table when suddenly I see a pile of strawberry blonde hair making its way through the crowd, past the other kids. Its owner takes a turn toward me. I see it's Lucy emerging from between the tables. Surprisingly, Lucy walks right up to my table, holding her expensive-looking lunchbox.

"Asher?" she asks, "Can I sit here?"

I shrug.

It's not like anybody else is coming. Christian is in lunch detention again.

She glances around, then sighs and perches on the seat across from me.

"Why are you here?" It comes off a little harsher than I meant it, but I do mean it.

Her eyes widen a little like she wasn't expecting that.

"Okay...I just wanted to talk for a second," she manages.

"Okay, what do you want?" I ask. I've already eaten my

food, but I find myself watching her blue and white lunchbox.

She looks at me like she's wondering how to talk to me. "Well…I was wondering why you compared me to your Mom that day when the phone accidentally broke."

That crawls up my back.

I'm not talking about that with you.

"I didn't say that. You heard me wrong." It's not my strongest reply, but it'll have to hold.

She hesitates, but decides not to pursue it. "How come I don't really see you during the day?"

I have to choose my words carefully. Does she need to know my hiding place? "I don't know, I'm usually in the hallways on my way to class."

I'll change the subject. Girls like Lucy love to talk about themselves, so I'll just get her talking about herself. She'll be gone soon, and so will her questions. "Hey, Lucy?" I ask.

Her face brightens. "Yes?"

"How are Lexi and Leo?"

"They're doing great! Thanks for asking. What about - " Lucy's face immediately contorts when she remembers about Mia.

I look down at the crumbs on the table.

I hear her voice. "…sorry."

"Do you make sure your siblings are safe?" I ask.

Lucy sighs. "Yeah, I try my best to. Even though they annoy the heck out of me, I still love and care for them."

"That's good. Aren't you going to eat?" I ask her.

She remembers she's got lunch with her and unzips her lunch box, revealing a plastic baggie with a sandwich in it. There's a brownie, a water bottle, and a note.

How "cute".

My stomach growls. "What do you do on your phone?" I ask to quickly change the subject.

"I only really use it for calling and social media," she says with a hint of confusion. "What about –?"

I cut her off. "I can differ. I only use my phone for music."

"Oh, what music do you like?"

"Heavy Metal."

"What's your favorite band?" she asks.

"It's a band called Perturbed."

"Hmm, I think I've heard of them before." She spaces out for a minute, then suddenly pipes up, "OH, my father listens to them. I only know one song though, I think it was called 'In The Midst of the Fire.'"

Interesting. Actually interesting.

"Hey, that's my favorite song of theirs!" I say with a little more enthusiasm than I expected. We're interrupted by the lunch bell. The cafeteria empties like a tidal wave, sweeping us all away.

XXXV

Asher

105

Friend or Foe?

The dismissal bell rings. Most of the kids pouring out of classrooms are car riders. They collide and swish together down the hall like whitewater rapids.

I have to stay behind with the rest of the bus riders to wait until our numbers are called. One car rider hangs back for a second.

"Bye, Ash," calls Lucy. "See you tomorrow."

I turn to look at her. "See ya."

I look beyond Lucy and see a few *other* car riders close behind. They slink up close like Siamese cats with evil grins. They form a half-circle around us. I know I should take this chance and leave now, but they haven't called my bus yet.

"What are you doing with *that*, Lucy?" asks Monica. Her voice is calm and level, as though she were talking about an object like a book or a pencil.

It's so convincing, I almost relax for a second.

Then Monica looks at me, raising an amused eyebrow and laughing, pushing Harper. Some other random girl follows along with them, trying to be included. Meghan is nowhere to be seen anymore.

Harper pushes Lucy and laughs, too.

Fire flushes hot in my cheeks.

I back away, pull my hood over my head, and go on my phone to disengage from the conversation.

"He is not a thing, he is a human being," states Lucy icily.

"Okay, then," Harper says, pulling her hand back in an exaggerated sweep.

"Looks like someone's claimed her man. Off-limits!" Monica sneers.

The girls cackle, looking at Lucy to join in. She doesn't.

Monica pulls out her phone to aim it at me, but is surprised when the camera doesn't seem to be working. She looks up and sees Lucy's hand wrapped around the camera lens.

"Wait, you're *serious?*" asks Monica, incredulous. "Are you actually *talking* with him?"

"We're surprised he even talks at all," Harper adds.

I'm getting fed up.

I look out from under my hood and open my mouth to snap back, but Lucy beats me to it.

"STOP, you're being very rude," Lucy states plainly. The mean girl in her shows for the quickest moment. "Besides, I don't have to date the entire football team just to feel wanted like *some* of us." She shoves the phone backward into Monica's hand.

I'm surprised at how acrid that was. I glance at Lucy's face.

She looks like she might be regretting what she said, but she stands firm.

Monica balks.

Harper looks wounded. "What *happened* to you, Lucy?"

Lucy waits for them to walk away.

They're talking amongst themselves, processing what just happened. They soon start to laugh in the distance.

"Hey Asher?" I hear her straining to talk over the noisy crowd and list of bus numbers on the loudspeaker.

"Yeah?" I reply.

"Is it okay if I sit with you at lunch again?"

After all that, I'd feel bad not to let her.

"Yeah, sure. Hey - thanks for that."

Lucy grins at me full force. It's a bit much, so I pull my hood over my head and walk out toward the bus lot. "See ya." My bus always gets here on the first wave, so it doesn't matter if I heard the announcement or not.

106

Friend > Foe

O**ctober 31**

Another week has come and gone. I wonder if time is this blurry for everyone else, or if they're so caught up in their lives, they don't notice. It seems like life is just moving through a comic strip. Places you spend the most time in, like your house and school, take up the biggest spaces in your head. I spend a lot of time in this bathroom stall. I've just finished adding the 53rd tally mark to my collection when an announcement comes on. I open and close my fist to get the blood to pool while the voice drones on in the background.

"Attention, staff and students, we are going into a school-wide blackout at this time. I repeat, we are going into a school-wide blackout at this time. If you are in the hallway or restroom, report to the nearest classroom immediately. Teachers, please ensure the halls are clear and everyone is in the blackout position." The message concludes with a crackle.

This doesn't sound like a drill.

I quickly mop up the cut with a wad of toilet paper and put a bandage on it. I debate whether or not I have time to wash my hands. Since I was messing with blood, I decide to do it quickly.

I soon find myself in the hall. There is one teacher nearby taking a final scan of the hall before locking her door. She spots me and motions to me urgently. I comply, slipping in through the closing door. I try not to listen to it locking behind me. The lights are off, the blinds are drawn, and the narrow window in the door is covered.

The teacher guides me toward the group of kids sitting on the floor by the wall. During a blackout, you have to stay in the safest corner you can find, out of the line of sight of someone who might come to the door.

She perches on a low stool near us. She doesn't have to hush anyone this time, because nobody expected this, and nobody said on the announcements that this is a blackout *drill.* Those, we're used to.

Lucy is in the group and waves me over. She pats the floor next to her. She takes a piece of paper out of her pocket, scribbles on it, and hands it to me.

I unfold it. It reads:

I'm glad you're here. I was hoping you were in a safe place. Do you think this is for real?

I look at her and shrug. The other kids are looking at each other for cues on how to respond to this. Usually, they tell you when it's a drill. The teacher is stoic, but her eyes are distant, watching the door carefully. I'm not really scared at the chance to see Mia again.

The only people who have ever said they were glad to see me were my brother and sister. Is it possible I've found a friend?

107

Pity

November 4, just thinking on the bus ride home.

Lucy was tripping today at lunch. She was trying too hard to be my friend because she suddenly pities me. Pity is not awkward – it's more frustrating than anything else. It's disgusting. I don't need anyone's pity. If I tell you something, I tell you something, but I don't need anyone's pity. If you pity me, I feel sorry for you, because I don't want it. The problem that happens with pity is that when a person pities you, they go off and tell your story to everyone. Then everyone comes back around and starts treating you differently. They say, "Oh, I'm so sorry, I didn't KNOW..." Then they handle you with tweezers like if you'll break.

As if being considerate of others is this huge thing you only do for "special" cases.

People are fake. People suck.

Maybe I should feel a sense of comfort when I'm with Lucy, because someone actually gives a crap enough to try to understand me. I'm still keeping my guard up, though. I'm tired of getting hurt.

Movies

November 8

Lucy comes by again today during lunch. She isn't there for long, but we talk about movies this time. It goes by fast.

Hungry

November 11

This seems to be a regular thing now. Lucy is showing up at lunch almost every day. She seems less nervous today and offers to share a cookie with me. I don't want to get used to it, so I ignore my stomach and decline it. We talk about our favorite classes.

XXXVI

Lucy

110

Journal Entry

November 14

I don't have much time to write today, but I did want to just say this real quick before I get too busy and forget. I think I'm finally gaining Asher's trust because he looks at me differently now. I can tell he's still very protective of himself, but there's less anger in his eyes when he looks at me. I understand why, though. I just want him to know I'm here for him and he's not alone. I guess trying to fix his life for him was pretty naive. It's obvious that's not what he needs or even wants. I care so much, but I don't know how else I can show it other than just being someone he can count on. -Lucy Mae

XXXVII

Asher

111

Big Talk

December 12

"Lucy?" I hear myself ask amid the noise of the cafeteria.

Lucy started sitting with me at lunch once in a while, and now she shows up every day. I would never have believed it if someone had told me 6 weeks ago that this would happen.

"Yeah, Asher?" she replies absently, chomping on a french fry.

She's changed so much, but I still feel kind of hollow when I say, "There's something I need to tell you."

Her eyes drift from the distant doorway back to me and lock onto my face. She straightens up in her seat. "What's up?"

I'm really about to tell her my all-time secrets, but I think she can handle it...right?

I push past the lump in my throat. "It's about my parents..."

Too late to turn back now.

Lucy takes a sip of juice and folds her hands politely,

waiting for me to continue.

I can't believe I'm actually saying this.

"My parents are really addicted to alcohol and drugs... and they seem to have gotten worse after Mia passed away..."

I just shared more than I thought I would.

Lucy just nods.   She even seems to take it in stride, not making a big deal about it.

I find myself continuing. "Almost every day I get beaten... the only relief I've found has been in cutting. I do it all the time."

Her face begins to change.

I said too much. Who else is she going to tell this to?

She notices my reaction and tries to reassure me. "It's okay, Ash, I'm just trying to understand. What do you mean by *cutting*?" She doesn't sound scared or repulsed - more concerned.

I pull up a corner of my sleeve, where I know the smaller cuts are. She's not ready to see the big ones, and I'm not sure she ever will be.

Lucy gasps quietly, so I know she saw it.

I pull my sleeve back down before anyone else sees.

She looks up at my face and half-whispers, *"Was that on purpose?"*

I nod.

Obviously.

Lucy really is sheltered. She's still trying to process it. She whispers again, *"Why, Asher? That looks like it really hurts."*

"It's just a way to deal with things. When you get into situations you have no control over, you start to get creative with how to escape them." I don't know how else to explain it. "When bad things happen over and over, you go numb.

This is the only way I can really feel anything at all."

She sits in silence. "I'm really sorry, Asher."

Strange thing to say.

"It's not like it's your fault," I answer. "My parents are basically trash, but somehow I still love them. Every fiber of common sense tells me to get as far away as I can. Mia was the only thing keeping me going, but now..." I drift off, fixing my eyes on a fly. It's perched on the edge of the overfilled trash can, rubbing its little hands together to drink from the stench.

"What do you mean they're trash? Isn't that a little harsh?" Lucy asks.

I don't even think about my answer. It just comes out, like I'm telling it to the fly. "Not harsh at all. Back when my parents first met, they weren't any better than they are now. My father was a drug dealer and my mother was a prostitute. To make things worse, they spent every penny and sold the majority of what we owned to get more drugs. Cocaine, meth, and now fentanyl. The fentanyl gummies were what ended up -" It's still too soon and the thought chokes me. Tears are threatening to come up, but my weakness is not for her to see. I pinch and twist on my leg and my attention comes back to Lucy.

Should I really continue?

I look at her.

Her face has gone pale with shock, as someone who has heard way more than they bargained for. She picks up her sandwich and takes a bite to help her think.

I guess I can't blame her, but my voice keeps going. It's surprisingly easy. "My brother is named Duncan and he was like an idol to me - he was everything I wish I could be because he had a decent job and a decent life despite being stuck with my parents. Once he had enough money saved up, he decided to leave some to me and walk out. That's the day I had to become a man and take care of Mia. Duncan probably chose the right idea since I haven't seen him in a while. That must mean he's having a good life." I pause again.

Lucy is listening so closely, her hand is barely clutching her sandwich. It looks like it's about to fall. She realizes I've stopped talking and waves it delicately at me, ushering me to continue. That evil flicker in her eye faded long ago - that one the mean girls have when they're fishing for blackmail. I've been around her long enough to know that she's okay to talk to, especially since I know the type of family she comes from.

I continue. "I always try to care for my parents even though they haven't shown me any real affection since Duncan lived with us. When Mia was still alive, she was my top priority. I had hope that she could be the one to make the family different but no...my parents decided to leave their gummy bear edibles out. She had no idea what she ate, and it..." I force myself to say it because I need to hear it. "...killed her immediately." I let one tear run down my face, hot and fat. I have to pinch my leg again to help me move past it and bring my focus back to Lucy.

The look on her face says everything. Guilt. She looks like she is going to be sick. I've been through enough to learn to bypass guilt and see through lies, but this guilt seems different. It's not that wishy-washy guilt that people try to get rid of by throwing money at it. Her face looks like she's actually feeling this with me.

She finally speaks in a semi-croak. "I never knew you were

going through this pain… if you could have told me earlier, maybe I could have helped…"

"No," I reply. "I've been through this my entire life. Nothing will change the way my parents act. My sister was buried in a trash bag because that's all we have left. If that didn't do it, nothing ever will. I've been so angry at everything. My parents, Principal Terry, Christian Clawthorne, and everyone who makes it their lives' mission to put me into the ground. I've often thought of just doing them the favor."

I said too much again.

I don't think Lucy caught that last little bit because she doesn't react to it. She just adds her own story, "I've felt angry at everything before too. One time, my mother was watching my siblings knock down everything in my room while I was trying to sleep in the same room. To make matters worse, my dog was in the room and started going crazy with them! They trashed my entire room and I had to clean up everything even though it was a school day and I had to get ready for school. I gave them all the silent treatment for two days straight. Eventually, they apologized."

The bell rings before I can answer. I wonder if she realizes how dumb her "problems" are. I'd trade her for them in a second. The crowd surges, builds up at the double doors, and spills out into the main hallway.

XXXVIII

Lucy

112

Journal Entry

December 22, 6:06pm

I have so many things going on this Christmas, and yet it seems pointless now. All I can think of is Asher. What will he do? Does he have anyone to wish him a Merry Christmas or Happy New Year? How am I supposed to go about my life now knowing that he's literally fighting for his own life every single day?

The way Mia died should not happen to anyone, ever. What kind of parents leave fentanyl-laced gummy bears lying around like that? Of course a little kid who doesn't know any better is going to eat it. That is the saddest thing I have ever known in my entire life. She wasn't in school, so they were able to hide her death from the cops. Poor Mia. Lexi really loved her like a sister.

Obviously, Asher is not in a safe place, but I don't know what to do. I could invite him to live here, but my parents would have a problem with having a boy living in the house. They'll probably say it's inappropriate, even though they like Asher well enough. We don't really have space, either. The only spare room we had was used for Leo when Mom learned she was having twins.

THIS IS HORRIBLE. If I call the cops and tell, they'll come and take Asher away, which is the one thing he never wanted because that means they'll throw him in the system. Kids in the system bounce around from one home to another, and their lives are ruined forever. The only good thing that would come of it is that they might lock up his parents, but I would never want to betray his trust like that.

Despite everything that's happening, I'm proud of Asher for speaking up to me and telling me his life story. Only problem with that is now I feel guilty for every word he's saying. None of those things have ever happened to me, even in my worst possible moments.

I was so mean to him on the first day I met

him. I wish I could take back all the rude remarks I have ever said to him. But he's my friend now and that's all that matters. I should protect our friendship no matter what.

113

BAD BAD NEWS!!!

December 23

"Lucy Mae." Mom's voice speaks firmly and clearly from downstairs.

That doesn't sound good.

I bookmark *Coldhearted*, get up from my bed, and walk out to the balcony from my room. I peer over the rail, feeling my heart thump faster. They're both looking up at me from the living room.

Wait, IS THAT MY–? How did they even get that!?

Mom's holding my journal.

Definitely NOT good.

"Please come here. We need to talk to you," adds Dad.

Oh no, no no no...they've read it. I'll have to play it cool and act like I don't know anything.

I do my best to chirp cheerfully as I come down the stairs. "Coming!" I find myself barely brushing the handrail with my fingertips and trying to glide, but promptly almost fall. Thankfully, I catch myself. The adrenaline spike makes my legs weak, so I just grab the handrail and clomp down the stairs like a normal person. I stare at the wooden steps, carefully placing one purple-socked foot, then the other.

This is SO not going to be good.

Mom's eyes are not at full power like I expected. It's actually worse. She looks disappointed. She's holding up my journal. "Why didn't you tell us any of this?"

I thought I was going to get yelled at. Now I'm just the most ashamed I've ever been in my entire life.

All I can do is look down at my socks. "What?"

"Lucy Mae Clark. You knew this entire time. Not only who Asher is, but from the sound of this entry, you also knew about the real reason Mia died. This means Asher is in very real danger. Shame on you for not speaking up," she informs me. "Your father has been trying to find any kind of contact information for Asher's parents and has not had any luck. Do you have Asher's phone number?"

I won't look at her. Instead, I trace the white polka dot pattern on my left sock with my eyes. "No. I'm sorry, Mom." It's the best I can come up with right now.

Dad's voice floats quietly over to us from his place by the window.

Though he's trying to be discreet, I can hear his phone squawking from here. "9-1-1, do you need fire, police, or medical?"

He responds, "Police, please."

"Please hold." The operator clicks off and there is a brief silence.

Another click. Another voice comes on the line. "Stoneville Police."

"Good evening, my name is Bill Clark. I'm calling in regard to the death of a minor by possible drug overdose."

The officer asks, "Do you have an address?"

"No, but I have some names and the area where they live," Dad offers.

"Let's start with what you have," says the officer.

XXXIX

Asher

114

Wellness Check

Friday, **8:00 PM**

I'm walking home from Food Lizard, one bag in each hand. Perturbed plays in one ear. I always keep the other one open so I can hear what's happening around me. The drums mark my pace, and the guitar riffs unconsciously influence my movements. I find myself air strumming with one hand, bag sliding off onto my wrist. I glance for cars and step off the sidewalk to cross the street.

As I approach the driveway, I see something different. There's a cop car parked outside the house, lights off. My stiff gait slows to a stop.

That's not good.

The grip I have on my bags tightens, crinkling the plastic.

There's another car, too. Gray. Unmarked. Maybe it's a civilian car?

I dare to hope for a second.

Duncan!?! Nah, there's no way. I really ought to just keep right on walking and pretend I have no idea who lives there. That would be the smart thing to do.

My heart is pounding.

I haven't seen my brother in forever. Maybe he's come back.

My internal debate is cut short when Mom appears in the window. She moves the blinds from inside the house and peers out at me like a ghost. She motions me inside with one hand.

Wow. This is the most we've talked in months. This must be serious. Maybe Dad had a heart attack.

Two cops are standing in front of the door. Dad is wedged like a rat between the screen door and house door, pointing a finger out at them.

I wince at my father's voice. It's slurred, but he furrows his brow hard to help him enunciate. "HEY! You ha-*hic* NO RIGHTS en'rin' *my house!*"

The officer probably expected this. He draws a deep breath, straightens up, and puts his hands on his lean waist just above his belt. "Sir, we have some questions for you and it is in your best interest that you cooperate, please. A report has been made about the possible death of a minor at this address. In order to perform this wellness check, we will need to enter your home whether you like it or not and verify that your children are alive and well."

After what I just heard, my head is swirling.

The only one I told anything to was Lucy. Did she actually call the cops...?

The weight of the groceries shifts in the bags I forgot I was holding. The music in my ear now sounds like noise. I shift both bags to my left hand, then use my free one to take the earbud out and drop it in my pocket. I drift the remaining distance towards my house.

One of the officers hears me coming up the path and turns

to greet me. "Hello, I am Officer Walker. What is your first and last name?"

"Asher Gryphon," I mumble in disbelief.

Then I hear - Mom's voice? It rings surprisingly clearly, but sounds foreign bouncing off the gray sky. "Please let my son in the house! I do-not give permissions f'you to talk to 'im!" All heads swivel as Mom makes her way toward me, slinking out past the rat in the door.

Dad looks at her and grunts, then turns his eyes back on the cop.

Mom shuffles across the gravel like an old vacuum cleaner. When she reaches me, she leans in; not quite close enough for a hug, but still invasive of personal space. Her arms wrap around me without quite touching me. It makes my flesh crawl. She taps my back awkwardly. Her whispers puff haltingly in my ear, "Make-sure to say...ever'thin's fine, okayplease?"

A familiar wave of disappointment washes over me.

Nothing at all has changed.

I look at her sunken eyes and stringy hair. All I can do is ask, "What *happened* to you?"

I turn away as her face starts to fall. I drift past the cops toward the door.

Dad makes a motion to move over and let me through, but his gelatinous beer gut, barely covered by his dirty wife-beater shirt, takes up most of the doorway.

Officer Walker tries talking to me again. "Asher, we need to ask you a few questions, if you'll come this way -"

My father suddenly lunges at the cop. He stupidly smashes a bottle of beer on the officer's head. With a dull crunch, it breaks apart into heavy shards. "WHO said 'nothing 'bout my chil'ren?! What'sh this about?" Then his back stiffens and he gets louder because he knows what's coming next. "YOU HAVE NO RIGHT. THIS IS MY HOME. YOU HAVE NO RIGHT."

I watch him.

Everything he does is utter bull–

The other officer shoves past me and is on Dad immediately. Within seconds, he has Dad's left arm twisted painfully around his own back, and he's leading him away from the door toward the police car.

Dad howls as loudly as he can. "POLICE BRUTALITY! YOU HAVE NO RIGHT. YOU HAVE NO RIGHT!"

The officer holding him clicks the first cuff on his right wrist. "Sir, you are under arrest for assaulting an officer. You have the right to remain silent. Anything you say can and will be used against you in the court of law. You also have the right to an attorney. If you cannot afford one, the court will appoint one for you. Do you understand?"

Dad isn't listening because he's stuck on a loop. He talks over him, and it sounds like a trashy daytime TV show. "YOU HAVE NO RIGHT. THIS IS MY HOME. YOU HAVE NO RIGHT."

Officer Walker, now off to the side, raises both arms, assessing the amount of beer dripping down his uniform. He angrily flicks his hands to try and get some of it off, then feels the top of his head. He brings his hand back down to check for blood. This time he addresses Mom, who is still hovering outside on the driveway. "Mrs. Gryphon, we are here to check on your children. Failure to cooperate may result in their immediate removal from the premises."

I take advantage of the moment and slip inside the house.

Dad's voice now trails from the hood of the police car where he's been thrown. "WE ONLY HAV' ONE CHILD, THE ONE YOU SAW RIGHT IN FRON'NA YOUR FACE, AND HE IS FINE." Then the loop starts again. "YOU HAVE NO RIGHT! THIS'S POLICE BRUTALITY."

You're the one who broke a bottle on his head, idiot. What did you think was going to happen?

Shaking my head, I enter the dark of the house and set the groceries down on the counter. I come back to watch from behind the screen door.

Officer Walker moves out of view. He's circling around the house with one hand ready by his holster, just in case. I can hear the echo of his radio crackling on the back side of the house, near Mom and Dad's room. It's been real quiet here, so I can hear him say, "This is Walker. Requesting K9 back up at 7777 Greg Dr."

The radio crackles back, "Roger that."

That's not going to be good. It sounds like he's where Mia is.

Even though I have spent the last few years terrified of this moment, now that it's here, I'm surprised at how peaceful I feel. Everything in me wants my waste-of-space parents to pay for what they've done. They deserve to. If dogs show up here, they're going to find at least one thing that will put them in prison by tonight. That's if they don't find Mia. I close my eyes and let the noises outside melt into quiet darkness.

I'll have to mentally prepare myself. They're definitely going to take me and I'm going back into the system.

I open my eyes and realize that I don't really have much to take with me except for my brother's CDs. Usually, the social worker has you fill a trash bag with your stuff before they take you.

Ha. Trash taking itself out.

I'm surprised to feel the corner of my lip curling.

This is so bad, I might as well laugh at it.

Before too long, red and blue lights flood the house.

My heart begins beating a little harder. My lips crunch together like an asterisk. I move to the window so I can see.

Dad's now in the back of the patrol car.

One down, one to go. Honestly, I'm kind of rooting for the cops. I don't care what happens to me as long as Mia gets justice. What was that saying – be sure your sins will find you out? It was something like that. I don't remember.

The window is partially rolled down, so Dad's twisting his neck to somehow sit higher and funnel his voice out through the crack. "HEY! What you think you doin' in my house!"

The officer that arrested Dad is in the driver's seat. He stares straight ahead and slowly rolls the window back up. The door pops open and he steps out, leaving Dad alone with his yelling.

Dad gets even more infuriated. The car wobbles slightly at his muted meltdown.

Three other cop cars are here, all with lights flashing. The backup officers all get out of their cars quickly, one of them with a dog.

Officer Walker is still back behind the house. I can hear him say, "Bring Ajax over here. This looks like a grave."

A second voice confirms it. "Dig it up and look inside."

115

With Faint Sunlight Comes A Darker Dusk

From my place at the window, I watch a Stoneville county car pull up and stop behind the collection of cop cars in the driveway. A tall shouldered lady steps out. She looks like a pale cartoon character with big red hair and too-red lipstick. She closes the door of her car with a crunch and makes her way over the gravel in her tiny shoes. She's clutching a legal pad in one hand and a pen in the other.

She approaches one of the cops hanging back by the patrol car and addresses him. They're too far away to hear, but she's showing him her badge and trying not to be obvious that she's asking questions about this...scene.

The cop says something into his radio and Officer Walker soon appears to talk to her.

She brandishes her ID again.

Officer Walker nods, then crosses his arms as he explains what's going on. He seems to be speaking very matter-of-factly based on his eyebrows, alternating between knitting together and arcing up into his forehead.

The red lady clicks her pen and scribbles some notes on the yellow legal pad. She thanks Officer Walker and walks back toward her car. She takes out her cell phone, dials someone, and puts the phone to her ear. Her hand floats up to her forehead and she glances over in my direction, but I know she can't see me back here. Her old leathery face is grim as she repeats what the cop told her. She pauses to listen, nodding.

I turn away from the window and look around at my home.

This is probably the last time I'll be here. It was a complete dumpster fire, but it was my dumpster fire. It's all I had.

I flick out a blade and absently filet the delicate skin on the tip of my index finger. A sliver of optimism surfaces from within, and I'm surprised.

Hope I land somewhere halfway decent when they take me away. Maybe they'll feed me.

The blood beads faithfully from under the slice and I put it to my lips to seal it off. It stings.

I'm not sure how much time just passed, but I decide to look out the window again to see where the red lady is. Now there's another county vehicle and a man stepping out of it. The man is wearing a brown suit, but he looks way less weird than red lizard lady. In fact, he's the exact opposite; he looks like a brown paper bag. I watch them greet each other and start walking toward the door.

Soon, the knock comes, polite and unassuming.

Funny how I used to be so scared of that knock when I had something to protect.

I open the door and get a good look at the red lady. The name tag clipped to her belt peeks out from under her blazer. She shows it to me. It reads *Diane Rogers*. She's obviously from DSS. She gives me a pity smile, red lips stretching across her reptilian jowl. "You must be Asher. I'm Diane, and this is my colleague, Mr. Frank Jones." She motions to her left with her legal pad and steps aside so I can see him.

Mr. Jones nods gruffly, speaking through his thick brown mustache. "How d'you do." I don't like him; his gray eyes are steely and distant.

Diane, the red lady, stoops a bit to "get on my level". She reaches across the threshold and barely touches my shoulder with her free hand. "Asher, is it okay with you if we speak privately?"

I cringe away from the touch.

Just don't, lady. I know why you're here. Let's get this over with.

They'll probably go through their list of questions and work them into the conversation to try and make me feel comfortable.

My chest feels tight. Can we please get on with it?

"Yes, ma'am." I answer. I shrug. "Not much choice, I guess."

She looks mildly stung. "Okay, great. Is there somewhere inside where we can all sit?"

Convenient way to see the living conditions for your little assessment.

I push the feeling down and lead them both inside the house. The male social worker makes me a little nervous. I turn on one of the lights, which burns dimly, revealing part of our ratty little house, crumbling walls, dingy floors and all. I look around and realize I'm actually all alone for real now. Dad's gone, and so is Mom; I saw when the cops found Mia's body, so Mom was immediately arrested.

Two for two. Good.

I point at the bean bag, the broken couch, and a folding chair. "You can sit here." I shut the door, and the screen door makes its muffled slap outside.

Diane is dressed way too nicely for this. She must be new, which explains why she called the other one.

I watch her eye the couch, then gingerly perch on the very edge of it, as though trying to touch as little of it as possible. She looks around the room too, then at me, calculating.

She's trying to figure me out. I hate when adults do that.

Mr. Jones chooses the opposite side of the couch and sits down gently. His phone dings, so he pauses to pull it out of his pocket and check it.

"I know you must have a lot of questions for us and are wondering why Mr. Jones and I are here today..." she begins.

Nope.

I chose the bean bag chair, so I sink a little deeper into my hoodie. My breath is stiff and I don't really want to look at them.

The man looks up from his phone, then at me. He puts it back into his pocket and leans forward onto his legs, propping himself up by the forearms.

Diane continues. "Would it be okay if I asked you some questions?"

I snort bitterly.

Why bother asking? You're going to do it, anyway.

She lets out an uneasy breath and exchanges a glance with Mr. Jones.

He nods as if to encourage her.

"Okay. Let's get started, then," she says. "Do you live here with Mom and Dad?"

"Yes," I reply in monotone.

She nods somberly, acting like she understands. She asks, "Do you have any siblings?"

That one stung a little harder than I expected it to. My eyes crunch shut to block the memory from coming back.

Too slow.

Mia's limp little body. The trash bag. The shovel. The air feels like it's crushing in on me. I use a nail to quietly dig as hard as I can into my freshly sliced fingertip. The wickedly sharp sensation is enough to distract me for now so I can answer her. "Yes, I did."

"Oh, I'm sorry, Asher. Did your sibling pass away?" Diane asks, glancing at my hands.

I nod without looking at her, because if I say it out loud, I'm going to lose it. My face and eyes are burning. A tiny twist of my nail in the cut brings my attention back to the present.

Diane says, "Okay, thank you for sharing that with me. We don't have to talk about that right now. I just have a few more questions for you, okay? Do you mind if I see your arm? You look hurt."

I yank my sleeve down as hard as I can and shake my head. *NO.*

Mr. Jones watches me quietly and doesn't say anything.

Diane tries it another way. "Asher, I have a difficult question for you. Please do your best to answer it. Have your parents done anything to you that physically or mentally harmed you?" she asks.

I can see right through this.

I find myself staring at a blank space on the wall. I feel like I'm in a tunnel and I can't seem to stop staring.

Lady, you have no idea.

It probably looks like I'm ignoring her. She starts to shift in her seat since I'm taking too long to answer.

I know it's not her fault she's clueless. She has no idea what I've been through. I'm sick and tired of it. I think this is it for me. I'm not living in fear anymore. It feels weird to say it after hiding for so long, but I'm finally letting the truth out, even if that means they'll take me away.

The word is heavy, but I push it out. "Yep."

She visibly relaxes the tiniest bit and jots down a note on her legal pad.

My thoughts play like a movie projector on the blank wall.

If I want them to pay for what they did to us, I'll have to take the hit and go into the system. It's worth it for Mia. I can't wait to see them in court so I can flip them off with both hands. For taking any joy I could possibly find and stomping it into the ground. For destroying our childhoods – not just Mia's, but mine and Duncan's. I will make sure they see both fingers, both hands. I hope they rot in prison. Laughably, there is STILL the chance that DSS will put me back with my parents despite everything, but it's a risk I can take now. I have literally nothing left to lose anymore, so I don't care.

"Can you tell me a little bit about that, please?" Diane asks, pencil hovering over the paper expectantly.

"About what?" I forgot what she asked before.

"Any cases of abuse...?" She prompts.

I look right at her, and she seems surprised. "There's not much to tell. He's a drug addict and a drunk who has been beating the hell out of me and everyone else here for years. My older brother Duncan couldn't take it anymore, so he left. He sends us money when he can, but we don't have his phone number or know where he is because Dad would probably kill him."

It feels so weird hearing that out loud for the first time.

"Once Duncan was gone, I had to always take the brunt of everything so my little sister wouldn't -"

It chokes me. It's over. The cry that comes from inside me has no sound, so hollow and hopeless it is. I cover my face with my sleeve and lean my head forward to hide under my hood. After a too-long span, my lungs finally catch up and drink in as much air as they can. I can't control the small weeping sob that comes out of me. I sit in silence for a few moments.

Please just go away.

That seems to be enough for Mr. Jones. I hear him standing up, followed by Diane.

From underneath my hood, I hear the whoosh of a trash bag.

116

One's Goodbye Left Unsaid

I know Lucy won't see this but I'm going to write it anyway.

Dear Lucy,

You are the best friend a person could ever ask for and don't let anyone tell you that you aren't. You made my ending a little more peaceful than if I never met you. Even though time was short, I'm glad I got to meet your family and eventually become your friend. Thanks for bringing some hope back to me, which is something I have been afraid to feel for a very long time. Even though my parents sucked, I know I have a choice in how my life turns out. I'm going to be the best version of myself I can be, for Mia's sake. I'm glad you changed and became a better person, even though that means you are no longer a "popular girl". I'm probably not going to see you again, but please don't forget me. I won't forget you.

Goodbye Lucy...

XL

Lucy

117

Journal Entry

J**anuary 1, 12:00am**

I wonder if Asher is safe right now? We never got to say goodbye to each other... I hope in the future I get to see Asher again, and that he's living a better life. Asher changed me for the good and I will never forget the impact he's made in my life...he really taught me that not everyone has the same life, and you never know what someone is going through. Most importantly, he made me realize that the superficial things we often worry about are not so bad when you think about it. My biggest worry was being popular, while he was just trying to find his next meal. I'm glad I got a chance to come out of my own head and see what's really important.

I thank you, Asher, for making me a better person.

Goodbye Asher...

XLI

Epilogue

Asher
February 20
*I've been living at a foster home and going to a
different school for the past month and a half.
They're not the worst family I've seen, but it's not
like I will get the chance to find out – they're
moving me again, and today I will meet the next
family.*

118

Tired

I'm slouching in the back corner of the social worker's car with my hood pulled over my head. I wish I had my phone and my music again. I trace my old scars with an absent-minded finger while I wait to find out how my life will go next.

The car door clicks from outside. I look up and watch it swing open. My caseworker looks in at me, waiting for me to get out and follow her to "my new home".

Who knows how long I'll be at this one.

I grab my back pack and get out of the car. The sun is harsh and hot, even under my hood.

The outside of the first-floor apartment is dingy white. Three ragtag steps lead uncertainly up to a faded red door. The social worker knocks on the door. It's only a few moments before there's a tinkling of a chain and thump of a deadbolt. The door slowly creaks open. I look through the widening crack.

It's a younger skinny guy with hair like mine. His clothes are baggy and he's wearing slides on his feet. The eyes are tired, but glad to see me. They look vaguely familiar, but their oldness makes them hard to recognize. "Hey, kid," he says.

My eyes snap wide open. I pull my hood off.

It *is* him.

"Duncan." Wordlessly, I throw myself on him and hug him as hard as I can.

He hugs me back just as hard.

Advice to the Hurting (From kids just like you)

"That's the funny thing about it. We don't feel it like regular people do. I have a really high pain tolerance. People that look at us when we cut ourselves think we're doing it for attention. After awhile when bad things keep happening, you just go numb. We're actually just doing it so we can feel SOMETHING. It helps us remember we're actually human, that we're actually alive. I hate that it has to come to this, but I need to know if I am." -Asher (Brooklynn, transcribed by Natalie)

Reflection Question:
What could you tell someone like Asher that is going through this situation? Clearly, Asher is very smart, but hasn't quite figured out how to get past this habit to cope with emotional pain. Cutting is all that he knows to do to escape, and telling someone else about it would make him feel exposed, making it very hard to trust anyone. Encouragement and reassurance does help when it comes from a genuine place of love and

caring, so what can we say? We're all Lucy until we start to give a crap and actually pay attention to those around us.

There was a quote that my 6th grade science teacher had on her wall. It said something like this...

If you see that somebody needs a friend, be that friend.

I feel like that's why we wrote *The Art of Giving A Crap*. To show how you can be that friend and stand up for them in a way that doesn't require a confrontation. When Lucy was really nice to Asher, he decided to tell her everything. This really gave her a glimpse into what other people go through. To those that are going through something similar to Asher, I recommend having someone to go through these tough times with you. And try praying. I believe personally that God will protect you because He loves you. Just try it. And the next time you see someone going through a hard time and they need a friend, put yourself in their shoes and **be that friend**.

-Angel Duran

For anyone going though this pain similar to Asher's. I want you to know to look inside yourself, find an accomplishment you're proud of, and if you don't have any, set out and make that your mission. If you aren't able to accomplish that today, then try tomorrow or the next day and the next day. Nothing can stop you from what you want to become and/or do, as well as seeking help when it is needed. **No one can ever truly be alone.** There will always be someone that's there for you no matter the person. Pain like this should never have existed but that's just the sad reality, that's why people are here, to help you in your time of need and to help steer you into making good choices that can benefit you and many others.

 -Kenshin Lee

As someone who has dealt with similar issues involving self-harm and abuse, I would like to say that you are not alone. You will never truly be alone in the world unless you are the last person alive. In many situations for people like myself, we grow up way too fast. We aren't mature and quiet because we are "old souls," we are this way because we were forced to be. No one deserves to be cheated out of their childhood. Mental illness tends to be swept under the rug, or just viewed as attention seeking. Personally, I don't like battling my mind the moment I wake up just to get out of bed, I don't like not being able to look in a mirror without hating everything about me, I don't like snapping at the people I love for no reason, I don't like becoming violent because of a minor inconvenience, I don't like experiencing violent intrusive thoughts at random, I don't want to hate myself, I don't want to feel like I'm insane and need to be locked away from others, I want to sleep soundly at night. Nobody wants to deal with any of these things, Nobody wants to live their life as if they are drowning. Self-harm is an addiction, you feel as if you have to do it just to feel human again, you do it because you think you're not enough, or to keep yourself from hurting others. In many cases, it gets to the point where you like it. You enjoy the cuts, burns, and the pain of hunger. It becomes a need if it

goes unchecked. Constant suffering until you can hurt yourself again, whether that be by physical injury or drug use. If it goes on for too long, it will kill you. It's a horrifying thought for most, but it does happen. Even unintentionally. People who struggle with suicidal thoughts and/or ideation tend to try and find something to hold on to. This is basically a last ditch effort to survive. This is your brain trying to keep you alive, although it hasn't helped much if it gets to this point. So please, talk to someone. Find every reason you possibly can to stay alive. There is hope, no matter how difficult it might be to find. Don't be ashamed of your scars, they are proof that you survived absolute hell. You don't deserve to suffer. Don't give in, dying isn't going to make it better, remember that you have a life to live. You have people to love. Don't give up. Be proud, you will survive. People like us need to support each other, we need to help each other find the light again. I know it seems impossible not to lose yourself to the pain, I've almost lost myself too. We need to keep going. We need to show everyone that we can survive anything they throw at us. Get up, go live your life. Find the light and help someone else find it too. My scars tell a story, yours do too. But our story doesn't have to end with those scars. It should end on a good note. So just do me a favor, survive. Live your best life. Never be ashamed of who you are.
With much love-Ash Ruiz ;

Personally, when I am in a similar situation I like to draw or read; it lets me escape the reality of things for a while, till I'm calm. And of course whenever you are ready to face that problem, you can face it with a clear head. When I draw, I

have an inspiration behind it, whether I'm doing it to escape reality or not. It affects the way it comes out along with the inspiration. For me, a lot of my inspiration is not the best - it is usually when I'm super upset and/or in a not-so-good head space. But I get the thought behind wanting to harm yourself. But if you are able to: number 1) get rid of things that you could harm yourself with, it helps if you don't have anything to do it with; And 2)talk to someone. I know it's hard, but if you have anybody at all that you can trust with information like that, tell them. You might not think it will help, but it will. Not all things need to be spoken about. If you need someone to talk to, find that person, whether that be a friend or a teacher. Either will do, just someone that will listen, and not make dumb comments, or ask more questions. Just someone who will listen. And believe me, it will not be easy to talk to them about personal things like that, but it can help. Just be kind to yourself
-Taryn

I do not have many friends and many others have disliked or made fun of me. It was hurtful at first but because of my few true friends which have stuck with me for who I am and are always there for me it has made it not sting as bad and I have come to accept that you can't live up to everyone's standards or expectations so stop trying to be someone you are not. The first lesson of becoming a good person who has a happy life is to accept yourself. By this I mean stop imitating others to gain popularity and just be who you are and how you enjoy to be. In Asher's situation, I would try to get him to open up then help him understand that he can change how his life is and have a happy ending, it would just take time. "Time and good true friends who you can share everything with, heals almost any wound or at least makes it less painful." So in all honesty, my best advice is just be true to yourself and others so you and them can find friends who make you see joy in the world. Remember, you could *say* everything to someone to try and make them feel better but in reality it's actions that do the most work, so instead of saying something, I would *do* something. - Kenneth L

Take Action

> "We are all a product of our childhoods, and **we have two choices:** we can choose to repeat what we saw or *not*, for better or for worse."
> -Mr. Cheezers

If you know of anyone that's suffering from abuse or neglect OR you are struggling with something yourself, please use the following resources:

Emergency: 911

Suicide & Crisis Lifeline: Call or text 988

National Domestic Violence Hotline: 1-800-799-7233

Crisis Text Line: Text "DESERVE" TO 741-741

Lifeline Crisis Chat (Online live messaging): https://988lifeline.org/chat

Self-Harm Hotline: 1-800-DONT CUT (1-800-366-8288)

Essential local and community services: 211, https://www.211.org/

Get matched with a therapist: BetterHelp.com

Real-time chat assistance: Mendora.ai

National Mental Health Hotline- 866-903-3787

Suicide Hotline: 988

National Alliance on Mental Illness: https://www.nami.org/help

NAMI Helpline: 1-800-950-6264
  Or text "HelpLine" to 62640

Sources:
  "Get Help Now - Resources for Crisis & Immediate Help | BetterHelp." *Betterhelp.com*, 2019, www.betterhelp.com/gethelpnow/.

NAMI. "NAMI HelpLine | NAMI: National Alliance on Mental Illness." *Nami.org*, 2015, www.nami.org/help.

Special Message from Natalie Wilkinson

The story you just read is fictional, but the pain Asher went through comes from a very real place. Asher represents the combined experiences of a group of kids that have had to deal with more tragedy, heartbreak, and grown-up problems than my generation rarely saw at the turn of the century.

When we were kids, we were into pizza, arcades, and movie theaters. We played outside and used house phones. The Internet was just barely starting to hit the mainstream. I don't remember us having social media other than AOL Instant messenger, and you had to wait for the dial-up connection. I learned to mess with HTML in 9th-10th grade, when MySpace and Yahoo Geocities webpages were the things to do. I still remember the day someone asked me if I had a Facebook and I said, "What is that?"

I don't remember things being quite so complicated - so *dark* - but now as I look back, I wonder if it always was and I just didn't know it. If there was a character I could relate to in this book, it is definitely Lucy, and I feel really lucky and blessed for that. I was far too nerdy to even attempt popularity, but I always had parents that loved me, had my back, and protected me and my brother. I know now it was something I took for granted for a long, long time.

Fast forward a bunch of years to my 8th grade English Language Arts classroom in a rural North Carolina town, far from the palm trees and pavement I grew up with in Florida. Even as an adult, I lived much of life pretty much thinking that people are inherently good, blissfully unaware of how much pain and evil there is in this world. I knew vaguely about there being a Dark Web and took the required school trainings every year on human trafficking, abuse, neglect, and blood-borne pathogens, but somehow they still felt like distant issues, something I could play in the background while I did laundry and dishes.

I was about to have my eyes opened. I soon learned I had been named as a trusted adult by one of my students. I thought that was nice and continued about my life as usual, until this student pulled me to the side and shared her story with me. She broke my heart, and I cried right there standing in that hallway. I never would have known this kid had so much on her plate just by looking at her. Here was this great kid - so smart, so kind, so funny, and overall just awesome, with such a great pain in her spirit.

School-wise, all she needed was some time, some peace and quiet to collect herself and get her work done. Once I gave her that, she excelled quite easily. Had there been a chance to adopt her, I would have right then and there. If she ever needs anything, I am still here and always will be. How could I not?

Once I learned what this kind of pain and loneliness looks like, I started to spot it in other kids, and it was really sobering.

Back in the classroom, student memoirs started trickling in for a class assignment, and I remember reading some that made my brow wrinkle pretty deeply. These kids all seemed happy and perfectly fine on the surface, yet they carried adult-sized burdens of physical and emotional abuse. It was disturbing. With their permission, I removed all identifying details from their stories and used a few of them as references for this novel when we started the Young Author Project. The team members still don't know who those kids are, but I'll never forget.

This novel aims to speak to every school staff member that reads it and highlight that disconnect for them. If it succeeds for one person, I think we accomplished a good thing, because from awareness comes change. The best classrooms are not the ones that hit all the check boxes perfectly. It's the ones led with love first, then excellence.

That leads me to the next part of my special message. It won't reflect the views of all our team members. I only speak for myself, and you can certainly skip it if you choose. It's the best message of hope that I have to offer, not just for kids like Asher, but for anyone willing to read it. I share it with my heart in my hand.

* * *

Penn Jillette, the famous magician who works with Teller and also happens to be an atheist, said something remarkable in a YouTube video that I'll never forget.

For the curious, here's the link: (**https://www.youtube.com/watch?v=owZc3Xq8obk**)

> *Penn said it is a genuine act of hatred for a Christian not to share Christ with someone if they truly believe that Hell is real.*

Digest that for a second. Penn himself does not believe, but he acknowledges and respects those that go outside of their comfort zone to proselytize, which is to share their faith. It's to share the urgency and reality of Hell, like warning someone that's heading for a cliff that they need to stop and turn back.

That's where I'm coming from. Nobody that knows me will be really surprised I've included this, because it's the air I breathe. The greatest act of love I can do for you, dear Reader, is to share with you the most urgent thing I know.

Read this one good time and think about it. If you decide to move past it with a grain of salt, I won't take it personally at all because it's not about me. It's about you and where you'll spend eternity. If something distracts you, come back and at least read this message one good time.

I'll simplify it to the bare bones:

1. There is none righteous, no, not one. (Romans 3:10)

2. We have all sinned and fallen short of the glory of God.

(Romans 3:23)

3. When we die, we go to either heaven or hell. (Matthew 25:41)

4. If you've ever told a lie, stolen something, looked at someone with impure thoughts like lust or hatred, taken God's Name in vain - you are guilty and face judgment from a thrice-Holy God when you die (that's literally everyone. Galatians 5:19-21)

5. The wages of sin is death. God is just and will pay out judgment to each person according to what they have done. (Romans 6:23)

6. Sin cannot be in the presence of God. (Yes, I said "cannot". This is one of its few valid uses. Revelation 21:27; 1 Corinthians 6:9-11; John 3:3)

7. God loved us so much, He sent His Son, Jesus Christ, to take the punishment for our sin. He paid our death penalty with His own Blood so we would be free to go to Heaven with Him when we die. (John 3:16-21; Romans 1:16-17; 1 Corinthians 15:1-4)

8. Repent of your sins and put your trust in Jesus, and you will have everlasting life in Heaven. (Mark 1:14-15)

9. Christ's shed Blood and resurrection paid for our sins. That's why on the cross He cried out, "It is finished!" That means "paid in full." It's like someone paying

your parking tickets for you so you'd be free to go, but on the greatest level there is.

10. God is Love, but God is also a just Judge. All will answer for what they have done. Every knee will bow and every tongue will confess that Jesus Christ is Lord. Hell was created for Satan and his angels, and those who continue to follow him will end up with him in Hell, and it's not a party, it's eternal torment.

Jesus Christ is our only hope of salvation. Repent of your sins, turn from them, and trust in Jesus. I'm not telling you that this will make your life magical and easy and solve all your problems. People that say that just want to get rich off you. What I'm telling you is that realizing you're a sinner facing judgment, repenting of your sins, and trusting in Jesus with your life will bring you salvation. That's it.

Go into your room, close the door, and talk to Him. Though you won't hear Him speak to you audibly, everything He wants us to know is in the Bible. Ask Him to help you in your new walk with Him, and He will. True repentance shows on the outside; as you grow in your faith, you'll find yourself disliking the sin you once ran to more and more.

Anyway, that's all I wanted to say. If you made it this far, thanks for reading. On the following pages you'll find some of the references mentioned above in case you're curious. I included the verses before and after for full context.

With all my love,
   Natalie

***

List of References

Rich Maurer. "Not Proselytize." *YouTube*, 13 Nov. 2009, www.youtube.com/watch?v=owZc3Xq8obk. Accessed 23 July 2024.

Bible Gateway. "New King James Version." *Biblegateway.com*, BibleGateway, 2011, www.biblegateway.com. Accessed 16 July 2024.

All Biblical references used in this section are from this webpage.

For additional resources and information, visit:
www.GotQuestions.org
www.NeedGod.com
Romans 3:9-19
⁹ What then? Are we better *than they?* Not at all. For we have previously charged both Jews and Greeks that they are all under sin.
¹⁰ As it is written:
"There is none righteous, no, not one;
¹¹ There is none who understands;
There is none who seeks after God.
¹² They have all turned aside;

They have together become unprofitable;
There is none who does good, no, not one."
13 "Their throat *is* an open tomb;
With their tongues they have practiced deceit";
"The poison of asps *is* under their lips";
14 "Whose mouth *is* full of cursing and bitterness."
15 "Their feet *are* swift to shed blood;
16 Destruction and misery *are* in their ways;
17 And the way of peace they have not known."
18 "There is no fear of God before their eyes."

19 Now we know that whatever the law says, it says to those who are under the law, that every mouth may be stopped, and all the world may become guilty before God. **20** Therefore by the deeds of the law no flesh will be justified in His sight, for by the law *is* the knowledge of sin.

Romans 3:21-26

21 But now the righteousness of God apart from the law is revealed, being witnessed by the Law and the Prophets, **22** even the righteousness of God, through faith in Jesus Christ, to all and on all who believe. For there is no difference; **23 for all have sinned and fall short of the glory of God,** **24** being justified freely by His grace through the redemption that is in Christ Jesus, **25** whom God set forth *as* a propitiation by His blood, through faith, to demonstrate His righteousness, because in His forbearance God had passed over the sins that were previously committed, **26** to demonstrate at the present time His righteousness, that He might be just and the justifier of the one who has faith in Jesus.

Matthew 25:31-44

The Son of Man Will Judge the Nations

31 "When the Son of Man comes in His glory, and all the holy angels with Him, then He will sit on the throne of His glory. **32** All the nations will be gathered before Him, and He will separate them one from another, as a shepherd divides *his* sheep from the goats. **33** And He will set the sheep on His right hand, but the goats on the left. **34** Then the King will say to those on His right hand, 'Come, you blessed of My Father, inherit the kingdom prepared for you from the foundation of the world: **35** for I was hungry and you gave Me food; I was thirsty and you gave Me drink; I was a stranger and you took Me in;**36** I *was* naked and you clothed Me; I was sick and you visited Me; I was in prison and you came to Me.'

37 "Then the righteous will answer Him, saying, 'Lord, when did we see You hungry and feed *You*, or thirsty and give *You* drink? **38** When did we see You a stranger and take *You* in, or naked and clothe *You?* **39** Or when did we see You sick, or in prison, and come to You?' **40** And the King will answer and say to them, 'Assuredly, I say to you, inasmuch as you did *it* to one of the least of these My brethren, you did *it* to Me.'

41 **"Then He will also say to those on the left hand,'Depart from Me, you cursed, into the everlasting fire prepared for the devil and his angels: 42** for I was hungry and you gave Me no food; I was thirsty and you gave Me no drink; **43** I was a stranger and you did not take Me in, naked and you did not clothe Me, sick and in prison and you did not visit Me.'

44 "Then they also will answer Him, saying, 'Lord, when did we see You hungry or thirsty or a stranger or naked or sick or in prison, and did not minister to You?'**45** Then He will answer them, saying, 'Assuredly, I say to you, inasmuch as you did not do *it* to one of the least of these, you did not do *it* to Me.' **⁴⁶** And these will go away into everlasting punishment, but the righteous into eternal life."

Galatians 5:19-26

¹⁹ Now the works of the flesh are evident, which are: adultery, fornication, uncleanness, lewdness, ²⁰ idolatry, sorcery, hatred, contentions, jealousies, outbursts of wrath, selfish ambitions, dissensions, heresies, ²¹ envy, murders, drunkenness, revelries, and the like; of which I tell you beforehand, just as I also told *you* in time past, that those who practice such things will not inherit the kingdom of God. 22 But the fruit of the Spirit is love, joy, peace, long-suffering, kindness, goodness, faithfulness, 23 gentleness, self-control. Against such there is no law. 24 And those who are Christ's have crucified the flesh with its passions and desires. 25 If we live in the Spirit, let us also walk in the Spirit. 26 Let us not become conceited, provoking one another, envying one another.

Romans 6

Dead to Sin, Alive to God

6 ¹ What shall we say then? Shall we continue in sin that grace may abound? **²** Certainly not! How shall we who died to sin live any longer in it? **³** Or do you not know that as many of us as were baptized into Christ Jesus were baptized into His death? **⁴** Therefore we were buried with Him through baptism into death, that just as Christ was raised from the dead by the glory of the Father, even so we also should walk in newness of life.

5 For if we have been united together in the likeness of His death, certainly we also shall be *in the likeness* of *His* resurrection, **6** knowing this, that our old man was crucified with *Him,* that the body of sin might be done away with, that we should no longer be slaves of sin. **7** For he who has died has been freed from sin. **8** Now if we died with Christ, we believe that we shall also live with Him, **9** knowing that Christ, having been raised from the dead, dies no more. Death no longer has dominion over Him. **10** For *the death* that He died, He died to sin once for all; but *the life* that He lives, He lives to God. **11** Likewise you also, reckon yourselves to be dead indeed to sin, but alive to God in Christ Jesus our Lord.

12 Therefore do not let sin reign in your mortal body, that you should obey it in its lusts. 13 And do not present your members as instruments of unrighteousness to sin, but present yourselves to God as being alive from the dead, and your members as instruments of righteousness to God. 14 For sin shall not have dominion over you, for you are not under law but under grace.

From Slaves of Sin to Slaves of God

15 What then? Shall we sin because we are not under law but under grace? Certainly not! **16** Do you not know that to whom you present yourselves slaves to obey, you are that one's slaves whom you obey, whether of sin *leading* to death, or of obedience *leading* to righteousness? **17** But God be thanked that *though* you were slaves of sin, yet you obeyed from the heart that form of doctrine to which you were delivered. ¹⁸ And having been set free from sin, you became slaves of righteousness. ¹⁹ I speak in human *terms* because of the weakness of your flesh. For just as you presented your members *as* slaves of uncleanness, and of lawlessness *leading* to *more* lawlessness, so now present your members *as* slaves *of* righteousness for holiness.

²⁰ For when you were slaves of sin, you were free in regard to righteousness. ²¹ What fruit did you have then in the things of which you are now ashamed? For the end of those things *is* death. ²² But now having been set free from sin, and having become slaves of God, you have your fruit to holiness, and the end, everlasting life. ²³ **For the wages of sin *is* death, but the gift of God *is* eternal life in Christ Jesus our Lord**.

John 3:3

³ Jesus answered and said to him, "Most assuredly, I say to you, unless one is born again, he cannot see the kingdom of God."

John 3:16-21

¹⁶ **For God so loved the world that He gave His only begotten Son, that whoever believes in Him should not perish but have everlasting life.** ¹⁷ For God did not send His Son into the world to condemn the world, but that the world through Him might be saved.

¹⁸ "He who believes in Him is not condemned; but he who does not believe is condemned already, because he has not believed in the name of the only begotten Son of God. ¹⁹ And this is the condemnation, that the light has come into the world, and men loved darkness rather than light, because their deeds were evil. ²⁰ For everyone practicing evil hates the light and does not come to the light, lest his deeds should

be exposed.²¹ But he who does the truth comes to the light, that his deeds may be clearly seen, that they have been done in God."

Romans 1:16-17

¹⁶ For I am not ashamed of the gospel of Christ, for it is the power of God to salvation for everyone who believes, for the Jew first and also for the Greek. ¹⁷ For in it the righteousness of God is revealed from faith to faith; as it is written, "The just shall live by faith."

1 Corinthians 15:1-4

1 Moreover, brethren, I declare to you the gospel which I preached to you, which also you received and in which you stand,

2 by which also you are saved, if you hold fast that word which I preached to you—unless you believed in vain.

3 For I delivered to you first of all that which I also received: that **Christ died for our sins according to the Scriptures,**

4 and that He was buried, and that He rose again the third day according to the Scriptures...

Mark 1:14-15

¹⁴ Now after John was put in prison, Jesus came to Galilee, preaching the gospel of the kingdom of God, ¹⁵ and saying, **"The time is fulfilled, and the kingdom of God is at hand. Repent, and believe in the gospel."**

About the Author

This is the story of the Young Author Project.

The Young Author Project was born in May 2023. All except one of these Young Authors were in my 8th grade ELA class at Mount Pleasant Middle School during the 2022-2023 school year. In their own ways, each one demonstrated outstanding work ethic and talent while in class in Reading, Writing, Speaking and Listening - so much so that one day I thought it'd be a great idea for them to write and publish an original novel. They all loved the prospect, so I picked up the phone and called everyone's home to pitch the idea of their child becoming a published author before graduating high school. Their parents, all of whom I have come to know and cherish, were extremely excited and supportive of the idea. What started uncertainly as a "book club" soon became much more than I ever could have anticipated. This book has become an act of service and of love, not just from me to the authors, but from us as a team to our future readers and our community. We've been meeting almost every single Saturday without fail at the public library to write, discuss, and collaborate since the Summer of 2023, and we already have ideas for the next 2-3 books! I sometimes ask myself how I end up getting into these kinds of projects, but it's been the most fun I've had in a long time, and it's been amazing, to say the least.

I'll let them tell you more.
  -Natalie

ANGEL DURAN

My name is Angel and I'm going to attend Early College High School. If I'm being completely honest, I didn't think that I would be making any contribution to the project. I was just there because my sister was there and it would be convenient for us both to be in the same place. When my mom told me to actually help out with the book, I realized how beneficial it was for me. This is exciting because it's the first novel any of us have ever done. I have always wanted to write a book (even if my vision wasn't a fiction book) and this project helped me learn the process. Anyway, that's enough of me. Most of us have never had experience publishing a book before, so we have had the unique opportunity to learn how to do just that. We've been able to see the whole process from start to finish, since we started from scratch. I mean absolute zero. We had no funding, no ideas for the book, and no clue how to get started. We didn't know how to format prose for a novel, and we didn't have an editor. The first thing we did was buy a box of World's Finest Chocolates and start selling like crazy during the Summer of 2023. We were so successful, we were able to buy a set of 10 ISBN numbers, hire an editor, and even fund rewards for ourselves. During the Christmas holiday, we got to participate in an awards ceremony in which we received letters of recommendation for future endeavors as well as lots of other cool stuff. I was definitely pushed out of my comfort zone because there were many people that we had to talk to. How would we get the funds we needed without talking to people to see if they were interested? We had to talk to people so that this novel could be possible. Next you'll learn about how the idea for the book came about.

KENSHIN LEE

My name is Kenshin Lee and I am currently attending Mount Pleasant High School. I joined because I had a passion for reading and I was asked to join because I loved reading. It was something different and I had never written before and it was something new and at first I was hesitant about joining, but a couple friends who were attending the meets as well persuaded me into joining. I hope in the future we can write more as an amazing team and possibly publish more books for the future generations. Mrs. Wilkinson first got the idea for our story from a memoir activity we did in class. For this activity, students wrote and submitted their own memoirs. Some of them were silly and others were fictional. However, there were a few stories that stood out way too much to be ignored. They were heartbreaking stories of abuse, neglect, and trauma. With permission, our team got to read some of these memoirs anonymously as a reference. We were surprised to learn that these were people in our grade level, walking the same halls. We still have no idea who they were. There was no way to tell, and it began to change the way we look at others around us. The next author will tell you all about our goals in writing this book.

ANAIS DURAN

My name is Anais and I go to Early College High School in Kannapolis. I joined this group because I've loved reading since I was little, and books give me a magical sort of feeling, like I've left this world and entered another. I write a lot of random ideas I have into stories (that I usually struggle to figure out how to end) so having a team to help me write was a very exciting prospect. The team of people that we have are amazing, and that team also includes my best friend, so everything really added up into a situation that was pretty much impossible to say no to. We decided early on that our main goals in writing this book were to create windows and mirrors. What do we mean by that? When we create a *mirror*, we are creating ways for readers to see themselves reflected in the story and characters. They can find a way to relate to the story, which can be comforting and make the story so much stronger. On the other side of that coin, our endeavor was also to create *windows* within our book. What does *that* mean? As we go about our day to day lives, we are kind of stuck in our own heads. We sometimes don't really pay attention to things going on around us, or even know to look for anything different. Our book seeks to create a *window* into someone else's world for a change, so that we can understand a point of view that's different from ours. This is so important because it helps people to empathize with different perspectives. Windows can break down stereotypes and help to better understand what people could be going through. With this book specifically, we want to show that you don't really ever know what is going on in the lives of the people around you. You have to be mindful, and put yourself in others shoes. That's what windows are for. Originally, we wanted to apply for all kinds of book awards, but we soon decided it was more important to tell a good story than to win a bunch of awards. We started to write with more passion after that. The next author will tell you about some of the research we did to help us write this novel.

BROOKLYNN SATTERFIELD

My name is Brooklynn and I am attending Mount Pleasant High School. I joined because I have a love for reading but mostly I wanted to raise awareness of the subjects in this book. I have a big passion for writing a lot. I hope we are able to write more books in the near future. Even though this story is completely fictional, due to the sensitive nature of some of the topics we discuss in our book, we had to do a fair amount of research in order to ensure that we remained both authentic and compassionate in our delivery of this story. We got to interview various experts from DSS, who were more than excited to help us and learn all about this project. I don't think we'd ever get to thank them enough for their support and valuable insight that helped make this book possible. They are Sarimar Miller from the Department of Juvenile Justice, Elaine Miller from the Department of Child Services, and Shelly Lee, also from the Department of Child Services. We are so grateful to our school social worker, Ms. Christy Clary, to Deputy Yang in Concord, and to Kenshin Lee for connecting us to these wonderful people! The next author will give you the synopsis of our novel, in case you're one of those people that reads the back part of the book first.

TARYN JOHNSON

My name is Taryn and I am from Mount Pleasant High School. I joined this team because I enjoy reading. Having the chance to help write a book about things that are real world problems and that can even change people's lives is quite an amazing opportunity. I'm excited about this project because I get to spend time and have fun with amazing people! I hope that I will be able to tell people that I was part of an incredible group of kids that made a book to help others and change lives. I want to help people and make people feel happy. Our novel is titled *The Art of Giving a Crap.* It's about two middle schoolers living VERY different lives. Lucy lives a comfortable life; her biggest problem is fitting in. Asher is barely surviving in a chaotic household rife with abuse and neglect. Can they find a common ground, or are they just too different? Will Asher find hope amid his circumstances? You never know what someone is going through, even the person sitting right next to you. Next, you'll learn a little bit about the actual process we've been using to put this novel together.

OLIVIA DESANTIS

My name is Olivia De Santis and I go to Cabarrus Health Science Institute. When I got asked to join the Young Authors Project, I was ecstatic because not only was this a great opportunity, but since I could remember I had a passion for writing. This project means a lot because this is an avenue for those who often are hidden in the shadows. I hope that those who often don't give a second thought to what may be going on behind the scenes, start to actually stop and think. Now, as Angel mentioned before, we had no idea what we were doing when we first started this project. As a result, we kind of flip-flopped back and forth between platforms until we figured out a flow that worked for us. We started off on Reedsy.com, which not only gives you a place to keep your writing, but it also helps you search and find editors, illustrators, marketing specialists, and whatever else you can possibly need to self-publish a novel. This is where we found our editor, Miriam Spitzer Franklin. Because of our budget and limited progress on the book at the time, we got turned down by 6 different editors. We were so excited when the 7th said she'd help us and even work within our budget! Ms. Franklin is also a middle school teacher here in North Carolina, and has also published several books herself, which has made her an incredible resource for us to learn from. We will never forget her kindness! She had us move over to a Google doc so we could all make active edits. We were used to working on Google Docs as a team from our time in Mrs. Wilkinson's class, but when the document started to pass 300 pages, it began to glitch and crash all our computers. We had to create a separate document for shorter edits. Needless to say, it was a huge learning experience for everyone! (That's not counting fixing plot holes and grammar.)

MICHAELLA RUIZ

My name is Michaella Ruiz and I attend Cabarrus Kannapolis Early College. I joined the Young Authors Project mainly because I love writing, but also because I felt that this story could shed light on so many important things that are often swept under the rug because it's uncomfortable to talk about. I'm excited about this project because it's an amazing opportunity for everyone who joined to get their work out to the general public while also educating our audience about abuse and mental illness. I hope that this project can provide a window for people who may not quite understand that someone right beside them could be struggling and fighting for their life while also being something that those who are struggling can relate to so they feel less alone.

KENNETH LODER

My name is Kenneth, and I'm a student at MPHS. I joined this ragtag group of young authors because I had been invited and I thought it would be a fun project to tell a story that others don't see. I was excited writing this book because it was a reason to help others realize they are not alone and help them to speak out about their problems. I hope the readers will find a will to live and share their experiences to have a more tight and understanding community that have personally dealt with these problems and for those who don't understand to try and gain some insight and if not just have a book to read and enjoy. In some form or another, we all have personal experiences with these topics that we bring to the table, which also show up in various parts of the story. This book has a piece from each of us in it. It would not be the same without all of us, and that's what makes it special. We hope you read and enjoy our book, and if you do, we'd love to hear from you. Feedback is so important for doing good work, and we always appreciate it. Everyone is also invited to sign up on our mailing list so you can be in the loop for future books that come out. Not to worry, Mrs. Wilkinson doesn't have time to sell your email or Spam you, so you'll be pleasantly surprised at how efficient and sporadic the emails are. For more information, visit https://YoungAuthorProjec t.com and reach out to us there!

As a student who has experienced what other people have done without getting caught: we hope this book will bring at least a small amount of courage to the readers who deal with many problems that go constantly unnoticed and stand up to them at least in their way.

Thanks.

You can connect with me on:

🌐 https://youngauthorproject.com

🔗 https://buymeacoffee.com/schoolboost

Subscribe to my newsletter:

✉️　　　https://mailchi.mp/46bf22b59be7/young-author-project-mailing-list

Also by Young Author Project

Sign up on our mailing list and be the first to know of updates on these upcoming projects. (See previous pages for the link.)

COMING SOON

Duncan and Asher are finally re-united. How will they come to terms and heal from their shared past? Will their parents face justice at last?

COMING SOON

Marcus is a nice guy facing many unseen battles. Can Lucy help him through?

COMING SOON

One kid faces down an eating disorder. It has a name, and it has to die.